Night Diving

Night Diving

Michelene Esposito

Spinsters Ink Books
Denver, Colorado
USA

Spinsters Ink Books
P. O. Box 22005
Denver, CO 80222
USA

Cover photography by Marilyn Lande
Cover graphic design and type by Attention Media
Interior design by Gilsvik Book Production
Printed in Canada

Library of Congress Cataloging-in-Publication Data
Esposito, Michelene.
  Night diving / by Michelene Esposito.
      p. cm.
  ISBN 1-883523-52-4
  1. Lesbians--Fiction. 2. Coming out (Sexual orientation)--Fiction.
I. Title.
PS3605.S76 N44 2002
813'.6--dc21

                                        2002009237

Acknowledgement

I would like to thank the following people who helped to make this story in my head an actual novel:

Diana. There would simply be no *Night Diving* without Diana, who spent hours (many, many hours) reading, editing and sitting on floors with me surrounded by pages, working and reworking the plot—not to mention the endless phone calls and emails. Your patience, humor, honesty, skill and love are more than any best friend could ask for.

Dru. My life partner and love was always eager and willing to hear me read each chapter aloud as I wrote it. It was a gift to have such enthusiastic and honest feedback so immediately available. Dru, your support of my writing is so genuine. I know how lucky I am.

Judy Lynne Ray. She was there back when I was in grade school, encouraging me, serving as a role model, and taking me to my first writing workshop.

Joan Drury. For some important editorial guidance and for paving the way to publication.

My writing group. Susan, Kamal, Brian, Claudine, Jaime and Carol. For your general comradeship and specific feedback.

My editor, Paulette Whitcomb. For the final flourishes and many details—and for the fun conversations. I am grateful for all you have done to shape this manuscript.

Sharon Silvas, Nina Miranda and the staff at Spinsters Ink. For your professionalism and talent and for making a dream come true.

For my parents, Eleanor and Michael.

Chapter One

I'm sitting in my mother's hair salon with my hands on a manicure table, my feet in the vibrating footbath. My mother, Vivian, is across the salon, pulling some woman's hair through a highlight cap.

Tomorrow is the first day of my grandmother's wake, which is why I'm back in Long Island in the first place. This is my father's mother. My mother's mother died when I was three. I have absolutely no memory of her, just memories of my mother's memories.

The manicurist is Fran, a huge, blond Hungarian woman with rolling arms and calves, who also does the skin care. She used to do my bikini waxes back when I worked for my mother during college summers. She talks the whole time in a high, singsong accent as she scrapes the calluses (and the first six layers of skin) from my heels. It's like the dentist scene from *Marathon Man*, but then I've been fed a steady diet of this stuff since birth: There is no price too great to pay for beauty. Yes, but beauty is hundreds of dollars a year, stinging perm lotion, wax that dries on cotton that is then used to rip the hairs out of your underarms; beauty is using a toilet-seat cover for a bib when you've eaten that piece of birthday cake you shouldn't have and you need to throw it up quick in the ladies' room.

I'm not bitter, just heavier with underarm stubble, clogged pores and less lustrous hair. You know how it is, life is about choices. I've been telling my mother for years that I'm happier being myself and she keeps replying, in one way or another, that she can't wait until the time I don't have to let myself go to hell to separate from her.

This is the danger of too much psychotherapy and not enough insight. Your sharing can become the other's weapon.

My cousin Tina is sitting at the front desk, answering the phone and putting change in the wallet of an overly tanned blond woman with wet nails. It's about 9 in the morning and the place is already a zoo with three blow-dryers going, the shampoo girls at the sinks, and some new girl giving out coffee and fried-egg sandwiches from the deli next door.

I'm always jet-lagged the first day after I fly in from California, and somehow I always find myself in my mother's Mercedes the next morning, driving to the salon around 7, which, in case you haven't done the math, is 4 in the morning California time. I'm not quite sure why this happens, except that I *know* I'm not quite as put together as my mother would like, and the early-morning salon visits seem to bind her anxiety some-how. She'd of course hand me my head on a roller tray if she heard me say this—"Do you know what people pay me to do their hair? Only my kids . . ."—and she goes on about how wildly unappre-ciative my sister, Claire, and I are. She's right. I've seen it. Summers when women literally beg for an appointment—like she's giving out hearts to transplant patients. These women would run their way through the gamut of influence techniques when I'd be taking appointments at the front desk.

"I have a *very* important dinner party tonight and my roots are down to my ears!"

"I'm sorry," I'd say, "she's booked for the next two weeks but . . ."

"I *can't* go out of the house like this!" In a voice that clearly conveys this woman has been locking her unsightly self in the attic like Mrs. Bates for the past few days, and has just sneaked down to a phone while her husband's stepped out to check the yacht. She'll be dashing back up to the attic with a chamber pot under one arm and a loaf of bread under the other by the time the receiver hits the cradle.

"I can put you on a waiting list."

"Okay, forget the color. How about just the blow-out?"

Moving now from politeness through pleading toward fury.

"She's been working since 7 this morning. It's 6 now, and she needs to finish up."

"Let me speak to her."

This is a technique only the real pushy ones or the oldtimers use, capitalizing on their relationship with my mother and her inability to set limits, skipping over the lowly receptionist. Later, when they come in—and they do, because the word no is not in Vivian's vocabulary when it comes to work or family—they are contrite to find out I'm her daughter.

Fran and I are splitting one of the fried-egg sandwiches and she's filling me in on her son-of-a-bitch ex who conned her out of her house. I'm eating with the hand she's not filing. In between threatening her ex-husband (she made pipe bombs as a child in Hungary and certainly remembers how it's done), she comments on my nails.

3

"Are you biting your nails?"

"No."

"Are they breaking?"

"No. I'm just keeping them short," I tell her, knowing the next question is going to be, "Why?"

I look at her and pause long enough to tell myself, This is a kid who made pipe bombs in Hungary. She can take it. And I know she knows anyway.

"The girls," I say pointedly. "They don't like long nails." She nods at me slowly and then leans toward me and whispers, "Your mother, Rose, do yourself a favor, tell her you're not getting enough calcium."

On the way home that night, Vivian's driving and eating the chicken-cutlet sandwich that was supposed to have been her lunch. It's dark and cold with two streams of warmth shooting out of the dashboard at my face, the headlights cutting a trail home.

"Want a bite?" Vivian says, motioning with the cutlet. This is nothing short of a commandment in my family. "Thou shalt not partake of a morsel of food without offering up such morsels to thy beloved children." This becomes quite the fiasco in restaurants where, depending on the number of extended family members present, you can easily find yourself with a bread plate filled with up to a dozen bite-size pieces of everyone's entree, and your own plate looking like some small war was fought on it, with dead and wounded scraps of chicken and potato gratin clinging pitifully to each other, your roll taking cover beneath the garnish.

It comes down to this: If you love and are truly loved, you share your food. Food is love, love is food and we have no boundaries anyway, so why be a hypocrite at the dinner table.

I look over at my mother as she begins to tell me, in her impatient and condemning way, about today's behind-the-scene trials with the new shampoo girl. She's particularly irritated that she had to instruct the girl on the proper way to rinse color—you start at the forehead and work your way down to the back of the head, if you're interested. It is clear that, as far as she is concerned, this is not rocket science and she showed the girl once and is astounded that she didn't get it the first time. This is Vivian at her worst, exacting and sarcastic. What you don't immediately see is that she is much, much harder on herself. She expects herself to know something *before* she is taught. So, if you look at it from her perspective, she's actually cutting the rest of us a break. As she winds down from her tirade with a final, "I'll have to fire her if she doesn't get with it by Friday. I'm too busy for this," I see her the way I always do—like some small piece of mountain that knows, nonetheless, that it's a mountain. Her face has the pointy, carved features of a small strong woman and she is Sicilian beautiful still, even with her slack chin and neck.

She was young when she had me—just 20. For forever strangers have thought we are sisters. I look so like my mother that people easily mistake the black and whites of her as a twin for me. So I've watched her grow older with extra interest, always thinking, "This will be me . . . at 20 . . . at 30 . . . at 50." In that way it's comforting. Vivian has aged well. In other ways, of course, it's eerie, always reminding yourself you *look* like her, you *are* not her. Her tapered waist is not yours; her swift, big-knuckled hands are not yours; and her hair that goes from blond to red and back to brown again in the course of a year is hers to do what she wants with. The same goes for her life.

It's the little mantra I chant to myself during times of particular stress when I fear I will respond to some crisis in my life by becoming her, because sometimes it's all I can think to do. I have yet to tell her, tell anyone, that the day before I got the call that my grandmother had died, my girlfriend Gail had not only dumped me but fired me from my job at "our" restaurant. I have a friend, Becky, who thinks it's best to get all your crises out on the table at once, like some big spring-cleaning. I like her anyway.

▼

That next morning we're gathered around my grandmother's casket: Tina, my mother, my Aunt Moe and me. Tina thinks my grandmother doesn't look right—like there is such a thing as the right way to look dead.

"It's her lipstick," my mother says, in a voice so knowing my eyes move from Tina, whom I am expecting to unravel on the parquet floor any moment, to her face. "And her hair is all wrong. I told you I should do it," she tells Aunt Moe.

"You would do her hair?" I screech to myself. Wait, is this before or after they siphon out all her bodily fluids? And really, if you're going to do her hair, you should take on the make-up because *really* what you're after is a complete look, right?

I need some air.

"Where are her glasses?" Tina's voice has now begun to rise. "This doesn't look like my grandmother. Why did they make her face look so fat? She has a skinny face. Oh God!" And I'm thinking, this is a beautiful family memory: Tina, moving fast and furious toward hysteria, my mother calmly directing the morgue man, requesting my grandmother's make-up bag, and my Aunt Moe grabbing Tina by the shoulders and hissing into her face, "If you can't control yourself, get out." And she can't.

"Come on, let's go for a walk," I say, and lead her out of the funeral parlor with about eight of our relatives I haven't seen in two decades watching our exit with pitying but somehow approving eyes. After all, they would do the same for their grandmother—have a breakdown, that is.

We walk out to the funeral-home porch, where my Uncle

Jimmy and some of his brothers are smoking. I want to smoke too, but I'm worried about my father walking out and dropping dead onto some shrub lining the porch railing. After all, this is his mother and a man can be expected to take only so much.

Tina and I walk along the blacktop behind the funeral home and she starts in again. "Oh my God, what did they put in her? She looks so bloated. It doesn't look like her!"

"That's because she's dead," I say before I can stop myself. "I'm sorry," I say. I'm not that cruel. The fact is, I don't know what Tina would have done without our grandmother. My Aunt Moe is one of those people who is good at loving and bad at taking care. I don't think people like that should be allowed to raise children, but there's not exactly a test for that kind of thing. Our grandmother was the one who made Tina's lunches, bought the new schoolbag each September and put the Italian evil eye on the algebra teacher who tried to touch Tina's thigh during an "extra help" meeting.

We plop ourselves down on the curb that lines the back parking lot and separates it from the woods and the backyards of a row of tract homes. It's September and leaves have already starting falling from the trees even though today it is almost 70°. I look over at Tina, who is fumbling for a tissue in her pocket, and sniffling, all red-faced and blotchy, in that way fair-skinned blondes have of doing. She is 27, three years younger than me, but bigger-boned and rounder all over. Like my sister, Tina has the breasts and hips of my father's side of the family. A figure that made me feel invisible when we'd shop at the Smithhaven Mall together as teenagers. She is also the only blond Italian I knew as a kid whose golden locks didn't come compliments of Clairol.

I, on the other hand, have the looks seen in so many migrant farm-worker photographs I've noticed in airports recently. Those that look like they rounded up some poor undernourished and unsuspecting group of young women about to expire from sun-stroke after a day of picking strawberries, lined them up and said, "Cheese!" I realize that matting and framing a bunch of these photos and putting them on the walls of the American Airlines terminal is an attempt to pay tribute to the various cultural heritages in the great state of California. But as I rushed to catch my flight to New York, I kept thinking those exhausted girls would have rather split the money it cost to buy the film than pose for a photo session.

"Oh, Rose, she looks so strange in that box."

"Who picked that box?"

"What do you mean, that's a very expensive box. Do you know what coffins cost? Gramps spent $10,000 on that coffin."

I smile. That's my Tina. She always has the inside scoop. What someone *really* paid for that Beemer. What exactly happened the night Uncle Phil got caught cheating on Aunt Maggie. Whose tennis bracelet is diamond versus zirconium.

"I guess it's a nice coffin," I admit.

"It's cherry wood and he's getting three limos to take us to Brooklyn."

"We're still going to Brooklyn?"

"Oh yeah. He says she told him last night she wanted to be buried in Brooklyn in that plot next to his mother."

"She hated his mother."

"Well, we know that . . ."

"You think he's losing it? You know, Grandma's ghost giving burial orders from the Great Beyond . . ."

"No, he's just stubborn. I told him, what do you think? It's gonna look like when you were a kid? Brooklyn's a disgusting jungle."

We spend three days in the McFinley Funeral Home and by

the second day we have the drill down. Three hours sitting in a room with your dead grandmother, two hours at my mother's or aunt's house to eat—which is just the thing you feel like doing after spending the morning in a room with your dead grandmother—and then the rest of the afternoon and evening in the funeral parlor. I had no idea this mourning thing would last so long, so by the second day I'm wearing one of my mother's dresses, this blue-and-yellow checked cotton number. I protest when she pulls it out of her closet for me, the tag still on, but she turns on me with a sigh and says, "It's Anne Klein," in a way that clearly ends the conversation. I'm standing by the window watching the traffic when Tina tugs at my dress and whispers, "Hey, come over here with that tablecloth and sit next to me."

"Tablecloth isn't mine," I say, taking a seat between Tina and my sister, Claire, who'd come in early that morning with her husband. We'd set up a row of seats by the door so we could watch the seemingly infinite flow of relatives file in and out of the room. Women with big hair, lots of eye make-up, all impeccably dressed. Men in dark suits and Italian shoes, all looking like my father—a man dressed every day of his life by his mother or his wife.

"Do you know who that is?"

Tina nods toward a lone woman descending down the hall toward us. I shake my head.

"That's cousin Caroline. She came all the way from Jersey. Her grandmother died last year. Did you go to her funeral?"

"I was in California. I don't even know her grandmother," I say, suddenly feeling that nasty but familiar guilt creeping its way up my insides. Maybe I *did* know her grandmother? Maybe it was during the holidays and I was too preoccupied and busy and self-absorbed? I could've at least sent a Mass card. Of course, I have absolutely no idea where to get a Mass card in the Bay Area, but I could've had my mother send one for me.

"She's not even on Grandma's side of the family. And look over there, in front of Gramps, that's our third cousin Susan, from Staten Island. Her mother died this summer, breast cancer. And did we go? No. All I can say is, we have no respect."

Tina tells me this with eyebrows raised.

This, I assure myself, is why I live 3,000 miles across the country now. *This* is why I allow my mother to bring Corning Ware from the Redding Outlets to the various bridal showers and forge my name on the little gift cards.

By 8 that night I am listening to my godmother, my Aunt Joan, compare embalmers with Aunt Moe. "Lenny in Brooklyn was the best. A true craftsman. You're either born with that kind of talent or you're not. You remember how he made my mother look? She was beautiful." And it's about that time I decide I need more air.

I walk out into the parking lot and in back of the funeral home where I light a cigarette I took from my uncle's pack at the midday feed. The traffic is making flashes onto the trees, and I'm thinking about the time my grandmother cut me a doll's dress to sew one day when she was baby-sitting me and I sewed it onto her couch. This makes me sad but I don't cry. I haven't cried once— a fact that clearly has not escaped my mother, who has been watching me like some moving target since she caught sight of me coming down the ramp at Kennedy. She took my carry-on, handed it to my father and let her eyes wash over me.

"You look thin." She'd heard about bulimia in a family ther-apy session 10 years earlier and, especially with my being all the way in California, she's constantly on the lookout for some kind of Karen Carpenter warning signs. She still sends me care pack-ages filled with Rice-A-Roni, tuna packed in water, and other exotic items we can't get in California.

"I missed you too, Mom," I said, smiling and shaking my head.

I actually did okay for most of the wake. It wasn't that I didn't miss my grandmother. I just think it was too many things going on at once. The only thing that really got me was my father. He got up from his chair in the row in front of the coffin as we left for the break, kneeled in front of his mother, and the next thing I know he's weeping.

This tore me up. My aunts, my cousins, they were always just one step short of hysteria, but the only other time I'd seen my father cry was 17 years ago when my cousin died. It was like my cousin Eddy drowned and everything went white—flowers, dresses, coffin, faces, noise in my head—and I wrote a poem called *The Angel Child*, a Hallmarky, choppy poem by a 13-year-old who doesn't know thing one about what a 6-year-old looks like lying at the bottom of a swimming pool. The last verse talks about all these kids with wings bouncing on clouds and there's this other line reassuring my family that it's okay—the way a teenager who has only heard or read about death can reassure. My grandmother got a metal frame from the Wading River Drug Store and hung *The Angel Child* in her living room and I'd try not to notice it, because you know the only thing I remembered about Eddy? Him chasing Claire and me around the backyard with this big metal pipe and my grandmother chasing him around the dining-room table with a wooden spoon. Couldn't even remember if she caught him. By that evening when my grandfather came home, Claire and I had found a turtle in the backyard and we'd sat in the dirt poking it gently with a stick to see its face. And everything was okay by the time my mother pulled into the driveway and honked the horn and we crawled into the backseat of the Caddie smelling like dirt, sweat and macaroni sauce and she smelled like coffee and hair spray, familiar and safe. The leather seats of the Caddie had eaten a Lego I dug out and pressed against my arm, making little rectangles all the way home, and I never once imagined Eddy would die.

That's what I'm thinking, all those years later, you just never know when some swimming pool or potted plant falling from a 10-story ledge or some plague is going to snatch a beloved and make the body disappear into some foul-smelling box. I smash my cigarette out on the curb, watching the amber die to black, and stand up quick. As I round the corner to the front of the funeral home, I see my mother standing and talking to some woman with bright red hair, and as I get closer I can still only see the back of the red-haired woman but, by the way my mother is looking at me, I suddenly know it is Jessie.

I haven't seen Jessie for over 12 years. She had run away to Florida our senior year of high school. She was gone for eight months and returned looking broken and lost but, most importantly, gone. Her eyes that had held mine as we scrapped and clawed our way through childhood and adolescence together were somehow clouded over, and by the time I was leaving for college we still hadn't figured out what had happened, or at least how to talk about what hurt. After a while I stopped daydreaming over a book in my dorm room that she would knock at my door and finally look at me.

"Rose," my mother says as I approach the two of them. "Look who's here."

"Hey, Jessie," I say, and I walk up to her and give her one of those hugs I've given to about 37 second cousins in the past two days. I'm surprised, somehow, that she looks like a grown-up. The last time I saw her we were both 18-year-olds who looked 14. She has no make-up on and I can spot these little wrinkles around her eyes.

"Sorry about your grandmother."

"Thanks." And then I don't know what to say.

My mother says, "Jessie, would you like to come over to the

house and have something to eat?"

"You know, Mrs. Salino, I have to get off to work. Thank you, though." Then Jessie turns to me and says slowly, "It's good to see you, Rose. You going to be in town for a while?"

"A little while. You living here now?"

"Yeah, I've got an apartment here in Rocky Point, over by the high school."

"Well, give me a call at the house. Maybe we can get some coffee or something."

"I'm off at 10 tomorrow night. Will you be up?"

"Oh yeah, the coffee-and-cake crew doesn't leave till about midnight." And I walk her to her car where she writes directions on an A&P receipt. When I walk back to the funeral home, my mother is standing there waiting for me.

"You know, she finally went to college. Nursing school. She works over at Mercy. And George and Hannah got divorced last year. I don't know what Hannah was waiting for."

When we get back to the house, my mother and aunts busy themselves with trays of lasagna and eggplant while my Uncle Jimmy cuts a 12-foot hero into 2-inch slices and we are together again. The loud, swirling movement of my family. Children in laps, uncles carrying folding chairs, aunts pulling foil trays in and out of the oven, all the while talking to and over one another.

"Did you hear," Claire says as she cuts a loaf of Italian bread into a basket, "that Peggy's mother is dying, unconscious in the hospital for the last month."

"Doesn't sound like she's ready to go yet," Tina says from the kitchen table where she is pouring soda for Aunt Moe and other relatives whose names I don't know.

"Yeah, that's it. That's what I say. The woman's like 65 pounds and she just won't die," Claire says.

"Don't worry, Mom," Tina says to Aunt Moe, "I'd have that

13

pillow over your head. It'd be done before you know it."

"Did you hear that, Vivian?" Aunt Moe screeches. "Don't you dare leave me alone with her in the hospital. She'd kill me. Can you believe such a thing?" And we all laugh.

My mother works her way around the kitchen, wiping counters, holding her hand under a wooden spoon she brings up to my mouth for me to taste her sauce—a taste as familiar as the scratchy wood against my tongue. After I swallow, I look up into her face and smile and nod slightly and just then I am six again, walking the table in a circle, folding napkins into triangles for each place setting, poised at the open silverware drawer as she counts forks out into my open hands.

Still, I watch her, the same way I watched her after the first time she got sick. Looking for some sign of strain, looking for anything, all the things you imagine are the problem when you are nine and your mother has her first nervous breakdown, and you're still young enough to think there are monsters under your bed without the finger of bathroom light falling into your doorway like a shield.

The last few years she's been looking well and she is slower, even though she refuses to take the Lithium the doctor prescribed for her after she was sick the last time. She will not take "pills" or "drugs." As if we would give her some illegal substance off a Queens street corner. She is stubborn, my mother, and the strongest being I know. Any one of us would have supported the idea of a little rest. The woman is 50, works 10 hours a day, 6 days a week and then seems surprised when at some point her body can no longer maintain her manic pace. The thing is, the last time, before anyone caught on that she was getting sick again, she hit a street sign on a road she traveled every day to and from work. My father said she cried in his arms for hours and when she stopped she had that scared, glassy look that tells us it's happened again.

Chapter 2

When we were 10, Jessie had a bike named Benny, a hairbrush named Harry and a pair of red, white and blue Keds named the Kraft Twins. On weekends she'd sleep over and as I'd be drifting off at night, I'd hear her climbing up the ladder to my top bunk. She'd crawl in next to me and sing me a lullaby in some language she'd made up. In the morning, when my mother came in to wake us and found Jessie in my bunk, we'd always tell her the same thing—nightmares—and my mother would look at me in that way of looking through me, but that was all.

One day, while I sat at the kitchen table doing my homework, she said, "I worry about that Jessie, all those nightmares. Her mother should take her to a doctor."

"Yeah, I suppose," I said, and she let it drop.

Jessie came to Redwood Elementary in the fifth grade and Mrs. Bass put her at the desk next to mine. She had the unusual combination of curly red hair but no freckles. Her hair was cut to the nape of her neck and she had a pink plastic headband that looked as if it would shatter into a million pieces at any moment as it labored to contain all those wild curls. She slid into her seat without a look at anyone, and all through the math lesson I watched her tear her pencil eraser into this fine layer of reddish dust on her desk. When Mrs. Bass called snack time, I returned from the coat closet with my baggy of Oreos and she had started in on the pencil itself, peeling the yellow paint off in thin strips, snackless. I watched her, growing increasingly more anxious, as if at any moment she might start peeling her own skin off, one layer at a time. My own 10-year-old heart forgot its shyness and I heard myself saying, "Hi. My name's Rose Salino." She swung around in her chair to look at me or, more accurately, to scan me for danger. She had the look I remembered in Tina's eye the time she got the wasp out of our tree house. She'd caught it in a paper cup with a coloring book held tightly over the top. She watched that cup all the way to the door as if she feared the wasp would transform itself into some Waspman superhero creature and burst from the cup.

Finally, Jessie seemed satisfied that I was not packing any icepicks or machine guns in my baggy and said, "My name's Jessie. Spencer."

"You didn't bring a snack, huh."

"No. I got up late."

"Want an Oreo?"

She nodded, reaching in and extracting a cookie. We sat in silence for a minute, eating our cookies, subtly checking each other out for leprosy. "Let's go outside," I said looking at the clock. We have 15 more minutes." We headed out the back door and on to the playground. I started walking away from the jungle gym, across the baseball field. When I looked over at her, I noticed the seams sticking out on her shirt.

"You know," I said, when we had made our way to the other side of the baseball field, "your shirt's inside out."

She pulled her shirt away from her waist to examine the seam for herself and then let it go, kicking at the dirt with the Kraft Twins, and the next thing I know this blush moved up her neck to her forehead and these tears were sliding down her cheeks.

"Hey, Jessie, don't cry. Hey, don't worry. The other kids didn't notice."

"Yes, they did!" she said, plopping herself onto the grass, her head in her hands.

"They did not. Joey Burke would've been standing on top of the monkey bars screaming his brains out like some lunatic if he'd seen your shirt was inside out," I said urgently. My heart was pounding by then because I knew why she sounded so doomed. All you needed was some moron boy to make fun of you your first day of school and you were ruined. I looked around to see if anyone was watching us, but Mrs. Bass was helping some girls twirl a jump rope and everyone else was either on the swings or lined up for the slide.

"Come on," I said, "hurry." I grabbed her hand, practically pulling her across the grass for a foot or two until she must have registered the tone in my voice, and we headed off at a run to the sideyard of the school and kept going till I had us behind the cafeteria dumpster. We stood panting, our backs against the dumpster, listening to the cafeteria workers' voices floating out of the open back door.

"Okay," I whispered, "take it off. Hurry up." And as she pulled her shirt off and flipped it right side out, she caught my eyes with a look that stopped me dead.

"Let's pretend," she whispered into my face, her hands grabbing my shoulders. "We're secret spies and we're trying to save all these rare tiger babies from the bad guys who stole them to sell to the Russians." I was fascinated. She looked as if she would surely explode, as if we indeed had some wooden crate, alive with priceless tiger babies. I felt like I was spinning.

Jessie did that, filled herself up with a feeling like a hose running full blast into a filled-up metal bucket and then, wham! the bucket careens into the bushes and the hose is loose, whipping around full blast again. Jessie off again, on to something else. Thing is, it never seemed to faze her, to be crying one minute, singing some secret song the next, then breaking a branch off a tree and slamming it against the trunk, cursing for all to hear.

But that time was the first time. The day Jessie Spencer stood before me, her whole body poised to rush off to save tiger babies, her eyes bright and flashing. The first time I claimed her for my own.

By that summer we had fallen together like two halves of something whole. Jessie sat, the first Saturday after the school year had ended, on a railroad tie that lined the flowerbeds of our backyard the length of the side driveway leading to the shed, waiting for me to emerge with my bicycle. It was dusty and dirty, the bell rusty in places from spending more days in the shed than out. I walked the bike out of the shed and into the sunlight and squinted, saying, "I don't ride much, you know."

The truth was that I was terrified of that bicycle. A huge rosebush, 10 feet long and taller than me, ran along the driveway, opposite the flowerbed. More than once I had started down that gentle slope of blacktop, wobbly, the soles of my sneakers dragging, and landed, howling, in that rosebush. It didn't help that Claire, four years old then, raced up and down, the sparkling fringe of her handlebar grips dancing. Claire was still, thankfully, too young to recognize me for the klutz I was. My struggles with the rosebush were just part of her days, like baloney sandwiches cut into four squares she munched with me at the child-sized picnic table in our backyard and the hide-and-seek we played with Tina and Eddy in the twilight of our summer nights. My klutziness humiliated me, though, and confused me. I couldn't figure out why other kids could whip around corners, skidding sideways to a stop with the panting breath of success, while I always felt like a circus act, trying to guide the too skinny wheels along a thread-like tightrope.

"Want to go swing on the swings?" I said, stalling for time. This was a device that often worked with Claire.

"No, come on, Rose. I've got a dollar. I'll buy you a cone at Baskin and Robbins."

I saw us mounting our bikes in front of Baskin and Robbins, cone in hand, Jessie weaving back and forth across the parking lot, steering with one hand, impatient and puzzled as my pathetic self juggled the handle bars and cone, finally stuffing the scoop in my mouth and pedaling toward her, the cone like some horn sticking out of my face.

She stood up then and walked over to me.

"You ride, don't you?"

"Not real good," I admitted.

"That's okay, Rose. We'll go slow," she said, like some little mother. She patted my arm. "Don't be afraid. I'm a good rider. I'll teach you. Get on and I'll hold it from the back."

I imagined her, one hand on the back of my seat, running behind me, pushing me left and right as I threatened to wipe out, like the father I had seen in the park with his son.

"I am *not* a baby," I shouted, desperate with shame.

"You're not a baby," she said plainly. "You're my best friend."

Up and down, up and down the driveway with Jessie running behind me, laughing and calling, "That's it, that's it! Way to go,

Rose!" and then letting go and running right behind me the whole time, never letting me get five feet ahead of her. All morning, until sweaty and stumbling from exhaustion, our arms thrown over each other's shoulders, we swayed over to the little picnic table where Vivian had put two paper plates of sandwiches and Dixie cups of Kool-Aid.

"Can I go to the Baskin and Robbins, Mom, and then go swimming at Jessie's?"

"Why don't you swim here?"

"Her pool's *heated*," I said. Vivian had put in our pool with the statement that it didn't need to be heated. It was hot enough out in the summer. The truth, of course, was that she barely had enough money for the pool itself. It was like that with Vivian, lots of things, as good or better than the other kids, but not quite right, not all done.

She called Hannah, Jessie's mother, to make sure she'd be home, and then called to us from the kitchen window that I could go *if* we waited an hour after we ate our cones so we didn't drown from stomach cramps and *if* we rode into town on the sidewalks, "*walking*," she said, "and I mean getting off and walking across each street, Rose."

I walked into Jessie's house that first time, fingers sticky with melted Mint Chip, my body damp, my T-shirt clinging from the ride from town and from keeping up with Jessie, who bent down low over her handle bars and flipped the front wheel of her bike up curbs, pausing at every intersection as I dutifully walked my bike across each street, grateful for the steady, solid ground beneath my feet.

Her mother told me a story once about Jessie climbing out her window one night at the age of three. After the whole family searched the house for about half an hour, one of her brothers spotted her sitting up on the roof, singing softly to herself. They all started yelling and screaming from the yard for her to come down "right now," and according to her mother, Jessie just sort of looked down at them with this puzzled look and kept singing. Finally, her father had to go up to the roof and carry her in through the window.

It seems this was about the time they started tying her to her crib with shoelaces, which is a picture as vivid in my mind as if I was there, little chubby wrists and ankles pulling against the white cotton. In her mother's defense, Jessie, in her pajamas, was also taking the family dog for walks at 3 in the morning, routinely being brought home by the police, and hurling her little body into the swimming pool whenever she got the chance. Honestly, what do you do with a kid like that? And the truth is, she used to untie herself anyway.

Her house was a huge, sprawling split-level in the Mill Creek area, a wealthy section of town with high-hedged properties and manicured lawns. It was where Vivian had planned for us to live, but at the last minute she'd had to reconsider and we'd ended up where we were, a new development with lower-priced but still nice houses, of ambitious and hardworking blue-collar families.

Jessie pushed open the front door and I followed her in. The air conditioning hit my body like a wave. By the time we were up the stairs and into the living room I was shivering pleasantly, my arms cold and clammy.

"Mom?" Jessie called down the hallway where a TV blared a commercial for Downy Fabric Softener. There was a scratching and yipping from the kitchen and suddenly three black puppies came skidding across the linoleum floor at us.

"Babies!" Jessie cried and fell to the carpet, both hands petting and pushing over the puppies that were now hopping around her, yelping and panting, "Babies, babies," she purred at them. "Come pet them," she said to me, and I sat and scooped one into my lap, pulling it up to my face. It smelled milky and musky and wiggled in my arms.

We never had dogs and I was part scared and part awed, watching Jessie, now rolling on the floor, the other two puppies leaping over her, licking her face.

"They're so cute," I said, letting mine go and watching it climb onto Jessie's stomach and walk up her like a sidewalk. "Are they yours?"

"They're my mother's," she said. "She breeds Newfoundlands. These are all sold. In a couple of weeks we have to ship them out to the people who bought them."

"Where's the mom?"

"Right there." She pointed into the kitchen and what I saw made my heart jolt. I was standing before I knew it, my hand on the end of the staircase rail, poised to run for my life. I was terrified of dogs. And this dog was huge.

"That's Sadie," Jessie said. "Come here, Sadie." And Sadie slowly got to her feet and began to lumber toward us. She was, I was sure, some mix of black bear and water buffalo, definitely bigger and heavier than me, with long black fur and a mouth I envisioned snapping off my leg in one jagged bloody chomp.

"Does she, um, bite?" I asked.

"No way," Jessie said, surprised, swinging around to look at me. "Are you scared?"

"No," I lied, beginning to back down the stairs. "Make her stop, Jessie."

"Sit, Sadie," she yelled quickly, and Sadie plopped her rear end on the floor and looked over at Jessie, her tongue hanging out, as if to say, "Is that good?"

"It's okay, Rose. Sadie doesn't bite. She doesn't even growl. You can even pull her tail, see?" And Jessie reached over and gave Sadie's tail a sharp yank as I watched horrified, hearing the crunch of Jessie's arm between the dog's teeth. Sadie scooted her bottom over an inch and kept looking at Jessie, almost grinning, it seemed.

"They call Newfoundlands the gentle giants," she said. "The dog in *Peter Pan* was really a Newfoundland in the book. They changed it to a Saint Bernard for the movie. Saint Bernards aren't nearly as nice, really," she went on, as if she was giving some report, standing in front of our class. "Sadie's usually outside in her run. We've got her two sisters, too, Grace and Molly."

I nodded, seeing a whole herd of them milling around the backyard, feeding off a wallaby carcass.

"You still scared?"

"A little."

"Want me to put them out?" I nodded, and she got up, calling Sadie, and mother and pups followed her into the kitchen and out of sight, and I heard the sliding glass door open and then shut. "They're gone," she called, and I walked into the kitchen.

I looked around then, finally seeing Jessie's house. The kitchen was long, with black-and-white linoleum tiles and a stove that was glass-topped with the burners drawn on in white. Sliding glass doors led out to a backyard with a built-in pool on the left and three fenced dog-runs on the right; chaise lounges and various pool toys, an inner tube with a horse head, a multicolored beach ball and a snorkel were scattered along the lawn. The living room had one wall of bookshelves from ceiling to floor and a baby grand piano with sheet music stacked on the top and above the keys. At least a dozen Coca-Cola cans lay warm and flat on counters, shelves, tables and even on the piano bench; I also saw books, dog-eared, stacked under the coffee table, opened and upside down, on the kitchen table, and a *New York Times* part unfolded, part refolded, with a coffee cup on top, a layer of white scum floating on the cold brown liquid. It was 2 in the afternoon and a plate of toast crust sat in the sink.

"Where's your mom?"

I urgently wanted someone's mother to come in and get this mess cleaned up.

"Probably in her room, reading," Jessie said, opening the freezer and peering into it, as if reading some message off the ice dispenser. "Want a push-up pop?"

"Sure, " I said, knowing for certain now that this was another world, an unkempt world of furry but harmless monsters, like the one in the *Rudolph the Red-Nosed Reindeer* special after his teeth were extracted by the elf, where 10-year-olds monitored their own sugar intake.

"Here, take these," Jessie said, stacking cartons of frozen fried chicken, creamed spinach and other pre-made dinners into my arms. "I *know* we have push-up pops. Okay, wait, wait, move—I'm gonna stick this in the sink," she said, as I moved out of her way and she hoisted a plastic bag with something black in it, the size of a loaf of bread.

"What's that?" I peered into the sink, the outside of the bag growing frosty and wet.

"Puppy," she said, matter of factly, her head deep in the freezer now. "Got 'em!"

"That's a puppy?" I whispered, backing away from the sink. "You've got a dead puppy in the freezer?!"

"It came out dead. My mother's going to have an autopsy, see why it died." She handed me a wrapped push-up pop.

"Gross! Next to your food?"

"It's in a bag, Rose."

"Who cares why it died?"

"These are expensive dogs. She needs to know. Don't look at it if it grosses you out."

"Doesn't it gross *you* out?" I asked, as Jessie picked it up and shoved it back in the freezer along with the creamed spinach and the other cartons.

"I don't know." She shrugged. "I guess I'm just used to it."

"Yuck! You don't have like kittens or bunnies in there, too?"

"She only breeds dogs."

"That's good," I muttered, my body giving off little shivers as we stood there unwrapping our pops.

"Want to meet my mom?" And we headed down the hallway toward the sound of the TV. "Mom?" she called. The bedroom was almost the size of the kitchen, the bed unmade with a nightgown flung over the crumpled covers. Another sliding glass door out to a deck. The bed and a couple of tall dressers with books and socks and photos and change mixed together on the top, a layer of dust, like white fur, coating it all. Hannah, Jessie's mother, came out of the bathroom then.

"You must be Rose," she said, standing in front of me, smiling down at me, about nine feet tall. The first thing I thought was that she was the longest mother I had ever seen—long legs, long hair with streaks of gray swept up off her face and held by a tortoise barrette and falling down her back to wisps that swayed across her behind. She had on a pair of cut-off denim shorts and a faded tie-dyed T-shirt. Even her fingers, dangling like vines, the part of her body that fell squarely across my line of vision, were long. She was older than my mother, had wrinkles where Vivian did not, but even that first time I thought she looked like some oversized baby-sitter; Jessie's blue child eyes in a grown-up's body.

Over time, I got to know Hannah, watched her at the dinner table rattle on to Dr. Spencer about the ozone, or the dogs, or her novel that she'd been writing since before Jessie was born, with Dr. Spencer sipping his Scotch, nodding, sometimes absently, sometimes irritated and sometimes kind, and me watching her frosted pink mouth—the only place on her face with make-up.

Jessie's father was a surgeon, a big straight man, with no hint of cuddliness like my own father, older and sterner and scary to me for his quiet reserve and a voice that spoke in orders, every question and statement like some important request for instruments in an operating room. Jessie always grew strangely smaller around him, her funny faces and bursting energy wrapped tightly away when he entered a room. His office was a white stucco building two blocks from the Baskin and Robbins, and we'd see people coming in and out on our way to get a cone. We went in a few times when we wanted ice-cream money, but it was usually Joyce, his nurse, who would pull out her wallet and give us a five-dollar bill. She was slim and taunt and reminded me of a freshly made bed in her white nurse's uniform. She wasn't married and obviously didn't eat ice cream, otherwise she'd have known we could buy cones for a week on five dollars.

Jessie had two brothers—Butch, who was 19, and Chuck, who was 17—but their rooms were on the bottom floor and they wandered in and out of the house as if they weren't quite sure they actually lived there. Sometimes, when Jessie and I first met, I'd see them coming in and out of the house with some girl or car part. I wasn't used to brothers, especially ones as old as Butch and Chuck. I heard them arguing a few times with Dr. Spencer, once about their hair and another time about being out all night. By mid-summer, they'd moved out and rented an apartment together in Rocky Point. I can't say it made much of a difference, the way they seemed like extras in a movie.

I often thought what that house needed was a mother and day-dreamed about lending out one of my aunts—even Aunt Moe would be an improvement. Hannah, who got lost in her own kitchen, finding herself paging through an Eddie Bauer catalog, our tuna sandwiches half made, the bread bare on the plates, the bowl of tuna salad waiting expectantly to be lunch, seemed too glasslike for the real world.

I watched Hannah, like some *National Geographic* special on rainforest tribes, a mother so alien to me, fascinating. And I watched Jessie worry over her, her face stern, her finger to her mouth, shushing me as she opened the front door when I came to play on mornings after Hannah had been up all night with a migraine or just depressed. Hannah's depression was a real illness, one that came with orange, plastic prescription bottles kept next to the kitchen sink and in her medicine cabinet; bottles with her name written on it, 'Hannah Spencer' and '2 in the morning with food' and long, funny names, names like Valium, Pamolar and Elavil. Unlike Vivian, who seemed to disappear from me for periods of time, years apart, Hannah seemed to *be* this thing, this depression, soft and cloudlike, slow and swaying. She was unpredictable, and Jessie and her father had seemed to settle into a routine of working around her. Because you could never know what you'd find in a room filled with Hannah, they had grown flexible: Gleeful and praising when she set steak and Béarnaise sauce on the dinner table, aglow with accomplishment and a pure, feathery joy, and all shoulder shrugs and resigned low voices when, at 6 in the evening, Dr. Spencer came home from the hospital to find her still in bed and the house a shambles of half-done projects—the dishwasher open and partially unloaded, milk warm and sweating in its plastic container on the counter, books and catalogs and opened mail everywhere, the stereo on and the record spinning, flinging tiny particles of dust in the air.

The difference between our mothers always seemed capsulated to me in the way Vivian and Hannah wore tie-dye. Vivian wore tie-dye as a fashion statement; Hannah, as a political statement. Vivian would examine its pattern and colors and declare you could most certainly make the identical garment for 50 to 75 cents, and churn out about 100 in no time at all at a significant, and most importantly, tax-free profit. Hannah would examine the same garment and spend about two days assessing the shades for their proper placement on the color wheel, chronicling the history of fabric art, in between steeping mugfuls of herb tea.

Vivian strategized. Hannah contemplated. And while it was true that poor Hannah wouldn't have lasted a day in my mother's world, trampled by the pace of Vivian's frenetic accomplishment, I can tell you Vivian doesn't know how to begin to find the door to Hannah's world. In between the lines of Vivian's casual, veiled jabs at Hannah, jabs that equated contemplation with laziness and freedom with neglect, was an envy and hunger for that door, one of the places in my mother that I wished I didn't see.

That afternoon we dropped our shorts and shirts in inside-out heaps on Hannah's bedroom carpet and headed out the sliding glass doors to the pool. I kept glancing up from the pool at first, to the kitchen and bedroom, expecting to see Hannah watching us through the glass. I finally gave up. Sadie, Grace and Molly lounged at the edge of the pool, watching us swim like surrogate nannies, and I swam anxiously, my eyes open under water, still distrustful of their burliness, on the lookout for Sadie who I was sure was waiting for the right moment to pluck me out of the pool like some trout and drag me, my body leaving a thick streak of wetness, across the backyard, where under a tree she would share me with Molly and Grace.

We swam all afternoon until dinnertime when Vivian called, and Jessie and I begged for me to spend the night. Vivian came by with a little bag of pajamas, a change of clothes and my toothbrush, and I ran from the pool to her for a quick hug that left her whole front dark. I watched happily as Vivian and Hannah disappeared into the kitchen talking about us, the words *growing* and *darling* and *hungry* floating out the sliding glass door and to the pool before Hannah pushed the door shut.

Night Diving

▼

When I think of Jessie and me, more often than not it is in that pool, pictures in my mind like photos in an album. It was one of those big, built-in pools with a diving board at the deep end. On the summer nights that were the hottest, the kind where the humidity wraps around you, all thick, Jessie and I lived in that pool. Jessie always had a special love for the water. That summer we started to play this game we called Little Mermaids, from the book we'd read in our summer library club, the kind where you got little stickers in a theme to place on your cardboard file, with the names of the books you read on one side and a picture on the other—one summer an ocean picture with stickers of whales and fish and boats, another summer a farm picture with stickers of cows and a farmer and his wife. All that first summer we pretended we were mermaids for hours at a time, emerging all wrinkly-fingered to eat dinner in our wet bathing suits, sitting on towels to keep from getting Hannah's kitchen chairs mildewy.

Once we got to junior high, we graduated to this game we called Night Diving that we only played after it got dark. We'd go out to the backyard and turn off the porch light so that the only light was the one big headlight-like brightness that shone out of the deep end of the pool. The way the game worked was that you'd dive off the diving board and swim underwater as far as you could before you ran out of breath. Both of us could make it to the other end, and then it was a matter of how far back we could make it. I usually got to the end of the shallow end, right to the place where the warm, heated water started to get cooler as it got deeper. We'd do it over and over again, diving in, the pool water sucking up our bodies and wrapping around us like some soupy cloud, the chlorine smell all around and the darkness of the water like being at the bottom of the sea, us swimming toward that one light that turned the blackness of the water into neon.

I always dove in head first, as far out as I could, but Jessie would do these handstands on the diving board or these back flips I had to shut my eyes for, even though I would still imagine her cracking her head on the board, blood spilling out like cherry Kool-Aid in streams from her head.

We'd go back into the house finally, wrapped in towels, shivering as the air conditioning hit our bodies, and climb into sleeping bags, alternating who slept on the couch and who slept on the floor, with our hair wet and big T-shirts on, exhausted. It was one of those junior-high summers during one when Jessie told me in a downcast whisper, as we were sliding into our sleeping bags, about Dr. Spencer coming into her room late at night. She was crying and I climbed out of my sleeping bag and slipped my arm around her waist. What I remember is my mind racing and then whispering into her hair.

"Lock your door." And looking straight into her eyes, "Tell your mother."

Jessie nodded and the next day I asked, "Did you do it?" and she nodded again. It became this thing that faded off somewhere I couldn't see but changed us anyway. We still lived and grew up together in this world of tiger babies, mermaids and night dives. We just didn't talk about it, neither of us knowing how to gather and place our words.

Chapter 3

My father is the smell of gasoline, powerful brown arms and hands, prickly cheeks. He loves Vivian so quietly and easily it's as if he doesn't notice, doesn't care that she's a handful. Once when I was eight she told him she wanted a built-in pool for Claire and me in the backyard. We were eating toast and scrambled eggs at the kitchen table, the morning sun making stripes along our plates. Vivian, who had been up since 4, was folding a load of laundry at one end of the table. He started to protest. We don't have the money. We have a perfectly good above-the-ground pool with a beautiful redwood deck he had meticulously sawed and nailed and stained.

"You can like it or not, Tommy," she told him. "One day you'll come home and there'll be a big hole in the backyard."

One day there was.

Tommy has only himself to blame. I've heard Vivian tell the story endless times about how on their first date, when they were both 18, he told Vivian, "I'm going to marry you."

"You're crazy," she said. "You don't even know me."

Two years later he did, and nine months later there was me. There are pictures of Tommy with me, looking like a 16-year-old boy with a new Mustang. Tommy is a plain, good ol' guy, responsible, accommodating, even-tempered. I figure the even-tempered part was what drew Vivian to him. There's hardly an even-tempered bone in Vivian's body. What my father has, he has by virtue of hard work and a lifetime of doing what's right. On their wedding day the plant he worked at as an airplane mechanic closed down. His uncle loaned him $3,000 to buy a Shell station.

I'd go to work with him sometimes when I was five, six and seven and wander around looking up under cars on lifts, handing people the change from their gasoline, and playing with the adding machine in the back room. He was handsome back then, with his hard arms and dark eyes, and he'd flirt with the old ladies and smile shyly at the young ones.

We always locked up for 10 minutes at lunchtime and walked over to the deli for sardines and white bread and mustard to make sardine sandwiches. He'd open the soda machine with a key and get us two bottles of Coke. He so lovingly prepared those sandwiches, the smell of the sardines and gasoline around us and the glass Coke bottle sweating in my hand, the whole time telling me how good lunch would taste.

When we closed up at night, we'd both stand at the big sink in the garage, me on an overturned bucket, dipping a hand into the soap cream so he could wash away the grease, and I could imagine, in those moments, how it must be to have his thick hands. We'd dry our hands on a clean rag, and he still always had little slits of grease underneath his fingernails.

He'd open the cash register with this key that made the drawer fly open with a bell, and he'd put all the bills in a brown leather zip-up bag, leaving the coins and the drawer open. One time I asked him why he left the register open.

"Don't want them breaking my machine when they rob me."

We'd climb into his pickup and I'd wait for him to say, "Put on your seatbelt," just because I liked hearing it, gruff and loving, his hand waiting on the ignition key to hear the click of my belt.

He can fix anything he can get those hands around, anything he can pry apart or unscrew with the force of his arms. Feelings, foggy and misty, elude him.

I had this Thumbelina doll when I was five, with a pull cord on her back and a music box in her tummy that played a little song I can still hear . . . *Thumbelina, Thumbelina, tiny little thing, Thumbelina dance, Thumbelina sing, Thumbelina, it doesn't matter if you're very small, 'cause when your heart is full of love you're nine feet tall . . .*

One summer I started giving Thumbelina baths in my plastic wading pool and by July her insides were rotted and her pull string hung limp. Tommy came home from work and I thrust the doll at him wordlessly as Vivian explained the cause of her demise.

"We'll have to do surgery," he said.

We sat out on the back cement stoop, the sun an orange, the cement still warm from the day, as he cut her open and pulled the goopy stuffing and the little plastic box out of her insides. He took a green rectangular sponge from under the kitchen sink and pressed it into her, then pulled the cloth tightly together and sewed her up, his hands fumbling with the needle. Her held her up to me smiling. Her plastic arms and legs hanging off her rectangular body, Thumbelina and I went off to bed, but even with the shades pulled it was light in my room, so I ran my fingers along her stitches and sang her song to her until she fell asleep.

▼

I was nine the first time my mother got sick, leaving me with an emptiness that clawed at me like some little trapped animal. It was as if some faceless man had taken her away in the middle of the night and because I could not yet feel where she ended and I began, had taken me with them. I awoke one morning to find her shell and a hugeness that grew louder and louder and more panicky inside me. The first aloneness.

I was beginning to grow that winter, in that awkward prepubescent way. Clothes were suddenly too tight around my hips and too loose around my waist. My hair, long and curly and frizzy, was a constant reminder of how out of control I felt. I have never asked Vivian what it was like for her those first few times. I know now that there must have been a gradual decline, the signs along the way that we now see to warn us, but then I didn't notice until the change was complete. For me, she was my mother. Someone I could hear pulling towels out of the linen closet as I awoke in the morning. This constant, powerful and ever-moving force of my days and nights. She was everywhere, straightening bedspreads, closing drawers, her fingers in my hair, pulling it neat and smooth. There was a time when I thought she didn't sleep. I would wake in the middle of the night, sit up in my bed and call, "Mom, can I have a drink of water?" and then wait in the dark for her to appear with a plastic bathroom cup. Nothing would dare hurt me. I was certain every being on the planet was as in awe and terrified of her as I.

Then one day I come home from school to find Aunt Moe's car in the driveway. She is a nurse, back then working the afternoon and evening shift, so as I walk up our driveway I can feel my heart pounding up against my coat. The house is still and I stand in the foyer for a moment before I bound up the stairs two at a time, almost knocking my aunt down as I round the hallway to my parents' room, gasping.

"Where's Mom?"

"In her room. She's sleeping. She's not feeling well," she says quietly, reaching behind her and closing the bedroom door. My throat feels like it is closing too, tears rising. I want in that room.

"Rose, she just fell asleep. Now come downstairs with me and we'll find you a snack."

"No." Our eyes lock and my aunt is angry and something else is in those eyes that I now know is fear.

My Aunt Moe is a big, lumpy woman with a crooked nose and hair frizzy like mine. My mother took her out sometimes and showed her the best clothes for her and cut and styled her hair, but the next day my aunt always showed up looking like the survivor of a week-long hostage situation. I knew she was harmless—actually would have taken a bullet for any of us—but she was as out of control as my mother was over-controlled and it frightened me to be alone with her. On the one hand, I knew she would not let anyone hurt me. On the other hand, I worried she'd be too busy rooting around in that overflowing pocketbook of hers to see the enemy approaching. At that moment, though, all I could see was that door.

"Don't you dare say no to me. Turn yourself around and get down those stairs."

In one move my hand's on the doorknob, turning it, and I'm standing in the room.

"Mom?" She's asleep or she has been. She lifts her head from the pillow and must see my terror because she starts to sit up.

"Come here, Rose," she says, and I'm next to her, practically on top of her, trembling. She murmurs into my hair, "It's okay, it's okay, honey, it's okay," in the voice that always has quieted me before but that day does not.

"Moe, will you get her a snack? There's some date nut bread

that she likes and cream cheese on the second shelf of the fridge," and then she takes my face in her hands and looks at me hard. "Mommy's going to rest a little before dinner." I look back at her and can see that look she gets when she's concerned and protecting us. And with that I feel I can leave her.

I find myself sitting at the kitchen table watching Aunt Moe nervously opening cupboards and drawers, standing too long in front of the refrigerator, moving like some nightmare in silence, and at some point I realize she is talking to me.

"It wasn't just that he'd throw her down the basement stairs," Aunt Moe is saying as she spreads cream cheese on bread and puts the plate before me. "It's that she'd get back up and elbow past him, he'd still be standing in the doorway, and she'd yell right into his face, Rose, not two inches from his nose, she'd yell, 'You leave me alone, Tony. You're not my father. I'll go out with who I want.' And down the stairs she'd go again and what else could we think? There's Tony, he's got fifty pounds on her, and she gets right back up again and right into his face, yelling, 'Tony, you son of a bitch, Daddy will kill you when I tell him.' Oh sure, you could understand her calling him a son of a bitch, but sane people, Rose, any person playing with a full deck, would know to at least put a locked door between you and some guy who just threw you down a flight of basement stairs before you call him a son of a bitch, even if he is your brother. And like I said, it wasn't just that, it was the days they'd come home from work and find their clothes thrown all over the front lawn and more coming out the windows and Vivian, she'd be screaming, 'Animals! You're all animals! I spent all day Saturday doing this laundry and you throw it all on the floor like nothing!' They'd be standing there, all six of our brothers, watching the clothes coming out the windows, just shaking their heads. 'She's crazy,' they'd say. 'She's gotta be crazy. She knows we could kill her, any one of us.'"

I don't know why she's telling me this. I can't picture my mother any other way than the way I've always known her. The woman that Aunt Moe is talking about is a stranger and the woman up in my mother's bed could be that same stranger, or some other stranger, even scarier than the woman my aunt is describing.

Aunt Moe is sitting now across the kitchen table, coffee cup in hand. I look at her and know something is terribly wrong. It is 4 in the afternoon, and I have seen her too many times, screeching up our driveway in her Lincoln, jumping out and calling from the front door, "Vivian, I'm late for work. I'm leaving those Hostess SnowBalls Tommy wanted and those pillows. Call you tomorrow, love." And the door would slam. I could get up from the TV and fish around in the pile she left and there it would all be, the SnowBalls, the pillows and other random items she had taken from the hospital, bedpans, antibiotics, little packets of Tylenols, toilet paper. I heard my Uncle Tony tell my mother once that Aunt Moe liked her best, that all he ever got was the toilet paper. My mother had denied this, stating she had seen my aunt with a bag of Ring Dings from the Hostess Outlet in the back seat the last time she went to visit him. My uncle was right, though. My Aunt Moe loves my mother the best. I can tell: She looks at my mother the way my mother looks at me.

I know, as I eat my sandwich and stare into the backyard, that my aunt isn't going to work and in my family you only miss work when there's something terrible. She is still talking in this frantic voice, on and on, and partly I am not listening and partly I am, because her voice is familiar and I am starting to feel desperate for familiar.

"What I'm telling you is my sister has been pushing from the start and who knows why, 'cause it's not like she ever got a chance to know anything better. We weren't the only house on the block with eight kids and no money. Our Mama didn't care, ah maybe she did once, but eight kids, six of them boys, one baby dead, you get tired, Rose. Our Mama got tired way before Vivian was even born. With Papa living in a dream world, someone has to be practical, Rose, and, Rose, practicality is tiring. So you should know it was chaos by the time Vivian came along. What you have to imagine is big heaping laundry baskets full of socks and undershirts. By the time a woman washes all that, you can't expect her to starch and iron shirts. You asked Mama to iron a shirt, she'd say, 'Here, give me that,' and she'd sit on it to make it flat while she's pulling the ends off string beans. Vivian would get crazy. 'You're disgusting!' But she wasn't. She was tired. Then when Vivian was 16 she went into a regular cleaning frenzy. The house was transformed. I'm telling you this so you'll know where it came from, so you shouldn't be so hard on her."

Aunt Moe pulls me from the kitchen chair onto her lap. She holds me with her soft, lumpy arms and I melt into my aunt's lap in that way small, quiet girls have of doing.

"Look, I know it's hard with her. *Rose, empty the garbage,* even when it's not full. *Rose, brush your hair*, drawers always having to be straightened and closed. Beds always made. But Italian shoes at $60 a pair and little cashmere dresses. You're her princess. She's needed that for you, Rose. A calmness, you know? A calmness. And a certainty your life would be different. And her life, too. You've never lived in a house like that. You don't know. You only know nice. She still talks about that house like it haunts her."

I lean into my aunt's breast, thinking of plastic on living room couches, how nice and cold it feels in the summer, how it sticks to my legs.

"Your mother is very sick or exhausted. What I mean, Rose,

is it's very important, very important that your mother rests." And she looks at me as if she has just seen me, has just realized to whom she is talking. Inside, I am falling inside like snow, like flakes that hit the pavement and dissolve into slickness, into nothing. "Your father will be home in half an hour. He's picking up Claire. He's picking up pizza."

Aunt Moe climbs into her car and blows me a kiss from the end of the driveway and I watch until her car disappears.

I sit in front of the TV. *The Brady Bunch, The Partridge Family, F-Troop* and still no pizza. I am hungry. I go into the kitchen and stand staring into the pantry, finally deciding on peanut butter and jelly.

Peanut butter on one side, jelly on the other. I smack the two pieces of bread together and for that instant I am happy and proud. This is the way I've always had my peanut butter and jelly but I've never really done it by myself before. I'll just sit on the counter and watch TV. But I stand staring at the sandwich on the plate, knife in my hand, knowing I cannot do it, not as good. Not four perfect squares. And so I stand there. Not wanting to cut, knowing I am hungry, but also knowing I just can't eat some crooked sandwich—not today.

But Mommy is tired and I shouldn't bother her. Aunt Moe said so. Mommy is tired and needs to rest. I stand there.

Finally, I go up. If she is awake I will ask her. If she is asleep, I will wait for pizza. Upstairs her room is dark. I switch on the hall light.

"Rose?"

"Mommy?"

"Get the door."

"What, Mommy?"

"There's someone knocking at the front door, honey. Go down and see who it is."

I put the sandwich and the knife down on the nightstand and listen for knocking, not hearing it.

"Rose?"

"I'll get it, Mom."

I run down the stairs then stand, staring at the front door. I switch on the porch light and slowly open the door. I stand, scanning the front yard, watching the wind make shadows with the trees. That is all I see. I slam the door and run upstairs.

In the half-light I can see her, lying on her back, eyes closed.

"There was no one there, Mom."

"Hmm, honey?"

"No one at the door. Mommy, could you cut this for me?"

I pick up the plate, reaching out with it. She opens her eyes and looks at me.

"I can't do it," I say.

She shifts over to one elbow and reaches for the knife. I put the plate on the bed. I watch her cut, once, twice, and hand me the plate, falling into the pillow, closing her eyes.

"Come here, Rose."

I climb onto the bed and she reaches out, curling an arm around me, pulling me against her.

"Mommy loves you." And we lie there for a moment. I can smell her in her pillow and on her nightgown and yet to me she seems somehow foreign. "Go down and watch TV, honey. Did you do your homework?"

"Yes."

"Good girl. Bring it up later. I want to see it."

I pick up the plate from the bed and start downstairs, then stop at the nightstand light, staring at the sandwich. It is crooked.

"Answer the door, honey. Someone's knocking again."

I don't know how to tell my father, when he finds me sitting in a corner of my dark room with my uneaten sandwich, why I didn't answer when he called for me to come down for pizza. I am clearly at my limit, though, and he tells me I can skip my bath, knowing how much I hate baths, how I spend many a dinner attempting to weasel an extra bathless day out of my mother. I can't explain to him why that concession doesn't make me happy either; why I sit cross-legged staring at the grimy soles of my feet, crying until he finally picks me up out of my chair, taking the pizza from my hand and placing it on the paper plate, and carries me to bed. He pulls only the sheet over me and sits on the bed.

"This day is over for you," he says, rubbing my back softly, and I look up at him and hold him tight in my gaze, the whole time crying wordless, angry sobs that turn to muffled sniffles and, finally, sleep.

The following night my mother still lies in bed, soft and vague. I pad up the steps to my parents' room. I sneak into her room, a room that seems to stay dark even in the day, and just stand, leaning up against the door, watching her breathe until some aunt's hand pushes open the bedroom door and reaches in for me. My aunts seem to be everywhere. Aunts with red eyes loading the dishwasher and folding clothes out of the dryer while they talk to my father in whispers that are loud enough to betray their fear. Aunt Moe in blue scrubs, feeding a cousin spoonfuls of Gerber. She spent the first night on the living-room couch, her head on the hard throw pillow, a crocheted blanket half covering her. Claire spends a week at my grandmother's, taking baths at night with Tina, sharing the double bed in her sewing room, their little heads at either end. My grandmother has tried, with her promises of warm chocolate pudding and doll dresses, to get me to go, too, but I'm too big to scoop up and I threaten to scream.

That morning I walk past Aunt Moe who is sleeping on the couch, into the kitchen, see the dishes on the counter and dash quietly out the back screen door she has left unlocked. My mother

41

checks every door every night as if some deranged killer would check the door, find it locked, and think to himself, "This is a house where the children are cherished and protected. I'll try the next one."

I am irritable. Aunt Rose with her rambling and the clutter she carries in that big old pocketbook of hers only makes me more so. I want my mother. I want to be sitting up on the kitchen counter with my mother pulling my hair into a perfect part and two pony-tails. I want to fish through the mayonnaise jar of covered rubber bands with plastic balls and flowers on them and pick out my favorites, even if I have to put them back because she tells me they don't match.

Chapter 4

We were 12, knots in our hair, lanky, sporting the training bras Vivian had taken us to get at Gimbel's the week before. The bras came in cardboard boxes with pictures of girls with long straight shiny blond hair and pale pink skin. We wore those bras like a secret, waiting, waiting because we knew the possibilities.

Dr. Spencer had a subscription to *Playboy*. The magazines arrived every month wrapped in brown paper, and he kept them neatly stacked in a metal cabinet in their bedroom.

"Wanna see something?" Jessie asked one day and led me into the room. The door of the cabinet rattled when she opened it, and she took a magazine out, pulled open the centerfold, and then did the same thing with another magazine, and another. Right then and there I knew the world was divided into two worlds: Women with breasts that swung to their belly buttons and the rest of the women in the world. I wanted to turn the page and see what else there was but I didn't want to seem like a total pervert, so I sat there, speechless, my eyes darting from one set of breasts to the next.

"What's the matter?"

"Nothing."

"Forget it."

Jessie sighed and put them all away, mistaking my awe for prudishness.

I got over it. We graduated from the centerfolds to reading the fantasies, sprawled on the floor with cans of Coca-Cola and bags of Nacho Cheese Doritos.

"Here, here, listen to this one . . ."

Somehow I knew not to ask how she knew the magazines were there in the first place, knew that Dr. Spencer didn't accidentally leave one lying around the bathroom. We especially liked the question-and-answer sections; it was there that we learned about aphrodisiacs. We rummaged through Hannah's kitchen in search of tins of caviar and oysters and settled on sardines and hard-boiled eggs, sitting on Jessie's bedroom floor and eating them with our fingers.

"You feel anything?"

"I'm not sure."

We sat there in silence.

"Let me try something," Jessie said and leaned over and by the time I realized she meant to actually kiss me, she was doing it.

"Hey!"

"Come on. Try."

And since she said it like I would only be the biggest bummer known to man if I refused, I nodded. It's not like I was raised by wolves. I knew what a French kiss was and pretty much all the other stuff that came after that, but it's one thing to *talk* about it and it's another thing to do it. Still, it felt good and Jessie seemed to know what she was doing, seemed to be liking it too. But when she put her hand down the front of my pants I freaked a little and I had to go and ruin it.

"I don't think we should be doing this."

"Why not?"

"Jessie!"

I started shaking my head at her. Partly I was feeling a little jealous that she clearly knew what she was doing and I was fumbling around like I had ten thumbs, and partly it wasn't exactly escaping me that we were two girls making out.

"We shouldn't be doing this."

"But I want to."

After that we started boiling our own eggs—and the Mill Creek Market carried caviar and tins of oysters. We agreed they were disgusting but swallowed them like the purple Robitussin that Vivian gave me for fevers, convinced they were the cause of the tingling that ran up our backs, our breathing when we'd take turns touching each other, leaning up against her bedroom door so no one could walk in and find us. And we waited, waited to see what our chests had in store for us, hoping against hope that we'd luck out better than our mothers, though we knew genes were not on our side.

▼

We were in the sixth grade then, on the second floor of our elementary school—the big kids, changing classes for the first time. We had different homerooms and mostly different classes except for art every Tuesday and Thursday, and gym every Monday, Wednesday and Friday.

Gym was blue, snap-up regulation uniforms in a polyester blend. We'd line up for teams looking like a row of inmates, Jessie and I shoving some pliable, unpopular girl between us when we counted off—one, two, one, two—for teams. Once the game started—usually kickball in the gym in the winter and field hockey or softball outside when the weather got warmer—we'd wait with the tense watchfulness of hostages for Miss Olsen, the gym teacher, to turn her back, and we'd dart out the gym door into the hall. We always went to the same place, the women teachers' bathroom on the first floor. We'd sneak into the last stall, the one that had a ledge of green tile we could sit on by the frosted windows, with the stall door locked. Then we'd sit in silence, except for the occasional whispers, until some teacher came in to pee. That was the best part, hearing a teacher in the other stall, hiding, bug-eyed, barely breathing until we heard the bathroom door swing open and shut with a thump. Then we'd head back to the gym.

It gave us a thrill we couldn't explain and we did it over and over, creating stories in which we were girl spies, gathering secrets from the Russians, secrets written on damp paper towels, deciphered from the Morse code of bouncing balls on the playground we could hear through the window. Once Watergate broke, we became Woodward and Bernstein (Jessie's family talked in heated urgent voices of such things at the dinner table), saving the country from Nixon, who was also stealing babies straight out of their strollers in Central Park to sell to the Russians who needed cute American babies because the ones we had seen in the film in social studies class were so unfortunate-looking.

The women's bathroom on the second floor, our other secret school place, wedged between our homerooms, was perfectly situated. The sixth grade lined up for lunch out in the hall and then descended down the stairs in two lines, looking like Madeline and her orphans. As the lines headed down the stairs, past the bathroom, we'd duck in the door and scramble up on the ledge, snap the lock in place and eat our lunch.

Jessie got $10 allowance a week, and it was supposed to be for buying hot lunch at school with a few dollars left over for our movies and ice cream cones, but she usually brought a lunch that she made herself. By then I had gotten over the shock of Jessie's lunches, looked forward to them, lunches completely lacking any nutritional value: a bag of Doritos, a sleeve of Girl Scout cookies, a couple of space bars. Vivian was still making my lunches then, a mortifying ensemble of healthy food: a sandwich, a piece of fruit, three cookies—in a paper lunch bag with my name on it. It was enough to make you die of embarrassment. I could see, I was sure the entire class could see, that this was clearly a second-grader's lunch—*three* cookies when everyone got a full sleeve, and *no* chips. For that reason alone I was grateful for the bathroom lunches, systematically flinging my sandwich and fruit into the trashcan on our way to the stall.

I couldn't say when or why exactly we stopped eating in the cafeteria. We never said it, not even to each other, but at some point it didn't feel safe. Not dangerous, like we'd get beat up or anything. It was just a sense we had to lie low because if the other kids got a good look at us, they'd figure out why we weren't getting picked for teams, or why it was only us and Alex, the one black kid in the school, at our table in science class.

Alex had arrived in midyear, a face full of eyes, with glasses that magnified those eyes until if you stared at them too long he started to look like a bug. His father was a scientist at the Brookhaven lab, working on some secret project for the year. It was all Jessie could do to not tie him to the leg of our science table and torture him for government secrets. She'd ask him, over and over, about what his father was doing and Alex kept telling her, "I don't know," which just confirmed for her the top-secret nature of it all. We only had science class with Alex, but I wasn't used to having to share Jessie's attention by then. I was quietly jealous of him and annoyed at Jessie for not seeing that our association with

Alex was doing nothing for our social standing. Alex was cool, though, in the most goober of ways. He was in the science club and had his own Bunsen burner he carried around in a leather case. He'd walk down the hall looking like some very short but very busy businessman off to another important meeting. With Alex in our group we always got our science projects done early, we'd get As, and we got to watch him melt things or cut open a worm.

The other boys fed off poor Alex like a school of sharks, teasing him, tripping him and taunting him with cries of "Beetle Face!" and "Queer!" shouted down the empty hall so the tormentors *knew* you couldn't tell yourself they were shouting at someone else.

One day Jessie and I rounded the corner to see Alex flying out of the boys' locker room. He looked like something sprung out of a slingshot, skidding across the freshly waxed hall.

"Alex," Jessie yelled to him, and old Alex changed course in midair like some heat-seeking missile, straight for Jessie. I think he would have hid behind her, peeking through her legs like a one-year-old, if he hadn't caught the tiniest bit of a grip.

"What's going on?" she asked.

"Nothing," he said, looking anxiously back at the locker-room door.

"What happened, Alex?" she asked again, and he looked at me pleadingly, saying wordlessly, "Call her off, Rose."

"They take your lunch money?"

"No."

"They took his jock strap," I said. I had seen the ditto Mr. Roth, the gym teacher, had handed out to all the sixth-grade boys the week before, just a glimpse in social studies, but I could make out the whispers during the film we were watching.

Jessie sighed, "Oh for God's sake," like she was his mother or something. "Wait here," she said, and before either of us could say a word, she was in the locker room.

I think it is safe to say that was the beginning of the end. I stood watching the door swing shut and my short life flash before my eyes, and my new, long life—a life filled with high-water pants, bathing caps, sticky olive-loaf sandwiches and friends who wore Husky Sears Wranglers—rise before me. I was so busy worrying about whether I would really like beauty school when it became impossible to return to Redwood anymore, that it didn't actually occur to me that they could be killing her in there. But Jessie came out of the locker room untouched, the jock strap balled in her hand, and shoved it at Alex.

"Now hold on to this." Then to me, "Burke is one moron."

Seemed she got it away from him pretty easily and then went at him, wrapping it around his neck, the cup like a gag, strangling him before the guys pulled her off. By lunchtime it was all over the school, even though they'd all been dressed. You'd think she'd gunned down a Burger King the way kids moved out of her way the whole rest of the afternoon. Then behind her back they started whispering. Just a hush when we walked by at first, but it grew into the word *lesbos* penciled on our desks, and elbows that found their way into our sides in the overly crowded coatroom in the mornings.

Jessie was like some animal that had tasted blood. It seemed to me she was looking for a fight. She'd get this wildman look in her eyes and get right in some kid's face, barking, "What'd you say?" The fact that she had beat up a boy was bad for everyone. Burke couldn't call her out because she was a girl, and yet he had to get back at her because she'd made him cry. I was so angry with her.

▼

Mr. Fred, our art teacher, was large and egg-shaped, a belly that wrapped around his middle all Jell-O-like and wiggly. He seemed to need to gather that middle up in his hands like a lady lifting a long, flowing skirt as she walks upstairs. In the art room, Jessie and I sat at a table we had claimed for our own in the corner by the window, puffs of hot air shooting up from the heater into our faces when we gathered our supplies from the shelves lining the window. He would sail from table to table, like some cruise liner. His belly always arrived first, bumping into the table like a docking ship bow.

Every May the middle school had its annual art show, with a prize for the best project from each grade. The theme was music, and Jessie and I decided we would do the scene from *The Sound of Music* where Maria and the von Trapp kids run through the hills singing *Do-Re-Me*. We created a papier mâché mountain and went through tubes of paint getting the color of the grass exactly right. We made the tiniest Liesl, Gretl, Kurt—all seven of them—from pipe cleaners and dressed them in white and green-flowered fabric that was Vivian's old curtains, just like in the movie. The real kicker was going to be the tape player we rigged up under the mountain to actually play the song when the judges walked by.

We were so enthralled with our work that we started eating lunch in the art room instead of the bathroom and staying after school, even on Thursdays when Hannah had her writing group and we had a clear shot at the metal cabinet.

Sometimes we were the only ones in the art room after school. That was when Mr. Fred was supposed to be supervising students at all times, but he would disappear for a half-hour, return smelling of cigarettes and coffee and offer us a Twinkie or a Ring Ding from the package he'd gotten out of the vending machine in the teachers' lounge. The moment he'd leave, Jessie would run into the supply closet to take something—markers, tubes of paint, colored tissue paper—and I didn't understand, when she was so fond of him, why she'd steal from him.

Mr. Fred sent us home one day with a ditto, still smelling purple:

MILLER AVE. MIDDLE SCHOOL
IS PROUD TO PRESENT
MULTI-MEDIA ART GALLERY

FRIDAY 8PM MAY 12, 1974

Vivian took me over to Gimbel's the Saturday before to buy a dress to wear to the show.

"You wanna come?" I asked Jessie that morning.

"No. My mom's gonna take me."

"She up?" I asked skeptically. Hannah seldom got up before noon on the weekend, and that week she was having one of her depressions. Jessie and I would walk to her house after school, through the path in the woods and over their back fence. We'd slide open the glass door into the kitchen. It got so I could see Hannah, her room dark with drawn curtains, all hair and covers, in my mind. I'd peer through the crack in the door Jessie left as she went in, tiptoeing, glasses of water, pills that left orange and pink dots on her sweaty palms. I'd wait in the hall like held breath, sure that some day Hannah would lose it completely, chasing Jessie and me around the kitchen island with some ax.

Jessie'd come out, eyes distant and hard, closing the door and walking down the hall like some little military nurse, always calling behind her, "She's better. She's better today," like I shouldn't even think of questioning her.

I never would have. I knew. I knew what it felt like to have this mother person, whose lap you needed to lay a sweaty head on, become something you could fall through like falling through a cloud, something fragile and tottering, a spindly table and porcelain figures. But when Vivian toppled, it was temporary; you saw it but it wasn't forever. With Hannah, it was a life condition, and how you saw it was with a lifelong stare.

It was two days before the Art Show and we'd have set up a couple cots in Mr. Fred's room if we could have, we were so determined to win the prize. Jessie would be talking away the whole time—"Mr. Fred, look at this! Mr. Fred, look at that!"—and I was getting one headache, but Mr. Fred didn't seem to mind and even kept asking her questions. And all this time she was stealing from him. And not just his art supplies but change from his desk drawer, one of his cigarettes, a mangy-looking book of matches. It was when she came back to the table sliding a half-eaten roll of Lifesavers into her front pocket that I spoke up.

"What if he catches you?"

She looked up at me wordlessly.

"Huh?" I asked. "How you gonna feel then?"

"Bad."

"Yeah. You sure will. Why don't you just ask him for a friggin' Lifesaver? You ask him for everything else. You think when he catches you he'll let us stay after school here anymore? You think he'll even want to be around you when he finds out you're a thief?"

This was a shittier thing than I'd meant to say and as she headed back to the desk I could see she was crying, but I didn't care. I liked Mr. Fred too, and if she was going to hoard him the way she did, she could be a little more careful. We weren't exactly flush in the friends department. She sat back down and bent over Friedrich, gluing his suspenders. I finally cooled off.

"You gotta stop taking his things."

"I know."

"Why do you do that?" And I wasn't really expecting an answer, but she says:

"He's nice and good, like clean white cotton, and funny, and sometimes I take the things out and just look at them and I feel like him instead of me and I feel better."

You know what? I knew that. I can't tell you how, but I did. I knew there was a place inside Jessie so hollow and black that she needed company. I could feel it when she'd climb into bed with me and fall asleep with an arm over my stomach and a fist tight around the end of my pajama top. I was scared enough of my own hollow black place that I peered through like a peep-hole. I knew Jessie's place was so big, if it was me I'd go screaming mad—like her nightmares—every minute of the day. Never mind a roll of Lifesavers, a handful of pipe cleaners. So I just said:

"You have enough things now, so don't take anymore."

▼

"That's nice, Rose. Goat?"

"Lamb," I said.

"I've got the Lonely Goat. His name is Barnaby," she said, proudly, holding Barnaby up for a better look. I shot her a dirty look. I was positive that the Lonely Goat was simply called the Lonely Goat, but because everything needed to have a friggin' name she kept insisting she could call the goat Barnaby. Had we been in the fifth grade, we probably would have come to blows over it, but being in the sixth grade we just gave each other the silent treatment, little hisses of *moron* and *retard* under our breath.

I watched Mr. Fred's kind but sad-looking eyes and soft voice and the kid-sized chair he scraped back from the table so he could sit and more closely check out old Barnaby. I watched the chair disappear under him and caught the other kids whispering, elbowing each other, all ugliness and treachery. They made fun of Mr. Fred, his jiggliness and lady-like voice. Any chair he sat in had cooties for a week, and some boy usually pulled his shirtsleeve over his hand to push the chair away from his table, breaking into snickers when some unsuspecting kid sat in it. Usually I had no backbone for this kind of thing, would play along with the other kids, throwing out some cruel tease at the victim to show I, too, was "in." Then I'd spend the whole rest of the day pushing away this creeping, sick feeling in my stomach.

That year, though, I—really Jessie and I—had become the object of those taunts. I tried so hard to do what had always worked for me, stay out of the way, be as invisible as I could. In the past it had worked. I'd had a few friends, other quiet, paper-doll-cutting, book-reading types, but even they had drifted away, scared off by the bright searchlight of attention, helicopter blades loudly chopping the air, that Jessie always drew to her—and now that we were inseparable, to me. I learned about choosing then, that things in the world were not like at home where if I really wanted something—shiny white sandals, the newest board game, another box of Crayolas with the sharpener because I'd used up all the silver one—Vivian would produce it. I wanted so badly to be liked at school, to push open the heavy glass front doors and not step onto the worn yellow linoleum tiles with dread. But I wanted, by then needed, Jessie, the world we created, all the secret places and plans and rolling laughter that made me feel like some pale green seedling digging its feet in the dirt, leaves opening to a sun, alive. I had to choose Jessie.

Jessie is prattling on to Mr. Fred like she's holding Barnaby's press conference.

"Barnaby lives on a farm. Farmer Hans has a hundred goats but he knows them all, Gwen, Frank, Larry, Marvin . . ." She

names them all, with Mr. Fred nodding, all oohs and ahas and
wows, on and on, and I leave to go to the bathroom. When I
come out, I can see them in the coatroom that's been made into
a supply closet, and I walk in. Mr. Fred has pipe cleaners, all different colors, and he's pulling them off a high shelf and lets us
pick some. We take more than we need because they're so pretty,
delicate and fuzzy.

We go back out to the classroom, leaving Mr. Fred to gather
the rejected pipe cleaners in their box.

We're so excited, in part I know because Mr. Fred didn't offer
up the pipe cleaners to the other kids. We get to our table, gloat-
ing loudly over our pipe-cleaner plans, and then Jessie gasps and
at the same moment I see it: The mountain, big punched holes in
the side, and all the von Trapp kids, beheaded. We swing around
to see Joey Burke, his face a contortion, laughing so hard he isn't
making any noise.

"Murderer!" Jessie shrieks, and she's running at him, a bull,
her head just missing a table corner as she tackles him, knocking
him to the ground, making a noise I'd never heard in my life, a
furious and wounded animal sound. I run to them to save her but
stop dead when I see, first, Joey Burke on his back, frozen with
terror, and then the scissors she's got two inches from his face.

"You fucking moron," she spits at him and draws the scissors
back.

"Jessie!" I scream. "No!" and I lunge for the scissors, pulling
her off him and we're a tangle on the floor, Jessie, purple-faced,
tears streaming down her cheeks.

"What's going on in here," Mr. Fred calls, and Jessie is sobbing now, her arms around me, and we're both breathing heavy
and jagged. I hold the scissors up over my head at Mr. Fred.

"He ruined our project for the show!" And Mr. Fred sees them,
the von Trapp kids, Barnaby and the rest of the farm animals,

scattered like debris across the table, and his face is in disbelief.

"Joey, get up off the floor and wait for me by the door. Now!" he thunders, no trace of the voice and mannerisms we know, and that voice sends Joey scurrying for the door.

"Jessie? Jessie?" he says, suddenly soft again, crouching down to us. She's shaking now. "Come here," and her hands slip from my neck as he gathers her up. He doesn't have to tell us: We scatter to our seats, heads in our arms on the tabletops.

"Stay in your seats. I don't want to hear a word. I'll be right back."

He carries Jessie away, Joey walking all crouched in front of him, like he's waiting for Mr. Fred to smash him into the floor like a bug.

In a minute the teacher next door is standing in the doorway, and I stare out the window, my head in my arms and, as my breath grows regular and slow, I am angry at every grown-up on the planet for not being aware of all the sneaky, whispered words, all the coatroom shoves, all the ugliness that led to that moment of scissors held up, catching a gleam of fluorescent light.

Chapter 5

Homeroom teachers come and wordlessly collect their charges and the room empties, four or five of us at a time. I put all the pieces of Barnaby, the farm animals and the von Trapp kids in a paper bag and burst out the front doors, daring someone to stop me. I'm down the walkway at a run, the bag bouncing against my leg. I don't stop running until I get to the path in the woods.

I plop myself down on this rusty old shopping cart someone's left by the path. Then I'm crying, the big ugly heaving kind of crying because I just don't give a shit if anyone hears me. I'm just that angry. I'm sick of it. I'm sick of making believe I don't hear when a bunch of girls giggle as I walk by. I'm sick of pulling Jessie off of boys bigger than she is who would love to knock her friggin' stupid head off her shoulders if it wasn't that she was a girl. And now scissors, *scissors*! I don't know for sure, but I don't think you go and pull a pair of scissors on someone unless you want to be shipped off to one of those juvie schools upstate.

And another thing. What about *me*? What about that every time she wins one of these fights, which is most of the time between the fact that she's a girl *and* a good fighter, I'm having to watch *my* back for the next month. That's what I'm thinking, and it feels like I'm shouting but luckily I have slightly enough of a grip to not actually be talking, because then I hear someone coming up the path, leaves crunching, and I quick wipe my eyes. It's Alex. He's shuffling along like he does most of the time when someone's not chasing him.

I don't know how long I've been sitting on that shopping cart, but I don't think it's been long enough for school to be over.

"Hey, Rose," he says, looking down at me. "Can I sit down?" Like we're suddenly so formal with each other!

"Sure." I'm rolling my eyes. "What are you doing here?"

"It's all over school—Jessie going psycho on Burke."

"Oh great, that is just so great!" And the juvie school upstate isn't looking so bad.

"Was she really gonna stab him?"

"Noooo." Though I'm not at all sure. "Ah Jesus, Alex." I sigh, my head in my hands, "How am I supposed to go back to school now?"

"*You* didn't go psycho."

"Stop saying that. She didn't go psycho. He'd been baiting her ever since she beat him up in the locker room, which, by the way, she did for you so I wouldn't be so quick to be calling her names."

"I don't think he'll be touching her. I think he'll leave her alone now."

"He's gonna want her dead now!"

"Rose, Mr. Burke came to pick him up and we were sitting outside when they walked out. He took off his belt right there in the parking lot and beat the shit out of Burke. Mrs. Burke stayed in the truck but she came out when Burke started screaming.

Someone ran for Mr. Fred but they pulled away before he got out there. If you'd heard the way he was yelling, you'd know he's not touching Jessie again."

"You're kidding."

"No kidding."

Poor Burke. I mean, he's a mean moron, but to be hit with an actual belt and in front of the whole school, I'd be a mean moron too. I'll admit I'm just the tiniest bit happy too, 'cause I know that tomorrow everyone will be talking about Burke and his dad more than Jessie and her scissors.

"You cut out of school early?"

"Yeah."

"You never leave school early, don't you have like computer club or debate club or Boy Scouts? Don't you have to walk your one-hundredth little old lady across the street for that super scout badge?"

He knows I'm teasing him.

"Fuck you, Rose."

And he jabs me with his elbow but I'm laughing, feeling suddenly lighter 'cause I think I might be able to show up at school tomorrow, and I know Alex came to find me in the woods 'cause he was worried about me, even if he's too much of a boy to tell me so.

The dogs hear me as I near the fence and are barking until they see it's me scaling the chainlink and break into a frenzy of shaking rear ends as I jump into the yard. I pet them, both hands, absently, "Hey girls, hey girls," and as I get to the sliding glass door I can see Hannah, the phone cord stretched across the kitchen, standing, leaning against the island and nodding, and Jessie hunched in a kitchen chair. I slide the door open and shut.

"I understand," Hannah is saying into the phone. "Yes . . . yes . . . What I'm asking is, why hasn't anyone noticed that these girls are afraid to eat lunch in the cafeteria, that they aren't there? Doesn't anyone take a head count? Oh, oh, okay . . ."

I go sit in one of the other kitchen chairs, next to Jessie.

"Who she . . ." I whisper.

"Shh," Jessie says, not taking her eyes off Hannah. That's when I realize Hannah is dressed. She's wearing actual grown-up clothes, stockings, long skirt, a turtleneck that hugs her slender shoulders and long waist. Her hair is pulled up in a loose bun, two tortoise shell barrettes and silver earrings, so long the ends swing back and forth when she nods. She looks like somebody's queen, regal, her voice measured as she speaks to whoever is on the other end of the phone. There's something else, though, something else I can't quite place. I've seen Hannah before in the same sort of clothes, a few other times, and she's always looked uncomfortable. She's looked like those eight-year-old boys in bow ties at my First Communion. That's it. She looks, her head nodding and lips pursed, like she's playing dress-up, like the baby-sitter telling you how you'll end up a midget if you don't eat all your string beans. Just not a real threat.

I'm rooting for her, though—for Jessie, really—praying she'll come through and at the same time knowing she's way out of her league. I'm tapping my foot on the table leg, growing more and more anxious for her.

"Oh, well, the doctor and I will talk about that. No, I'm sure Dr. Spencer will have someone in mind if she's willing to go . . ." And Jessie lets out a sigh of disappointment.

"God!"

I tell you, I feel like we're sinking, like the ship is going down, that by the time Hannah hangs up, Jessie's going to be finishing up grade school at Pilgrim State Psychiatric Hospital, never mind the juvie school. I wish I could throw Hannah some cue cards. She's practically sweating, her voice pressed and pleasing.

I hear the front door open and close. And it's Vivian. She's going about a hundred miles an hour, that look on her face that makes me want to take cover under the kitchen table. She's got her coat off and it and her purse on the island without missing a step and I watch her, trying to figure out what to expect, what she knows, what the school told her, what they even know.

She leans down between our chairs and kisses us both, in our hair, me then Jessie, and whispers, "You two okay?" We nod quickly, and then she mouths to Hannah, "Who's on the phone?"

"Mr. Fred," Hannah mouths back. Vivian walks toward Hannah, hand outstretched for the receiver.

"That's fine. Rose's mother is here and would like to speak with you also . . . yes . . . yes . . . thank you." She hands Vivian the phone.

"This is Vivian Salino." A pause and then, "Guess what? I don't give a shit what some lunchroom monitor thinks. You better tell that little son of a bitch that if he comes near either one of these girls again I'm coming over to that school and ripping his fucking lungs out. Do you hear me?"

Oh my God. I look over at Jessie and Hannah who are staring at my mother, their mouths hanging open. I shut my eyes, just imagining poor Mr. Fred, who I'm not sure has ever even heard the F word, grabbing on to the back of his chair for support.

"That is not my problem. I don't care if his father hangs him by his fucking balls every night while he says his prayers . . . Then he's a fucking animal, too."

I'm figuring Mr. Fred has definitely wet himself by now.

"You figure it out because you can tell that little lunatic that he's lucky Jessie got to him first, that *I* work with scissors every day."

Jessie and Hannah are looking at each other, smiles of incredulity, but I know Vivian's not nearly close to being done.

61

"Look, I appreciate that. What I'm telling you is that when I put my daughter on that school bus, I expect to go to work with a clear head, not worrying that some sick little bastard's gonna terrorize my child. This is not what I pay taxes for."

And a little burst of laughter escapes from me and I throw both hands over my mouth as Vivian shoots me one of her looks.

Jessie's on her knees now, in her chair, looking like she's ready to break into a cheer at any moment.

"And I'll be sending the school a bill for those art supplies I bought that the little monster destroyed . . ." I catch Jessie's eye and point over at the bag I left by the door.

"I can't believe it," Vivian says, hanging up the phone. "He's actually trying to tell me how I'm overreacting, that this kind of thing happens all the time."

Then Vivian and Hannah look at each other and Vivian grows quiet, coming to sit at the table with us. They're giving each other that mothers' look, the look mothers share when they're joining forces to interrogate their young, one switching on the imaginary light bulb over your head, the other flipping through the incriminating evidence on her yellow legal pad.

I look at Jessie to make sure she's caught on and am relieved to see she has, a blank, simple-minded *I don't know, Officer. I was out back pruning my begonias on the afternoon in question* expression already plastered across her face. I'm doing the final nips and tucks on mine when Vivian turns on me.

"So, what happened today?"

"Well, we were in art class, making our scene from *Sound of Music*," I begin, stalling for time. "And we weren't bothering anyone, Mom. We were just doing our mountain, at our own table . . ."

"Don't bullshit me, Rose. Jessie, what did you do to that boy that he had it in for you like this?"

"Well, Mrs. Salino, I was only trying to protect Rose."

I swing around to look at her. *Nice, good!* And then stare into my lap to listen and reorganize my face.

"If you wanna know the truth, I think he *likes* Rose, and you know how boys can be, and so yesterday at recess he came over to us while we were minding our own business, making our bead bracelets, and asks if Rose wants to go play kickball, which is kind of a baby game but the boys still like it. But Rose isn't a boy. Rose is a girl and so you know she doesn't really want to play, *so* I think his feelings were hurt . . ."

And my mother's looking at Jessie like Hannah forgot to give her daughter her medication that day.

". . . so I think then today in the art room . . ."

"So Jessie," Hannah interrupts, "this kickball thing was *after* you beat him up in the boys' locker room?"

Double-teaming her! I'm torn really, worrying that Jessie's going to get us both grounded, but proud of Hannah, who seems to be drawing strength from Vivian.

"You know about that," Jessie says dully.

"Yes," Hannah says. "And before you dig yourself an even deeper hole, let's review that you also told me in the principal's office today how you've been afraid all year to eat in the lunchroom, how the kids are teasing you . . ."

"Where *do* you eat lunch?" Vivian cuts in.

"In the ladies' room," Jessie blurts out.

"The ladies' room! Do you have any idea what kinds of germs grow in bathrooms and you're eating your food . . ."

I check out here, figuring she's good for at least two minutes of horror stories about children contracting oozing sores from toilet-paper dispensers.

"But we were afraid!" Jessie interrupts. "One girl had slapped me in the face when I was coming back from dropping my hot lunch tray at the dishwasher!"

Which was true. It was also true that Jessie had grabbed her by her braid and dragged her around the cafeteria for a good 30 seconds before some cafeteria monitor had pried her hand loose.

"Well, honey," Vivian says, "why didn't you tell us or tell your teachers?"

And I look up at her, thinking, ah yeah, so exactly why didn't we tell them? Thinking, we're dead, we're very dead.

"We were gonna actually, today. Weren't we, Rose?"

And I'm nodding, just one nodding maniac 'cause you know I just couldn't agree more, and Jessie quavers, "But then today he killed the entire von Trapp family."

"Sweetie," Vivian says. "Pipe cleaner people aren't alive. They can't be killed."

"Well, it *feels* like they're dead!" Jessie cries out, bursting into tears, which an hour earlier would have really got to me, but I can tell she's doing this for effect, even letting a little trickle of snot slide toward her mouth. Disgusting, but definitely a nice touch. "We've spent weeks on this and we were almost done and Rose had this little lamb and Barnaby was *so* cool, he . . ."

She starts in on the gory details of their slaughter, and with a flash of inspiration I go for the paper bag and begin pouring the contents on the table. We're getting into this now. "I had to paste these little beads on for eyes and we had to keep remaking the papier mâché for the heads because some of them were looking like coneheads . . ." and I'm holding each von Trapp kid up while she talks, body in one hand, head in the other, like I'm doing the seatbelt demonstration for TWA.

"I think they're gonna live," Vivian says to Hannah, rolling her eyes, both of them shaking their heads, obviously pleased enough with how cute and clever we are to forget for the moment that Jessie nearly stabbed one of our classmates.

"Okay, Rose," Vivian says. "Get your stuff. Let's go."

"Oh Mom, can't I stay and have dinner?" and she shoots me one of those *Do not even think of embarrassing me now by inviting yourself to someone's dinner table*—like I don't live there half the time anyway. Mothers do this, get all Miss Manners with their kids, smoothing their skirt, pleases and thank yous, in front of other mothers when at home it's, "Pick up those fucking clothes, now!" their heads all spinning, green slimy stuff flying out of their mouths. But before she can start in on me, Hannah says:

"Let her stay, Vivian. George's working late tonight so I'll probably just throw together some macaroni and cheese." And Jessie and I head out of the kitchen before Vivian has a chance to change her mind.

"Well, it's still cooking, it's still another plate to wash!" Like Hannah's taking the dishes down to the river. This is another mother-thing. Mothers like to make sure they get in one solid affirmation to each other for every contact hour. "After a long day, cooking anything is just that extra push. You know, some nights I'm so tired I just stop at Kentucky Fried Chicken, and I hate to do it but they have to know there are limits," Vivian says in a tone that insinuates she also lets Claire and me loose in the backyard to root for nuts and berries on those real killer days.

We disappear into Jessie's room and fall on the bed, all sighs of relief and then giggles. And then quiet.

"You okay?"

"Suspended tomorrow."

I tell her about Burke and then I say, "You could've killed him, you know, if you'd really stabbed him."

"I know," she says quietly. "You think I'm crazy?"

"I didn't say that, Jessie. I just . . . "

"'Cause I think, I mean I'm not sure, but I think I was gonna do it. I'm not sure if I was just scaring him."

I look at her and she's not kidding.

65

"You wouldn't do that," I say quickly. "You go to jail forever for that. You know that. Jessie?"

"Yeah, you're right, but I wanted to, Rose. Before I heard about his dad." Then, shaking her head, "Poor Burke."

When we go back out to the kitchen, Hannah is sitting at the table, drinking a glass of wine and paging through another of those Eddie Bauer catalogs that they must churn out once a week especially for their star customer, Hannah Spencer, the box of macaroni and cheese sitting unopened on the counter.

"Mom, we're hungry, it's 7," Jessie says, all irritable. Hannah leaps up from the table.

"Oh my God, I lost track of the time!" And that seems to have jump-started her into the fridge for the milk and butter. Satisfied, Jessie goes and sits at the table.

"You know, girls," Hannah says, "I was thinking we could make you a new project, something really cool." Hannah was the only mother I knew who said cool.

"He wrecked everything, Mom. Even the mountain has big holes in it."

"Could they be caves?"

"I don't know, I mean maybe, I guess?"

Both of us are clearly edging our way out of the kitchen. Hannah is unaware.

"I was thinking about it and there's no reason you can't make another project. Ernest Hemingway lost a whole novel on a train and that did not stop him. I was thinking that, given what's going on in school, we should make you some project that will symbolize strength and protection and the power of the female energy." She's losing us fast. "You can make these caves and have each house a powerful animal like a wolf, or a bear or even a Newfoundland." That sounds more like it.

"Yeah!" Jessie says. "Like Mutual of Omaha's *Wild Kingdom*."

"Sort of. I was thinking more of the PBS special on cave dwellers, but it's your project."

"I could glue Barnaby's head back on, and we could have different animals in each cave with babies."

"And a kid raised by wolves like Mowgli in *The Jungle Book*."

I am definitely getting into this now.

"But the show is the day after tomorrow and Craft Corner must be closed by now and we don't have anything to make the animals out of and . . ."

"Oh, but I think we do," says Hannah, with enough mystery in her voice to evoke the image of the three of us, big hulking rifles, stalking grizzlies through a forest. "Come here!" And we follow her into her room.

"How about *this*?" Hannah asks, pulling a full-length mink coat out of the closet.

"You're gonna cut up your fur coat?" I'm enough of my mother's daughter to register a tiny bit of horror in my voice, and Jessie gives me a quick shove with her elbow.

"It was my mother's and you know I would never wear fur. I've just been keeping it, trying to figure out a useful way to get rid of it. This seems to be it."

She brings the coat into the kitchen and we scurry around like Cinderella's mice, sewing and gluing, and it isn't until 8:30 that any of us notices we haven't eaten. I go over to the counter and make the macaroni and cheese, letting Hannah sew the eyes on Delia, Warrior Wolf.

It gets so late Hannah gets my mother to let me spend the night. We fall into bed about 11 and I lie there for a while, unable to sleep, listening to Jessie snore, Barnaby and Bob the Bear tucked in her arm. I get up finally to get some water, and Hannah is sitting in the living room, reading a book.

"Can't sleep?"

"Nope."

"What are you thinking about?"

And I want to tell her, want to tell her the truth about today, about Jessie and me, and get some grown-up, some grown-up who's not my mother and not going to burst a blood vessel when she hears, to help us out. Besides, I know somehow that Hannah's a safer choice than my own mother, Hannah who so clearly knows what it's like not to be all someone hopes you will be. I sit on the couch by her, letting her stroke my hair and close my eyes.

"It'll work out, Rose," she says, and my eyes fly open.

"What?"

"This thing with you and Jessie."

"What thing?" I say, like, What knife?

"Your special friendship with Jessie." She's being just vague enough that I don't know if we're talking about the same thing here, or if she's just working up to one of her Life Is a Spiritual Journey lectures.

"Think so?" I ask. "You think it will just work out?"

"Yeah, I think it will."

She says it like she knows, not know-it-all like Vivian and Jessie, but like she's just got some teeny, tiny version of one of her Angels whispering in her ear, all sweet and reassuring, and I look up at her, sort of sighing with relief.

"Go on to bed, Rose," she says mussing my hair, and I go back to Jessie's room and fall asleep.

Chapter 6

In a way Hannah was right. The other kids left us alone after that, way alone. They ignored us, really. For our part, we became more careful, checked locks on doors at home and waited until we were halfway down the wooded path that led to the Spencers' back fence on our walks home before letting our fingers weave together. We'd kiss in the hidden daylight, but anything more happened in darkness.

In the seventh grade, during Easter break, the Spencers took me along on their vacation to Florida. We stayed in the Disney World Hotel, the one where the Monorail ran straight through the middle. Dr. Spencer reserved three rooms, one for the boys, one for Jessie and me, and one for him and Hannah. There was a restaurant with white tablecloths and napkins, heavy silverware, and the waiter brought orange juice in the smallest glasses I'd ever seen. I couldn't stop thinking about those glasses. Dr. Spencer bought us thick books of tickets and every morning, as we finished our breakfast, he'd slide a twenty across the table from behind his newspaper at us. We'd use the money for frozen chocolate-covered bananas and E tickets—we'd run through the E tickets in our book the first day.

We had talked the whole way on the plane about Space Mountain and how we would ride it with our arms straight up. The first time we rode it, Jessie went directly from the exit to the ladies' room and threw up, emerging from the stall all watery-eyed and panting. The rest of the trip she waited while I rode anything that went fast, upside down or spinning. I'd see her waving from the ground as I swung by, and it struck me as funny that I was the one in the air, me the big coward, me with my still wobbly bike-riding.

Vivian had given me $100 to pay my way for meals, and luckily Dr. Spencer would have none of it. If I even tried to pull my wallet out at the table, he'd look at me from behind the tinkling ice of his Scotch glass and growl, "Put that away!" I nearly peed my pants. I used the money to buy little glass animals, one each day, from the souvenir shops that dotted the park.

We ran wild through the park all week by ourselves. Once we ran into the boys by the Swiss Family Robinson Treehouse, drinking beer under an umbrella table, but other than that, we made believe we were alone. Jessie wanted her picture taken with every Disney character who crossed our path, and I made her go into every souvenir shop to check out the glass animals. We had to be in the dining room at 7 every night for dinner, bathed and brushed, in a dress and shoes.

The tub in our room was bigger than the one at home, and we'd get back from a sweaty day at the park and strip off our clothes in two heaps on the floor.

"I stink," Jessie said, smelling under her arms. "Smell," she said. She did. "Let me smell you."

I was worse. We climbed into the tub, lathering the little bars of hotel soap between our hands and devoting considerable attention to our underarms. On the way down to the dining room that night, we stopped off at the hotel shop and bought deodorant.

"What did you buy, Jessie?" Hannah asked as we slipped into our seats.

"Deodorant!" Jessie said proudly, pulling the stick out of the bag.

"Put that away!" Dr. Spencer growled, shaking his head.

"You don't bring hygiene products to the dinner table, girls," Hannah said, shooting a sideways look at her husband, but her eyes were twinkling.

I don't know if Hannah and Dr. Spencer ever made it into the park at all. They seemed to spend the whole time playing tennis, in their room (doing you-know-what, Jessie explained), at the pool, or at the bar. One afternoon it was so hot, some pregnant woman fainted out in front of Cinderella's Castle, and we decided to go swimming during the day. We swam every night after dinner until the pool closed at 10. A few times we were alone, could glide quietly to the shallow end where it was dark and slip our hands into each other's bathing suits. We'd stand next to each other, leaning against the side of the pool, and take turns. We'd talk the whole time, in case someone came by for a swim, about the rides mostly, and if Jessie was touching me I always ended up with my eyes closed, the pool water holding me up as my legs let go. She'd start off saying things like, "Wasn't that great when the Bear came out singing in the Bear Jamboree," or, "Don't you think that the Tea Cups are the most fun?" in a voice loud enough to be heard in the lobby, but after a while it was just, "Haunted House, Tea Cups, Space Mountain, Tom Sawyer's Adventure . . ." like this was some perfectly normal conversation.

Jessie had her first orgasm in that pool, and I spent the rest of the vacation trying to catch up. "Mr. Toad's Wild Ride, It's a Small World . . ."

"It's not working," I said, opening my eyes.

"What are you thinking of?"

"I don't know." Truth be told, my mind kept wandering to those orange juice glasses.

We had sat naked the night before, our legs spread to the mirror with Jessie pointing, instructing.

"Now, right there, that's your clitoris. That's the part you want to touch for the good part."

"I know that," I said, annoyed. Ever since she's had her orgasm, which she'd named The Good Part, she was one Miss Know-it-all about sex.

When it was her turn she kept her eyes open, looking down at the water, watching the surface, babbling, "The Pirates of the Caribbean, Snow White's Adventure . . ." until her body jerked and all she said was, "Oh," a little cry of it and then, "You want to try again?"

In case you want to know, when we were there the Disney World Hotel didn't have anyone come out and lock up the pool at 10, and one night we were out there until dawn. We had moved ourselves to one of the chaise lounges for a different angle. About two hours later I hit pay dirt, Jessie snoring softly beside me.

"Wake up!"

"What?"

"I did it!"

"Did what?"

"The good part."

"Let me try."

The pool guy almost caught us. We scrambled out of the chaise lounge with Jessie pretty much yelling, "No pain, no gain,

Salino! Time for your weight training!" And then directly to the guy as we sprinted by him, "Watch for her. This one's gonna make it."

"That was *so* pitiful," I whispered as we waited for the elevator. But I don't think the guy spoke English anyway.

We were late for breakfast, and it occurred to me that my mother would have had security out looking for us hours ago, that we could have been kidnapped, raped and left for dead, and the Spencers wouldn't have realized we were gone until we didn't show up for breakfast. We dashed into the dining room and I tried to act normal, like nothing was up. I ordered three of those orange juice glasses with Jessie kicking me under the table when I asked the waiter for the third.

"You have to listen to your body," Hannah said to me, smiling. "Your body's obviously craving Vitamin C. Probably all that sun." Kick, under the table, and I nodded, gulping the last of it down.

We nearly missed our plane back home the next morning. Jessie and I stayed up the whole night, sitting out on the balcony smoking the pack of cigarettes we'd found out by the pool, the breeze wet and warm on our damp swimsuits. It was tense between us that night. Jessie hadn't wanted to do our usual routine in the pool, which I thought was selfish since I was still behind her a good six orgasms due to my late start. She was a brooding quiet I knew meant one of her outbursts was coming at any moment. She'd been out of sorts all day, had taken a nap after lunch but awakened screaming in her sleep, a sound that made me tremble and my heart beat hard.

Jessie had always had bad nightmares and talked in her sleep. A couple of times when I'd sleep over, I'd wake to a thump and Jessie standing in the middle of her room, fast asleep, a can of Coca Cola spilling onto the rug at her feet. I had heard something once about how someone could die of a heart attack if you woke them up when they were sleep-walking, so I'd lead her, mumbling, back to the bed, whispering, "It's okay, it's okay. You were just thirsty. It's not morning time yet. Go back to sleep." She never remembered any of it and actually got angry with me when I told her, like I'd make that kind of thing up. Eventually, I stopped telling her when it happened.

"What's the matter?" I asked, out on the balcony.

"Nothing."

"You're lying."

"It's nothing!"

"Sure."

"Screw you, Rose!" And she disappeared back into the room, a puff of air conditioning hitting my back and neck as she shoved the sliding glass door open and slammed it shut.

When I went back inside, she had all the lights off, lying still in the bed, tiny crying squeaks and sniffles. I stood by the door, waiting for my eyes to adjust to the light, standing still, then went and sat on the bed.

"Why are you crying?"

"They're fighting again."

"Who?"

"My parents. When I went by their room this morning to get ice, I could hear them. *Everyone* could hear them."

"What did you hear?"

"My mom, she was crying, saying, 'I hate you' and 'I know. Don't think I'm stupid.'"

"What? What does she know?"

"What do you *think*, Rose?!"

"What?"

She sat up then, her face contorted in anger. "She thinks he's having an affair with Joyce."

"Oh," I said, trying to imagine the starched Joyce looking like an unmade bed. I couldn't. "Is he?"

"Who knows."

By the time Hannah and Dr. Spencer came down to breakfast the next morning, we were done eating and the boys had gone to the game room for one last game of PacMan. I was sneaking my orange juice glass down the front of my jeans.

We heard Hannah's laugh first, a husky sound, and when we turned they were walking toward us, holding hands. I watched Jessie watch them, could almost see her face fall into smoothness.

"Good morning, ladies," Dr. Spencer said, pulling out Hannah's chair. "Well, we need to leave in half an hour. Are you girls packed yet?"

"Yeah," Jessie said. Hannah plucked a sugar cube from its bowl and dropped it into her coffee, stirring.

"Good vacation?" he asked us.

"Yeah!" Jessie said. "Space Mountain was the best!"

I swung around to look at her. She was one big grin, reaching across the table for a sugar cube she started sucking on.

"Jessie, honey, you know better than that," Hannah said absently as she stirred and stirred, coffee slopping over the side of her cup, making this moat in her saucer, stirring like she was going to whip that coffee into its gas form at any moment. Luckily I knew when to keep my mouth shut.

The flight was delayed and we ended up sitting in the airport for two hours. Hannah and Dr. Spencer headed for the bar and gave us the celery sticks out of their Bloody Marys. That took all of about five minutes and then we were bored. The boys were out by the gate watching a TV suspended from the ceiling, and Jessie and I finished off the bowl of dry roasted nuts. I watched Dr. Spencer, trying to see signs of his cheating, like he'd accidentally pull some white nurse's cap out of his back pocket, but it was just his handkerchief.

Jessie got up to switch our empty nut bowl for a full one from the bar, and Dr. Spencer reached across the table, brushing a few strands of hair from in front of Hannah's face. They looked at each other so intently, I thought for a second they were going to kiss right there at the table.

"Let's go to the store by the gate," I said to Jessie when she returned with the nuts.

"Okay."

"I think she's wrong," I told Jessie when we were out of earshot.

"Who?"

"Your mom. I think he loves her." I glanced behind me at the bar, expecting to see them in a passionate embrace, but they were just trading their empty Bloody Mary glasses for new ones.

"Me too," she said, smiling.

I had forgotten to get Claire a gift, and all I could afford after Jessie and I pooled our money was a Disney World baseball cap. I paid for it feeling guilty as hell. I had 14 glass animals, including one whole family and two cats I fluctuated between calling a single parent family and two sisters whose parents were run over.

"I'll give her the elephant, too," I said as we walked back to the bar. It was my second favorite after the giraffe.

"She'll like that," Jessie said.

I had packed all the animals, each carefully rolled in a dirty sock, in my carry-on bag, but when I got home and unrolled them on the coffee table, half of them were beheaded. Claire watched me, an episode of *Gilligan's Island* on the TV and my grandmother clanging around in the kitchen.

"I got you this one," I said, holding the body in one hand and the trunk in the other.

"It's *broken*, Rose! Don't you have anything else? Didn't you get any *ears*?"

I pulled out the baseball cap I had gotten her.

"See? It's got Mickey on the front."

"I wanted ears!"

"Well, I didn't have enough money."

"Mom gave you money to buy me a present!"

"Here," I said, rummaging through my bag, "you can have mine."

I handed her the ears Jessie and I had bought, matching ones with our names the guy at the store had sewn on in script and pink embroidery thread.

"It's got your name on it!"

"Wear it backwards!"

And I grabbed it out of her hand and plopped it onto her head. She looked like one Mouseketeer! Claire was cute that way. She looked like a squirrel, her full cheeks storing nuts, and her eyes giant with long lashes. When she was born, Vivian said the lashes were facing the wrong way and she had a big beauty mark on her cheek that Vivian had removed. Vivian said she was horrified when the nurse brought her Claire. She said she looked like a sea creature you see on those Jacques Cousteau specials, but she always ended the story with, "And look how beautiful you turned out!"

"You can just wear it like that."

"I look like a retard!"

We ended up bringing it to my grandmother, who sat in the den with us making little scissors-clicking noises, unraveling the stitches. Claire wore it the whole night and then stuck it on a shelf in her room.

▼

The summer between ninth and tenth grade we moved, only

15 minutes away but it was a new school district. We might as well have moved to Iowa. The house was in this brand new community, and when we moved in, we were the only house on the block. The kitchen floor wasn't put in for weeks, and the way Vivian was working everyday, unpacking boxes late at night, and the way Tommy was sullen and edgy, I knew it was Vivian's idea. I felt stranded, punished somehow, and hated Vivian. I wouldn't say it, was too afraid of her, but was certain she knew about Jessie and me and had moved to separate us. I sat up in my new room, a room that smelled of cut wood and fresh paint, feeling wronged and empty in a way that frightened me.

The day Vivian told me we were moving, I stood up, pressing the handle of the screen door, said only, "I'm going to Jessie's," and let the door slam and rattle behind me. She let me go. When I told Jessie, her eyes became big and full and we held each other, crying. For some reason I can't explain, at that point I remembered what Jessie had told me about Dr. Spencer bothering her, was going to ask whatever happened with that, and didn't.

There are some things that don't make sense when you turn to look back at them, no matter how many times. I didn't tell Jessie what I was thinking, or figure out why I remembered in the first place. But when the knock on her bedroom door came, and when the door opened to Dr. Spencer standing there, I caught my breath like he knew what I was thinking and had come to threaten me.

But the look on his face was kind, a look I had seen on him many times over the years, mostly directed at Hannah, but sometimes at dinner on the nights he had two Scotches before dinner and sipped through a third, amber and tinkling, and told us a patient had died. I never stopped being afraid of him for reasons that had nothing to do with what Jessie had told me. Maybe it was the starched shirts and ties, or the way he read his newspaper at the breakfast table instead of in the bathroom like Tommy, or monitored his children's table manners. I never understood that kind of father. I think he knew he made me anxious. He only corrected me once, when I was picking at my teeth at a Japanese restaurant. I didn't even have anything stuck in there; I kept dropping the food right at the opening of my mouth, unable to work the chopsticks. I'd never been in a Japanese restaurant before, sitting on blue pillows on the floor, worrying my feet stank. He only said my name, "Rose," but I must have looked back at him like he'd hauled off and slapped me beside the head, because his tone changed instantly and he said, "Would you like another Shirley Temple?"

Standing in the doorway, he didn't comment at all on what was really going on, how we were crying. I'd heard the phone ring, knew Vivian had called to tell them.

"I have two tickets to Westbury Music Hall to see Tom Jones If you two can be ready in an hour, I'll take you."

We said yes.

"I thought he was dead," I said. Tom Jones was someone Tommy imitated, singing and dancing in the kitchen during a commercial that offered 100 hits of the Sixties for $19.99. We had no interest in Tom Jones, but had caught each other's eye quickly and were thinking the same thing: We'd wander around for a few hours until Dr. Spencer came back to pick us up, like we'd done when our parents signed us up for tennis lessons. After our last tennis lesson, we had gone into the women's locker room, turned all the showers on hot, and filled the toilets with orange and yellow tennis balls. It was like eating lunch in the bathroom in elementary school.

We ended up going to see Tom Jones. I was so agitated and angry that the world actually looked weird, kind of fuzzy and closing in, and then the lights went out and Tom leaped onto the stage and these women started throwing bras at him. Tom danced around and over them and they kept coming, some landing on his outstretched arm like a version of horseshoes Tommy and my uncles played. In some strange way it helped. We bounded into the back of Dr. Spencer's Jaguar already talking, telling him about it.

Jessie danced and sang like Tommy that night, a full husky imitating voice, and we laughed so hard my stomach cramped and I slid from the bed to the floor hugging my sides.

Going to a new school, without Jessie, with all these new kids staring at me, gave me the runs. It was a small school and word spread that there was a new kid by the second period. It didn't help that every teacher thought it was his or her personal duty to welcome the new student to the school, remind the class to be courteous and helpful. Courteous and helpful are not two traits I've seen many teenagers aspire to. By the end of the day, though, a group of kind of popular-looking girls took pity on me and guided me to the back of the room to sit with them.

Still, I'd go to school without Jessie feeling like I had forgotten something—my lunch, my math book, my shoes, like those dreams where I'm standing between library stacks and notice my bare toes and the stares and snickers coming from a table full of popular kids, and slowly become aware that I'm either not wearing a shirt or I'm completely naked.

It was Jessie who started talking about liking this guy, Don, a senior at her school. I met him one Saturday when Jessie was trying out for the track team. He needed a bath.

"Could you have picked someone a little creepier, maybe?" I asked afterward.

"You don't know anything about him."

"He smells. I don't need to know anything else about him."

Obviously my opinion was highly valued because she went

out with him that next weekend.

"Where'd he take you?"

"Cassie's."

This was a bar in Port Jeff that I happened to know was where the potheads from Commack South went when they needed to refill their bongs and crawl out of their basements for some fresh air.

"That was a good choice. Anywhere else you would have had to hose him down first."

I didn't even bother asking her if she was getting high. I guessed I wasn't her goddamn mother. But I wasn't ready for her to hang up on me when I told her I had a boyfriend. She called back, crying, saying she knew Jack would be more important and I had to promise on both Sadie and her new kitten, Bo, that that wasn't true. Dish it out but can't take it.

As it turned out, Jessie made the JV track team and was either at practice or a meet on Saturdays, so *she* ended up being the one less available. I didn't like it but I had too much pride to let anyone know I was jealous of a pair of smelly Nikes. Don turned out to be an on-again-off-again kind of thing, and he didn't talk much when he was around, as most of the time he was stoned out to oblivion. I couldn't imagine what she saw in him.

Once we started driving, I'd go watch her track meets, sitting on the cold metal bleachers, sipping paper cups of hot chocolate. She was fast and she won a lot. When I think of Jessie back then, I think of her running, fast, with everyone else trying to catch her. She was always training, on humid suffocating days, in stinging cold rain, checking her time with the stopwatch that hung from a cord around her neck.

I was at her house during Christmas break one night when the Spencers were out. We hung out in the kitchen, blasting music and making daiquiris in the blender, and she told me her plan. We were so drunk that night we had to sit on the floor, right below the blender, taking turns crawling up the kitchen cabinets to switch it on, then one of us holding the glass with two hands and the other pouring, clutching the counter while the whole kitchen swayed. We made it up to her bedroom just in time for me to throw up and fall into bed giggling. The bed was spinning and rocking like the Tea Cups at Disney World.

And that's when Jessie told me her plan, that night, and asked if I would run away with her. I only remembered that later, though, and just little bits of all she must have said.

We woke up the next morning so hung over, with Jessie stumbling off to track practice, that we didn't say anything more about it.

New Year's Day, Hannah called. Jessie had run away, she said, left a note that she hated them both. I couldn't believe she'd leave without telling me.

Then I remembered she had.

Chapter 7

A week later she came back, a wild look in her eyes, so vacant and tense she nearly glowed in the shadows of the driveway. My boyfriend, Jack, pulled away, and when I turned to go inside, she was there. I was mad enough that I waited for her to speak first, but I'd have chased after her if she'd run off.

That New Year's Day, after Hannah called, I'd spent all of it driving around looking for her. I'd called Don but he was gone, too. I spoke with Don's mother about five times that first day, once in person, and got a whole new perspective on old Don. His mother opened the front door, Coors can in hand, and had bed-head at 3 in the afternoon—not the kind of parent that would notice her son stank. She wasn't particularly concerned that Don had disappeared into the night. He'd be back, she said; he'd been running away, off and on, since he was 11, and she had four other kids to worry about.

I drove home and paced my room. Dr. Spencer had called the

police. After a while, I just waited for the phone to ring so I'd know once and for all she was dead. Once Vivian came in my room without knocking and I nearly spat at her. For once she just walked out. And she didn't push it when I said I wasn't going to school on Monday.

So that night in the driveway, right about when I'm starting to think I'm having an hallucination brought on by heavy-duty stress, Jessie speaks up.

"Hi, Rose."

Like nothing. I could have smacked her.

"Come in the house."

It was drizzling and she had no coat, just stood in the rain, the light catching each drop that stuck to her hair and her clothes.

"Could we take a ride instead?" So we got in her car. It smelled like pot, old beer, Peppermint Schnapps. It probably smelled exactly like Don.

She drove us to where she was staying. It took us maybe 20 minutes to get there, a motel with one of those Rent by the Hour or Week signs I don't think I'd ever actually seen up close. The motel was a scatter of one-room cottages, gray and musty. Between that and the dark and the rain, it was so disgusting I couldn't find a single word. Inside, lying on the floor, were men's shirts, a worn leather belt and a pair of work boots. Jessie was saying from someplace far off that they were staying with Don's friend, Dan, who would get them both jobs at the Hostess Outlet where he worked. Clearly, Dan was making a mint there and knew how to share a good thing with a friend. I looked at her, her pupils dilated, slowly and slightly swaying, and didn't know where to start.

That's when I noticed the one unmade bed.

"Are you out of your fucking mind?!" And for a moment I looked around the room to see if there was anything of hers we needed to take, before I realized Vivian was fresh out of lye. "Let's go."

"I want you to come with me to my father's office," she said as we drove off.

"Why?"

"There's something I want."

"Okay."

I knew what she wanted to do—Dr. Spencer kept about $100 in fives, singles and change at the front desk—but anything was better than the motel. We drove down a dark road, our headlights the only lights around, and I looked behind us a couple of times to see if anyone was following us. We didn't say anything during the whole ride to his office, but my mind was racing and shuffling, trying to make sense of everything I had seen. I'll tell you, nights like that make you think the worst happens suddenly, without warning, and maybe sometimes that's true. But I think most of the time it's our own fault for not paying enough attention, not because we don't care, but because we don't know how to make sense of things, don't know what kind of help to ask for or how to ask for it.

I could feel Jessie in that car, slick with rain, slipping away from me when really she'd been clawing her way free from her big black hole right in front of my face all along.

It was close to 1 when we got to Dr. Spencer's office. Jessie turned off the ignition and the headlights, and we sat there in the dark.

"What are you doing?"

Reining in my voice to keep it soft.

"Getting out of here. I can't take it."

"Jesus Christ, Jessie, you don't even know these guys."

"They're cool."

"You've got to be kidding me! You're kidding me, right?

85

You've gotta be." Ranting at her. "*What* are you doing?"

"Getting out of here." She says it so quietly I look at her closely, her eyes puddled.

"What?"

"I can't take it. I'm getting out of here." And I can see she's shivering and I take her hand.

"Jessie, please don't do this. Wait. Another year and we'll be leaving for college."

"Another year? I can't wait another year! Look at me! You think I can stand myself in that house with him for another year? I promise you I can't. You stay if you want."

She throws open the door and runs from the car and I follow her, catch her as she rounds the back corner of the office. She tries to pull free from me but I've got her tight.

"Leave me alone, Rose. You don't understand."

"So talk to me."

"No, I'm sick of talking. I'm done talking!"

I don't know if she's still high or talking about her brilliant boyfriend, who has likely showered her with his full complement of sound advice. Other than the daiquiri night, I don't recall any actual conversations about this. I pull us under the awning, down onto the back steps. She's sobbing, saying, "I can't," over and over, "I can't," and all I can think is that I can't let her go back there, that I don't know what to do.

It's pouring now and the rain is gushing through a gutter that empties at our feet. We just sit there, holding each other, while the rain pounds the sidewalk, and I think how much I love her and how crazy she's acting, thinking I don't know what she'll do next and knowing she doesn't either. I see us sitting there and I want to tell both of us to ask for a hand, that we're way out of our league, that Jessie's only getting started, and that we're both going to get dragged through hell and back before this is over. And whose fault will that be? Jessie's for dragging, or me for not letting go?

I kiss her, hard, my hands holding her face, strands of wet hair between my fingers, until she kisses me back, pressing me into the door and all I know at that moment is that I love her so, that I can't feel anything else, that even the rain, the thunder and lightning are inside me. I am a storm, a force to be reckoned with in my desperate, clutching fear of being left, and as afraid as I am of losing her, I'm more afraid of me because I just don't know what I'll stop at. In the end, it doesn't seem to matter and I don't care, because when we stop kissing, she is smiling at me in that way that makes me feel like a fresh tide, lapping and cool.

"Come on," she says finally. "I'll take you home." And we walk back to her car with our arms around each other like when we were kids, breaking for Kool-Aid and sandwiches in the backyard. But when we get in the car, I pull her over to the passenger's seat, on top of me, and kiss her, long and deep, until she pulls my shirt up over my head, the slightest smile on her lips, and she shakes her head, lying, "It's okay, Rose."

It's Tommy who is awake when we get home.

"Jessie's spending the night," I tell him, and we head up to my room with him looking after us. I think he doesn't know what to say. Of course, Vivian wakes up and I have to beg her, outside my bedroom door, with Jessie changing into a pair of my pajamas, to please not call the Spencers, to please wait until the next morning. She is staring at me, up and down, and I know that look, checking to see if I'm okay, and even though I'm practically vibrating with all the feelings I don't understand, she lets us be.

I crawl into bed and Jessie's hair is a damp tangle on my pillow. She smells like Downy Fabric Softener and the rain and I lie there breathing her in. She pushes the covers away and says, "Sit up a sec," and we sit cross-legged, our eyes adjusting to the darkness.

She opens her mouth a few times to say something, then closes it.

"What?"

"Wait."

She swallows, then says, "I love you."

"I . . ."

"Let me finish."

I do not want to hear this.

"When I feel like I don't have one clear thought, like everything is going by so fast, I remember I have you. When I want to just go away and think that's what I really want to do, I remind myself that I'll miss you."

My heart is going a mile a minute because I don't know what else she's going to say next, and I want everything to stop. She might as well be rising off the bed, toward the window.

"Stay here," I say.

"No. You think my parents will let me stay here, that your parents will let me stay if my father says no?"

"Why can't you just wait?"

"You don't understand, Rose. I can't wait anymore."

"But why?"

"Because I'll kill him if I stay. I promise you I will. For a week before I left I got up every night and sat outside their bedroom door. I hate him too much. He knows, too. He hasn't touched me for a month."

I start to say she's just talking, and then I remember that motel room and know that anything is possible, that I am one giant fool if I think there isn't a whole lot I don't know.

"Come with me, Rose."

"With those guys?"

"Just me and you."

"Where are we gonna go?"

She says it's my choice. We'll pack a bag tomorrow, make

believe we're going to school.

I say okay.

When I wake up in the morning, she's gone. Vivian is standing by my bed, telling me someone set fire to Dr. Spencer's office.

Jessie calls that night from some gas station off the Long Island Expressway. I can hear the cars whizzing by. She says in a voice pressured and loud that she's leaving for Florida, the police are after them, she took Percocet and Vicoden from Dr. Spencer's office. I just stare out the window. It's still pouring, and all day and night I've been so tired, weary in a way that makes me want to curl up and disappear. She says good-bye so quickly I'm sure someone's hurrying her. I don't say anything about her leaving without me. We both know I was too scared to really go, and I have no idea what would make her stay.

▼

Soon after Jessie left, Vivian got sick again—vague, soft, teary. I came home from school to find her sitting at the kitchen table with a pile of sweatshirts, every sweatshirt in the house, including Tommy's. She sat there painting a flower on the front of each sweatshirt like some art therapist fairy godmother had descended upon her with the smooth squat bottles of paint.

I put my books down on the kitchen table and shuffled through the pantry shelves for a snack, trying to figure out how to act, what to say, and why I felt so irritated suddenly. I sat across the table from her with a bag of pretzels and she looked up at me.

"How was school today?"

"Fine. I have my SATs this Saturday and we're going out to lunch afterwards."

Actually, my friends and I were going over to the local pub to drink. Most of us were 18 by then, and Jack the Boyfriend was a budding alcoholic who seized any opportunity to enter into an altered state. He was high in second period, drunk after baseball practice, and brilliant enough to get away with it. He had gotten an early admission to Harvard plus a scholarship, and he was really just killing time.

I wasn't high in school or on school nights, but on weekends I would share a bottle of wine and shots of whiskey with Jack, thankful for the way it dulled and quieted my head. Jessie had been gone three months by then. Most evenings, after I'd been drinking and was lying in bed, the bed spinning, the alcohol would lower the drawbridge and my feelings, raging and ripping, would storm their way up that bridge and into my heart. I'd wake up in the morning, my head pounding and my pillow still damp.

One of Vivian's brothers was an alcoholic; a couple of times the phone had rung in the middle of the night, and Tommy had gotten dressed and bailed him out at the police station. Vivian hated Jack, the way he touched me like I was some part of him, his temper, his smart, disrespectful mouth; mostly the drinking scared her. And that was fine with me. I hated her then, did what I could to avoid her for reasons I couldn't explain. Sometimes I thought of breaking up with Jack, tired of his spoiled-brat tantrums and possessiveness, tired of his touching me, but then I would think of Vivian and decide not to. I think now it was the only way I knew to be angry at her, to get back at her without feeling guilty for being angry at someone who couldn't help getting sick. And I blamed her, in some way I couldn't articulate, for losing Jessie.

"How are you feeling?"

Vivian's eyes welled with tears. I got up quickly and pulled a chair up to her, putting my arms around her and holding her close while she cried softly, my hatred dissolving quickly into fear.

"What's the matter? What's the matter, Mom?"

But she couldn't say. She just looked at me, trying to make

herself stop crying. She didn't have to tell me she was scared. For the past month she'd been racing around like some wild horse until one morning I got up for school and went downstairs to the kitchen to find it dark, the coffee pre-made but unplugged, last night's crumbs still on the kitchen table, and that heavy feeling in the house again. And I knew.

This time she left, packing her little jars of paint in her suitcase, saying she needed a break, a rest, and took a plane to Sicily to stay with her cousins. We still have pictures of her, sitting on a donkey, picking olives, her cousins and some other people I don't know gathered around her. She is beautiful in these pictures, tan, her eyes strangely clear. She stayed there a month, stayed until the evening when she was supposed to be on a plane home, and she called Tommy to say her suitcase was locked in the trunk of a car and the lock was jammed, couldn't get it open.

Tommy went raging around the kitchen, yelling,

"This is fucking enough, Vivian! I've had it. Get home now!"

He slammed the phone down and looked over at me, loading the dinner dishes into the dishwasher. We'd been alone together for that month, me running freer than I ever had and yet knowing not to push my luck with him. He was barely keeping it all together—the gas station, Claire's lunches and soccer practices, my curfew he'd extended until midnight.

"This is bullshit," he said to me, disgusted. He was scared but also just fed up. He wouldn't ever say it, wouldn't betray my mother in that way, but I knew what he meant: That he was sick of watching Vivian spin around like some twister, shoving away both him and his efforts to talk sense into her, and then leaving him with this shell of a wife, this damp heap on the floor he had to pick up and soothe.

Vivian came home, and after a week went back to work in a paced and sensible way that made me anxious, like having to look

over your shoulder. It was the third time she'd been sick like this.
Her recovery always seemed to start this way, planned and practical, with good intentions, but it had always ended up somewhere
else, stretched to the breaking point. This time, she made files,
talked to clients on the phone in a voice steady and clear. She
made big Xs in her date book, two whole days, an hour at noon
and Xs at the top of each day that guarded the mornings until 9.
The pen made hard sounds on the pages, like lengths of fence
being nailed together.

▼

In May I'm accepted at the Claremont Colleges in California.
I sit at the kitchen table, reading the acceptance materials, all
these colored pages and choices, which dorm, which meal plan,
tentative major, orientation schedule. I look at the slick photos in
the catalog, serene teenagers lounging on lovely lawns, studying
in dorm rooms, smiling cafeteria worker spooning mashed potatoes onto happy student's extended plate.

The phone rings and it's Jessie, calling from a pay phone to
tell me she is waitressing, and that she and Don have rented an
apartment with some guy named Baloo, clearly another esteemed
Hostess-Outlet type of acquaintance. She is in Chapel Hill. She's
going on about a Pink Floyd Concert from the night before, and
about how hot it is in Chapel Hill. I sit on the cold tile of the dining-room floor, the phone cord pulled taut from the kitchen wall.
I am spinning inside, the sound of her voice, the pressure in my
chest, my mouth dry with anger at her selfishness. At the same
time it's like sitting in the movies watching the show happen in
front of you.

I don't know what I expected her to say when she finally
called. She's giving me the details of her apartment, two bedrooms, a balcony and a pool, and I'm thinking Jessie is gone

someplace so far away, where there are no parents, no curfews, no school, no me, no us, and where they are other things I know she isn't telling me.

"So, what's going on with you?"

Like she's just come home from a family skiing vacation.

I search for an answer, not knowing how to tell Jessie such big things: My mother being sick again, my being accepted to a college in California, Jack's drinking and possessiveness that are starting to frighten me.

The pay-phone voice comes on asking for 40 cents more, please. Please deposit 40 cents for the next three minutes.

"Hold on! Hold on!" she calls over the voice and the sound of the phone eating coins. And in the time it takes for the coins to fall, before I even hear her say my name and ask if I'm there, I know that Jessie is gone in a way I can't even fathom, and that I have felt lonelier talking to her in those few minutes than during the whole four months she's been gone.

"I have to go." And I hang up, slow and quiet like maybe neither of us will notice I've slipped away.

I walk out the back door where Vivian is planting the tomato plants she has gotten from the nursery the day before. She is barefoot, her pants rolled up and the hose running, making mud over her feet. I sit out on the back stoop, my mind a jumble, and think again about my father fixing Thumbelina. I wish he could pull out Jessie's pain and hand her back to me with her rectangular body and fresh stitches.

My father probably wishes he or someone could do the same for Vivian.

Vivian smiles up at me as she pulls a tomato plant out of its little plastic pot and deposits it in the hole she has dug. She has 10 little holes dug in two parallel rows, all neatly filled with a shallow pool.

"Who was on the phone?"

"Jessie."

Vivian lets the plant drop into its hole and stands up.

"Where's she calling from?"

"North Carolina—Chapel Hill—some pay phone."

"Jesus Christ, I don't know what's wrong with her mother! I'd be on a plane and bring you back here before you knew what hit you," she says angrily. And I know she is right.

"I talked to Hannah last week. She said the police said Jessie's 18 now. They can't bring her back if she doesn't want to come back. They said she'd just run away again anyway."

"I don't give a shit what the police said. I'd have your ass back here. I don't get it. She's an excellent student. Her parents adore her—not the best discipline and structure, but things seemed fine . . ."

"Things were not fine."

"What're you talking about?"

"Dr. Spencer molested her. He wouldn't leave her alone. That's why she left."

I unload it just like that, looking full into my mother's face, watching the horror rise into her eyes and color her cheeks as what I've said registers, as she sees I'm not kidding.

"Jesus Christ! Why didn't you tell me?"

"I don't know."

And it's true. I can't explain it, really. It was like something that was always there, hidden behind shoeboxes and sweaters in the back of some closet you never open, walk by every day but it's somewhere away in the back. It isn't until I hang up the phone, sit on the stoop with the sun making the top of my head hot and my feet cool with the hose water and mud, that it comes out, that I think to say it out loud.

"Are you sure? You know Jessie, she has that imagination of

hers. Maybe . . ." But she stops when she sees the look on my face.

"You should have told me. Jessie should have told me."

I just shrug. I don't know what to say to that.

"Rose," Vivian says. "Did he ever bother you?"

"No, Mom."

"Are you sure?"

"Of course I'm sure."

"And where the hell was Hannah?"

"I don't know," I say, my voice flat, toeing the mud. Vivian's looking like she's about to jump in the car and go after the Spencers with that spade she's clutching on to.

"You're *sure* he never touched you?"

"Yes, Mom, I'm sure."

And I want her to stop because my throat is getting tight like I'm going start crying and that's the last thing I want. I'm sick of crying about Jessie while she's off at some Pink Floyd Concert with Don and his Twinkie-making friends. "Never," I say again, so she knows I'm not lying.

"I don't want you going over there anymore."

That's when I lose it.

"Why would I go over there when Jessie's gone!"

And I'm crying and I'm so pissed that I'm crying that I'm making it worse with these big groaning sounds, my head in my hands, tears falling onto my legs. I feel Vivian sit next to me, hugging me, her face in my hair, whispering, "Shhh," and I lean into her.

"She'll be back, Rose."

As if she knows, as if she can see into the future.

"You don't know that."

"I do, trust me." And for once I hope she really does know everything.

"I don't care if she ever comes back!"

"Oh yes you do, Rose," she says, stroking my hair out of my

eyes, and I can't stop crying, wanting to tell Vivian the way I love Jessie and how scared I am of those feelings, so she can protect me and make it safe. I don't tell her, of course, knowing, even though I'm desperate for it to be different, that Vivian wouldn't understand, would be horrified—worse than the thing with Dr. Spencer. I also start to worry that I've told her too much already, not a week after she's come home. I had promised myself that I would be more thoughtful; wipe off the bathroom counter, empty the dishwasher and fill it again instead of leaving my dish in the sink, not give her those ugly looks when she annoys me.

My father comes around the corner, wearing a baseball cap, no shirt or shoes, his shorts covered with old and new paint. He's been painting the back shed and he's dripping sweat. He walks over to the hose, picks it up and lets the cold water run into his mouth, splashing it on his face and neck. He's tanned dark now on his arms and face. His chest and stomach are white and his forearms have these lines where his tan ends and his T-shirt sleeves begin. He looks at us, the water like a tube of light running over his mouth, and smiles this kooky smile.

"Hot," he says, then sees my tears. "What's going on?"

"Jessie called," my mother says, and he nods, moving now to turn off the hose, and then stands there wiping his mouth.

"She back?" he asks.

"No," I say. "She's not coming back."

And he nods again, kind but that's all. I don't expect anything else; I know there's nothing they can do. In a way it's enough, what they give me, which is everything they can give: Love, warm and solid, cocooned in the smell of tomato plants, spicy sweet.

I watch my father as he walks back to the shed, thinking I know he knows what it is like to have a beloved orbit around you just slowly enough to watch and yet so far away that only the tips of your outstretched fingers brush her as she swings by.

Chapter 8

Vivian was right. Jessie came home in August, a week before I left for Claremont, but it wasn't okay. They brought her straight to the psychiatric unit at Mercy Hospital, a transfer from some hospital in Florida where she'd landed after taking too many of some pills no one seemed to know the name of. It was there that a nurse saw the cuts, on her arms, stomach and thighs—not deep enough to need stitches, Vivian told me after she hung up the phone with Hannah, as if that should be a relief.

"Why?"

"I don't know. You'll have to ask her. She'll be back tomorrow."

I went to my room, closed the door and sat on my bed. My suitcase lay open against the wall, half packed with clothes that mostly still had the tags on them, bought especially for college, and with graduation presents, a travel iron, a reading light, the packing list sent from Claremont lying on top.

She wasn't coming with me.

That had been my carefully hidden fantasy since she had left, that she'd come back to Long Island, live with us until it was time to leave for college. It's not the kind of thing you tell anyone, but I had bought doubles of things when I could, two sets of towels and sheets, two tubes of toothpaste.

I pictured her sitting on a hospital bed, bird-like, defeated, and I couldn't imagine what to say first when I walked into her room.

▼

Hospitals buy the same linoleum as schools. They just take better care of it. I follow the signs to the two heavy white doors with the little windows, wire mesh embedded in the glass. There's a mixed message for you! "You're sane enough for us not to worry if you wander out the door, but just in case we're wrong we've installed this nice sturdy reinforced glass." No one's wearing hospital gowns. Everyone's in sweats. This is the unlocked unit. There's a locked unit upstairs where Jessie was for the first few hours after she arrived.

Lots of colored tape on the floor, little paths, orange tape leading to the nurses' station, blue tape leading to a TV room where a few people sit on a plastic couch, pink tape leading out to a terrace, people smoking. One woman, who looks about 40 with deep brown circles under her eyes and clothes that hang from pointy shoulders and hips, sits on a bench, crying and smoking. Another, much younger but with a face that's hard and yellow, like people who've ridden Greyhound buses their whole lives, like the cashiers in the A&P Vivian would point at saying, "That's what you end up looking like when you eat that processed food every night for dinner." I head down the hall, looking for Jessie's room, thinking Vivian's probably right, in general. But I can bet you those women lived through more than just one too many TV dinners.

The day is heavy and hot, the kind of August summer sun that goes down leaving sidewalks steamy and damp little tugs of breeze too weak to cool anything off.

She is on fire, a mass of springy red hair and ruddy-faced, a pinkish tan from the Florida sun. I stand in the doorway of her room for a moment. She's sitting on her bed, listening to a Walkman, the headphones like some hair accessory, pushing the curls from her face. She's wearing a Queen T-shirt and sweat pants. She senses someone there and turns to the doorway.

"Hey, Rose."

Tentatively.

"Hey, Jessie." And I feel like it takes me a day to get across the room, my arms awkward as I lean over to hug her. She smells like soap and the bleach of hospital sheets, stiff and blank. We hug tight. The force of that hug squeezes pools of tears into my eyes.

"You okay?" I whisper hoarsely into that hair and she nods, hard, not letting go of me. I am so happy to see her. I crawl up onto the bed and we sit there, cross-legged, looking in each other's faces.

"Your hair is *pink*, Rose." Crooked little smile.

"It's a cellophane. You like it?"

"I don't know. It's a little space-age. Only the part the sun's hitting is pink. The other part's brown."

"Yeah, it's supposed to be subtle."

We laugh, short nervous laughs that leave us sitting in awkward quiet. Finally I realize I'm holding my breath and sigh. Jessie looks up at me expectantly.

"Hannah said you took some pills."

Jessie nods, solemnly.

"That you tried to kill yourself."

"Yeah."

"Why?"

"I don't know."

"You don't know?"

"No."

I believe her, though I can't imagine someone doing something like that without even having a reason. She looks frightened then, like it was someone else who hurt her, her eyes darting around the room like whoever it was might return.

"You really wanted to die?"

"Yeah."

Then she looks up at me like she's just thought of something.

"Or at least stop the feelings. I couldn't stand it. I'd rather be dead. I felt like I was crawling out of my skin, like I couldn't stop crying, and I was so scared. I was so scared, Rose."

"Of what?"

"I don't know. And that's worse. It's just this big scared feeling like someone's gonna kill me but I don't know why or who and like my inside is this big hole and there's no one else in the world. I'm all alone."

I can see she's getting frightened, her eyes doing that darting thing all over the room, her face getting even redder.

"How do you feel now?"

"Better. The nurses watch me and talk to me. They gave me some medicine and it makes me spacey and gives me cottonmouth, but I'm sleeping at night now and I'm less scared today. The other patients are all fucked up too, so I don't have to pretend everything's okay."

"You're not fucked up."

"Oh yeah." And she pulls up her shirt to show me her stomach: Three lines of scabs, skinny and sharp, the skin swollen red around the scabs. That irritates me, because she does it like she's proud of it.

"Why'd you do that to yourself?"

"I don't know."

Flatly, dropping her shirt.

I strain to keep the edge out of my voice, feeling like a real witch for being angry at her when she's so clearly in trouble.

"I think you know," I say finally.

"I don't want to talk about it anymore, okay?"

"Okay."

"Want to go outside? I want a smoke."

I nod, even though I don't smoke. I'm surprised that she does. I follow her out to the terrace. The other patients outside all greet her, and she introduces me around. We go sit on a bench under a tree; they all go back to what they were doing. The one that was crying when I walked by earlier gets up and leaves. I have this mad urge to call her back and invite her over. She looks like what it used to feel like to sit alone on the bus in elementary school, like her life is this big long lonely bus ride, and I can feel this huge sadness I push away, almost swatting the air.

"I think I get to leave soon."

This catches me by surprise because I've kind of thought maybe she likes it here.

"We have a family session tonight and the doctor said I can leave tomorrow, probably."

"Are you going to tell them, Jessie?"

"What?"

"You know what, about your dad."

She won't look at me, looks out past the parking lot, her eyes fixed on the trees in the distance, but I know we're both thinking of Dr. Spencer's office, scorched stucco and the bottles of pills she took.

"Well, are you?"

"No," she says, her voice dull. "I can't."

"Why not?"

"It doesn't matter."

"Oh, I guess not. I guess it doesn't matter that your stomach looks like that, that you're in this place. Come *on*, Jessie. You need to tell Hannah so she can . . ."

"Can what? What do you think she's gonna do, Rose?" she says, turning on me, accusing, waiting for an answer.

"She'll tell him to leave. She'll make him stop."

But before the words are even out of my mouth, I know I don't really believe them. And that's her point. I don't want to find out for a certainty whom Hannah would choose.

"You want to come stay with us?"

"Don't you need to ask?"

"Vivian said to tell you to come."

"Oh, okay."

I remember that, us nodding, looking into each other's eyes like that fixed everything.

Jessie left the hospital the next day, and for the rest of the week Vivian and I hovered over her, Vivian cutting her hair, adding vitamins to her morning medicines, giving her chores to do and quick kisses on the top of her head. I got up one morning and found them out on the chaise lounges with their coffee, talking softly, stopping when they heard me pushing open the screen door. Jessie was crying, noiseless tears, blotchy face, and Vivian had her wrapped in her arms. She looked over Jessie's shoulder at me, her eyes wet and murderous.

I loved my mother so much that morning, an angry flame in the morning sun.

I was bussing tables that summer at an upscale restaurant in the Hamptons, The Duck Pond Inn, getting home at 2 or 3 in the morning, my feet aching, dreams of half-filled water glasses, little chunks of ice that wedged in the spout of the pitcher and then suddenly dislodged, water gushing out over the glass and onto the table, empty breadbaskets thrust at me by countless bodiless hands.

I also manned the dessert cart, four stories on wheels, taller than me, cakes and tarts and clear glass bowls of berries, deep reds and purples and blues. I quickly became The Duck Pond Inn's rendition of a closing act, wheeling the cart onto the floor like some unicycle on the high wire. Alfonse, the maitre-d', could toss a line of flaming Zambuca across the table in between coffee cups, which I thought was better than my act, but I sold more desserts than he sold Zambuca.

Alfonse was an elderly gentleman with a British accent who had grown up in restaurants, mostly in Europe. He would stand in the doorway, erect and stern, watching the waiters and me out on the floor, like some governess with her charges. He was someone who could give orders with the slightest nod of the head, or eyes that guided you to empty salad plates waiting to be cleared, a peppermill you neglected to offer, a tiny hair in the frosting of a slice of cake. I was the only female he allowed to work the dinner shift and by far the youngest.

The owners were professionals: a doctor and his wife, an attorney and some man who didn't seem to me then to have any real job, just investments. Alfonse gave them the same unforgiving stares and seemed to take them on like a band of unruly children who were *finally* getting the unwavering hand of discipline they so desperately needed to guide them. Most of this he did without a word.

It was Alfonse who showed me I have a gift for reading others, their needs, their wants, their soft fragile places, and how to stand back and watch, picking up subtle hints about what pleases them. I became his star pupil, flitting from table to table, a snapshot in my mind of each party's unspoken wants and needs . . . The woman at Table 3 needs another Manhattan . . . ducking into the kitchen with salad forks and soup spoons for one final shine with a dishtowel as a customer raised her hand, then her eyes pleasantly amused as I set the needed utensils in front of her before the request had even left her lips. I'd sneak a look at Alfonse, who was always watching, the faintest nod of approval in my direction.

Before the dinner shift, we'd gather in the dining room to taste the specials, and Alfonse would describe this sauce, that side dish, to the waiters, while I folded napkins into triangular hats and moved through the dining room, shining silverware, the bowls of soup spoons, the blades of knives, setting water and wine glasses at a straight diagonal from the tip of the knife, removing and filling salt and pepper shakers. The three waiters, all with other careers—teacher, graduate student, sculptor—listened to Alfonse with respectful amusement. I could hear them later, out of his earshot, during a lull in the dinner activity, talking softly— "It's only a piece of salmon, for God's sake, a *slice* of cake"—and wink at me when they caught me eavesdropping.

Lawrence, the teacher, had come home from the Vietnam War with a Vietnamese wife. I had met her and their little brown boy after a brunch shift. It was my first interracial couple, and I watched other people watch them like they were looking for something. I watched too, and I don't know what I was looking for either, except some kind of difference. One time I imagined her pulling this bowl of rice out of her purse, but after that I just didn't think about it, like someone would be able to read my mind and see what a latent bigot I was.

Lawrence was my favorite, after Alfonse, and he looked after me like a baby sister, taking my side with Murray the Big Fat Cook. You want to experience death by multiple skewer wounds? Just call a chef a cook. I wasn't brave enough to say it to his face, but I called him that in a whisper once we were out on the floor, to the waiters. Even Alfonse smiled, and it stuck. Mrs. Baxter, Dr. Baxter's wife, muttered it under her breath once after he screamed at her in front of a deliveryman for ordering double-cream instead of triple-cream Brie. He would throw taunts at me as I passed him with a tray full of dishes for the dishwasher.

"Those pants are getting kind of tight, Rose."

My face would grow hot with embarrassment. I'd stand in the walk-in box after the dinner shift and devour big chunks of broken cake, my fingers scooping strawberry rhubarb pie filling from its tin, as I stretched plastic wrap over the desserts and lined them up on the shelves.

"That's enough, Murray," Lawrence would say to him in a tone that made me think of him in the jungle, his eyes searching for the enemy, an entity I was never quite able to put a face to after meeting his wife and son. "White trash," Lawrence would say to me later.

"Yeah, well, it's kind of true."

"You look fine. Don't pay him any attention."

He'd pat me on the head like a kid much younger than my 18 years, and I'd head back out to the floor chanting softly, "Murray, Murray-the-Big-Fat-Cook, Murray-the-Big-Fat-Ugly-Cook, Oh, Murray . . ." Like a fourth-grader. But I'd calm myself down.

I did the same thing with Vivian, when she'd ground me for missing my curfew, but I had started doing it so long before, I can't even remember how old I was. I just remember climbing up the stairs after being sent to my room, and singing, little breaths really, "I hope you get hit by a truck, I hope it runs you over," hitting a high note on the you.

"What did you say?" Vivian would call from the kitchen.

"God! I can't even sing now?" It was all the defiance I could muster as I was so terrified of her, but it worked. A small little protest that gave me enough control to save face, the anger seeping out of me like air from a pinhole in a birthday balloon.

Something changed for Vivian and me that summer, the kind of understanding and compassion for another's pain you can get only from shared experience.

I'd heard Lawrence talk differently, and talk more, to the male customers his age who had been in Vietnam. I was aching from Jessie's absence, an empty place, a feeling like broken glass in my stomach. I learned how work could be a drug, distracting and preoccupying, filling emptiness or at least demanding attention somewhere else. So I worked hard and did not spend all day and night in the broken-glass place, sitting in the middle of ruins, absently fingering broken furniture, staring at smolderings of something so burnt that its identity can't even be made out anymore.

On some mornings after waking up, I'd lie in bed and just peek in on that ruined empty place, and it did seem as if some tiny clean-up crew had been working away, in their orange vests, the pain shoveled into big black plastic trash bags like so many broken plates, the big pieces gathered into piles they hauled away. Once I realized how time can do that if you only find a way to bear it, I understood how Vivian could act like work was some miracle cure and get hooked. It wasn't a knowledge I could put into words that summer, even to myself. I just watched her differently, just as worried, but with less bewilderment and anger.

Vivian opened a second salon that summer. Overnight it seemed to arrive, without warning, like the big yellow diggers that showed up to make our pool one morning, the diggers I suddenly saw through the kitchen window while I was eating my cereal.

There were the usual yelling fights for a day or two, Tommy's attempt to hold some ground.

"I am not going to stop at Home Depot!" he yelled over the phone to Tina, who was working receptionist at the new shop. Vivian had told her to call Tommy at the gas station and tell him to pick up paint to redo the facial room. She wanted a more tranquil color, robin's egg blue or the pale yellow of an infant's room. Tina held the phone away from her ear shaking her head, rolling her eyes at my father's rantings.

"Tell her she's a fucking nut job! We've been working on that place till 11 every night . . ."

"Okay, Uncle Tommy, okay . . . yeah, no, I'll tell her . . ." And then an hour later he calls from his car phone.

"Ask her does she want semi-gloss or flat?"

"You know I didn't even bother telling her he wasn't going," Tina said to me the next day when she told me the story, and we laughed quietly, fondly, together.

One week Vivian and I had the same day off, a Wednesday because restaurants and hair salons demand weekend work. We sat out in the backyard, in the chaise lounges, drinking coffee in our nightgowns.

"How much you make yesterday?" she asked.

"Ninety."

I had worked a double-shift, falling into bed in the middle of the night, dreams of a world where all glasses were half-empty. "How about you?"

Vivian looked over at me in surprise. I had never asked her how much money she made. Everyone seemed to pretend that the bills she pulled out of her bra, in the grocery store, the deli, the mall ("Oh, Mom, that is *so* embarrassing," Claire would snarl under her breath as we left a store), just hatched in there, multi-plying like little chicks.

"Five hundred."

"Five hundred! I don't make five hundred in a week!"

"No, Rose, ninety is good. Think of it this way, it's the same as double that, one-eighty, once the government takes its part."

"Oh," was all I said, but I'd heard it all right, I'd heard her say "good"—good enough, more than good enough. Words like the admittance into some exclusive club.

We showered and dressed and went shopping at the outlets and then had lunch on the porch of one of the most popular restaurants in the Hamptons. I had broken up with Jack back in July, something that took me a month to get up the nerve to do, hanging on to him, not wanting to lose anyone or anything else since Jessie's leaving. A series of sobbing, screaming phone calls left me feeling numb and guilty as I listened on the other end of the phone. A series of, "I'm sorry, Jack, I'm sorry," in a flat voice. A series of, "I'm hanging up now." In a flatter voice. I wanted to miss him, to feel heartbroken and to long for his company, but that never happened. It worried me and confused me, but by then I'd gotten good about not thinking about feelings.

"You'll meet some nice boy in college," Vivian said, a forkful of spinach salad in mid-air.

"Sure," I said. "One of those blond, tan surfer boys."

And we smiled, eyebrows raised.

I left for college with the three of us having mapped out Jessie's life like Vivian's vegetable garden, a row of eggplants here, the peppers there, the basil getting its own little bed so it doesn't take over the rest of the garden, just like it is possible to save someone's life, fix a decade of what was lacking with a reception-ist job at the salon, mending it with personal objects you place toward the front of a dresser, like the photo Jessie and I framed one night, sitting on my bed, cropping it and turning over the frame. The photo of Jessie and me at 13, slick as seals, bobbing in this big ol' inner tube, funny faces for the camera.

Tommy answered the phone when I called that day from college, three weeks after I'd arrived, from a pay phone at the end of the hall.

"She ran away again, Rose. Your mother called the police."

It was worse this time. They pumped her stomach and she needed stitches. There are no phones in the rooms on the locked unit, just this one pay phone. A patient would answer and then go off to find her and come back to take a message. She was in Group. I called seven times, three times in one day and the last time I slammed the phone down, almost knocking some guy to the ground when I flew around the corner, blind with tears.

Chapter 9

I drive to Jessie's that night very slowly. The Mercedes is a diesel and, as my father says, it can't get out of its own way. I'm also just one of those slow drivers. One of those bad, slow drivers. The kind people interrupt conversations to curse and pass. It's unfortunate because, honestly, I was given every opportunity. I got my permit the day after my 15th birthday, and the same week Vivian enrolled me in the AAA driving school.

It wasn't the instructor's fault. Mr. Cooper was a benevolent, clearly brave, pink-skinned, middle-aged man who would arrive every Saturday morning at 10 to drive me around the Island for an hour or two. I'd be terrified. I'd open our front door to see him standing there in his windbreaker, and my heart would start bouncing off my ribs. But I was 15 and you know how it is: It's very uncool to be scared at 15.

So I did what always worked just fine for me. I told myself it was my imagination and slammed the door shut on the feeling.

I'm still very good at this. You can almost hear the little lock snap.

We'd head down the walkway, get in one of those cars with two steering wheels and the big Caution: Student Driver sign bolted to the hood. I don't remember how long this went on, but it was long enough for a routine to develop where my mother would leave the $30 to pay him stuck to the refrigerator with a magnet, next to all her notes. Claire and I each got a note, like: *Claire—empty garbage, clean out spice cabinet, vacuum downstairs. Rose—empty dishwasher, fold laundry, dust living room.*

Now, to really appreciate this you have to know that we had a cleaning woman who came every week. At one point the cleaning woman actually came on Fridays, but we'd wake up to the same notes on Saturday morning. A few years ago I finally asked Vivian what the deal was, and she said she figured if she kept us busy we wouldn't do drugs.

Anyway, eventually I did get my license, and within the first month I caused a major accident. I was driving Jessie home after a basketball game and pulled out to make a left turn and just miscalculated how long it would take to get my 1963 Falcon across the intersection. And a guy rolled his car. I sat in our living room afterward crying quietly, tears smeared all over my face, and telling Jessie, "I could have killed him!"

"He was driving too fast."

"I could have killed him!"

"He walked away from the car."

"Oh God! How would I have lived with that?"

By then I was rocking back and forth on the couch and sort of ranting like an ad for Xanax, and Jessie went and got my mother. Vivian put me to bed, tucking the blankets around my head and whispering into my hair.

"Now Rose, go to sleep. That asshole could have killed you, going that fast. Don't worry; this is why we have insurance."

That stopped me all right. My eyes flew open and I stared into the blanket, the blue weave all blurry up close. Somehow, in one fell swoop, my mother had shifted the responsibility from me—the driver who had clearly made a mistake of judgment—to the driver who had been innocently driving along in his own lane. I didn't understand it all at the time, but I did understand that we were *not* going to have the conversation I so desperately needed to have at that moment: A conversation about how you live with yourself when you make a mistake so big, so permanent, that it forever alters yours and another's life. True, he had walked away. But he might not have. I needed to sit with that possibility and all the feelings that went with it—and not retreat from them. I needed to claim the act as my own and then forgive and then go on. I couldn't do it alone and Vivian didn't know how to do it with me; she couldn't possibly tolerate the pain and fear and self-loathing she would see streaked across her daughter's cheeks.

I woke up the next morning from this dream I still have, where I'm on a beach and all these people are wading at the shore-line or sitting under umbrellas, and it's sunny and warm. Then it's not. It's cloudy and windy, like it gets on summer afternoons right before it rains. Suddenly this huge tidal wave rears up and over the beach and over me, and I'm tumbling in the wild foam, and there's always this high cement wall that catches and holds the wave's tons of water, but of course, before I'm completely out of breath, I wake up.

Now, this is why sometimes I think my friends and I have probably had entirely too much psychotherapy for our own good. One day recently, we're sitting around at Felice Mundo, my friend Marcelle's restaurant, and I'm telling them about the recurring wave dream. They're also, all of them except my friend Becky, in recovery and used to being a little more direct and to the point than, if you ask me, anyone needs to be. Personally I'm a big proponent of the skirting-the-issue-tiptoeing-around-sensitive-topics school of communication. *They* go for the psychological jugular.

"I think," Joven says, stroking his chin like he's accessing his inner Sigmund Freud, "that the wave symbolizes your desire to lose control, and the wall symbolizes the overactive superego that smashes these desires over and over . . ."

"No, no, no, no, I don't think so," Bessie cuts in. "*I* think the significant part of the dream is the change from the sunny happy day to the ominous clouds, and *I* think the catastrophic tidal wave signifies your fear that you are unable to successfully navigate the ups and downs of your life."

And I'm thinking, What is *wrong* with you that you even bring these things up?

"Maybe you're both right," I weasel. "I mean, I've got the control issues, and I do worry that I'll be faced with a tragedy and I won't be able to handle it . . ."

"The real issue here," Marcelle says, with that French accent that makes it sound even more like a proclamation, "is fear of death. But so what? Who is not afraid of death? Crazy people, that's who. Am I right?" I love Marcelle.

Last year she was diagnosed with breast cancer. She had a mastectomy and at first they thought they'd got it all, but about three months later they found some cells in her lymph nodes. She had six months of chemo. They think they've got it in remission, so now she goes in for monthly checkups. Joven and I take turns covering for her at the restaurant when she goes in, and I'm usually so shook up the whole time, worrying that this will be the time they find something again, that I burn one or two entrees at a minimum. Sometimes I don't even know it, and Bessie and Dee, who are the waitresses, they have to say, "Honey, what does this look like to you?" tilting the plate for me to see.

"Like a very unfortunate mistake."

"Thank you. Can I get another?"

But so far, every time, she's been okay.

▼

I scan the mailboxes until I find the address on the receipt
Jessie gave me and park along the curb. It's one of those fourplexes
built in the Fifties or Sixties that's clearly a rental unit, because the
paint is one of those on-sale-this-week colors—a rancid butter-
scotch, in this case, and it's peeling. I walk up the driveway, past
a laundry room and carports on the first floor, and then upstairs,
where the apartments are lined up in a row, with Jessie's on the
end. I knock on the door feeling antsy as hell.

Truth is, I hadn't let myself think one full thought about seeing Jessie again. Every time I started trying to remember if her
hair was really short or medium length, what I'd say when her
front door swung open and she was actually standing there in
front of me—just the two of us and the dark—I stopped myself.
And I'm actually driving to Jessie's and still dodging, even reliving
painful memories to help me do it.

As I'm knocking, I hear, "Hey, I'm over here."

And there's Jessie sitting on the roof over the laundry room,
smoking.

She's sort of smiling in a nervous way. She's got on these blue
scrubs and shiny white sneakers and her hair is short. She's
thinned out. As she walks carefully toward me, it hits me again,
like earlier at the funeral home but stronger this time, that she's
not really 18 anymore. She too is older, with the coarser skin of
an adult. Then I realize she's got her hand out, wanting to help
me climb over the rail and out onto the roof.

Quite frankly, I'm not a roof-climbing kind of person. More
than that, I know Jessie knows this, as I have never been a roof-
climbing kind of person. There are roof-climbing types. You

know, the people who as kids built ramps to ride their bicycles off
of and the mothers don't realize what they're up to until one day
they look out the kitchen window to see their eight-year-old flying through the air, with a look of triumphant hysteria, straight
for some tree. Later these same kids grow up and drive Volvos.

"Come on."

Jessie is still holding out her hand.

"I won't let you fall."

I take her hand and climb over the railing and onto the roof.
I can feel the tightness of her grasp. As we edge out to where she'd
been sitting, I get that embarrassed but safe, grateful feeling you
get when you know someone knows you're vulnerable and is
watching out for you without making you have to ask. We sit
down beside each other and stare out at the night.

Her roof has a view of the street and the high-school football
field and track where some lunatic woman is walking alone, at 10
at night. We smile at one another with that kind of look down-
look back smile that gives you away every time.

"I really am sorry about your grandmother," she finally says,
and I reach out for the cigarette she's handing me. I get a mock-
ing, shocked look. "You're a smoker?"

"Sometimes," I say, taking a drag, wishing for about a liter of
wine to go with it and chastising myself for being so pathetically
nervous. I can't even tell you why I'm so damn nervous except
that I don't know where to start. You can't start from where you
left off because that was a dozen years ago and you end up feeling
like William Randolph Hearst clutching a sled, rocking back and
forth in some dark room, whispering, "Rosebud, Rosebud." Of
course I'd deny it, but to pull this off I'm drawing on all the social
skills and coolness training gleaned from my years of eating lunch
in a junior-high cafeteria.

"A sometimes smoker?"

"Yeah."

"You know, Rose, there are some things you either are or you aren't. Like you either *are* a cat burglar or you're not. You either *are* a Democrat or you're not. You either *are* a . . ." She's doing this with full hand gestures.

"Why do I think I know where this is going?" I hand back the smoke. "Jeez, Jessie."

"Well, I'm curious. I've heard things."

"And *whom* could you have possibly heard things *from?*"

"Fran," she says. "We split a sandwich from the deli last week, when your mother cut my hair."

"Fran is obviously the kind of woman who will split a deli sandwich with anyone. I don't think you can trust a thing a woman like that says."

This makes her laugh. Then we sit there, quiet.

"So, what did you hear?" I finally ask.

"You, some woman, last year, around Easter, your mother throwing a fit, something about how she didn't dress you that way . . ."

"*Raise*," I say. "As in she didn't *raise* me that way."

"Oh no, not Vivian, she definitely said *dress.*"

I shake my head slowly, looking down at my lap, realizing, with shy happiness, that she is giving me a hard time after all these years.

"Okay, yes. Last year, I'm on the phone with Vivian and she wants me to come home for Easter and I tell her I can't. I have other plans . . ."

"As in, I'm 29 years old and have a life that includes other plans?"

Her eyebrow's raised.

"Wait a minute. I am not the one still living in my hometown."

"Living, not hiding."

Then the smile slides off her face as she sees she has hurt me. She sighs. "Sorry."

"You're still angry with me."

"Angry? About what, Rose?"

"Don't do that."

Now I am angry, in that way where old feelings sweep over you like some wave you don't get a chance to ride. "If you weren't angry with me, you'd have returned my calls to the hospital."

And part of me is thinking this is definitely a Hearst moment.

"It wasn't that I was angry."

Tautness is in her voice.

"Okay. What were you?"

"Jealous, confused, scared and ashamed. I mean, Rose, *you* weren't on the locked unit, you were in college in California like a normal person."

"I didn't think you were abnormal."

"Then you have a very generous definition of normal. I'd say anyone residing on a locked psych ward with their wrists stitched up is having more than a bad day. It just felt too bad to talk to you when you were fine and I couldn't stay away from anything with a point."

"But maybe if we could have talked it would have helped."

"Believe me, Rose, I felt so hateful and repulsive back then, nothing you'd have said could have made a difference. It would have made it worse—together, understanding Rose keeping in touch with that crazy friend of hers."

She pauses. Then exhales abruptly.

"In case no one has told you this some time in the past dozen years, let me break the news flash: Sometimes you *can't* help someone. You can love them to death, but you still can't help them."

She doesn't have to say anything else. I know she's talking about Hannah as well as herself.

"I missed you, though."

"I missed you, too."

We watch the street. A lone car pulls into a driveway. The woman on the track is stretching one leg on the bleachers. I don't think either one of us knows what else to say. I steal a look at Jessie and she's deep in some thought. I just let her be. I'm sad looking at her, though. I know she's right about my not being able to help, but it's not that simple. We still aren't talking about the angry feelings. As we know, I'm a pro in the avoidance department. Jessie, on the other hand, must be some heavyweight champ in the feelings department, with all that therapy, so I figure it's up to her to decide the right time to have that conversation. Finally she speaks.

"How was college, anyway?"

College? College was so long ago. But I don't say that, of course.

"Good. I mean, I dropped out to go to the Culinary Academy my senior year . . ."

"I hear San Francisco is a great place to be a chef, all those restaurants, all that organic produce . . ."

"It can get crazy, though." I shrug. "I was the baker at the coffee-house at the college—work-study job—and I used to imagine what it would be like to be a real chef. I had these fantasies of getting written up in *Gourmet Magazine* and attending all these trendy parties. Then I got to the Academy and reality set in. I love it, though, even with all the craziness."

"So, who was this woman?"

"Gail? She was my girlfriend. We lived together for a couple years, and I was the chef at the restaurant she owned. And, I don't know, I thought everything was going okay. Then I find out she's sleeping with our organic farmer."

"Your organic farmer? You're kidding?" And I can tell she's loving this. "Ah, the perils of organic gardening. That is *so* California. That is so great. I'm sorry, go on."

"That's it. She leaves. She fires me. And the day she leaves, just the other day, right? Vivian calls me to tell me my grandmother's died."

"So you have no job?"

"No."

"But, you're like this hot-shot chef, right? You could probably get a job anywhere, right?"

"I don't know. Maybe. I didn't even have a chance to make any calls. When I found out she was having the affair, I confronted her, and she left to go spend the night at Leslie's—that's the farmer's name. And I just get changed and go to work. I figure she'll move to beautiful Sonoma with Farmer Leslie, I'll stay in Marin, and we'll just see each other at work."

"You really thought that?"

"I *did*. It was like our place, I was the chef when it opened."

"Okay, one thing: Did you have any ownership in this place, like did you buy in at some point?"

"I didn't see the need. If you were there . . ."

"Face it, Rose. You were a fool for love. You'll just have to get another job at another restaurant."

"Yeah. I just can't believe it, though. It was *our* place."

"You're like not as concerned about losing this Gail as you are about losing this restaurant, are you?"

"It was our baby."

"Maybe you can work out some weekend visitation thing."

"Very funny. You don't know, it's a pretty cliquey town. I'm actually a little worried about getting another position."

"Oh, come on! You cannot be the only chef in San Francisco who slept with a restaurant owner. You're being melodramatic."

"Oh yeah? I had this professor at the Academy, Marcelle Péron, she was this terrible alcoholic, drank these expensive bottles of wine through the dinner shift, and this is at Postrio! But they let it slide because she doesn't miss a beat. You can't get a Saturday night reservation for three months. Then one day, out of the blue, they fire her and she can't get a job anywhere. I mean anywhere you'd consider working. Not even the wineries. She got in recovery, but that was the end for her. It can be cutthroat like that. I could end up flipping pancakes at Bob's Big Boy."

"So, let me get the full picture here. You lose your girlfriend, your job and your, ah, baby, all in one day, and then your grandmother."

And her eyes are dancing.

"Yeah, I was thinking of maybe running myself over with the car on the way home." And we both start laughing, with Jessie pushing at me, pushing me over, chiding, "Poor Rose, poor, poor thing."

We crawl to the railing, Jessie holding me by the waist.

"Okay, now jump." She eases me down, toe to toe.

We find ourselves sitting on her living-room carpet, a strong breeze making the screen door rattle.

I sit with my back leaning up against a gray and ratty couch that smells like gerbils. Jessie always had these gerbils that she let loose in her room like it was some gerbil sanctuary. One day her cat caught and killed one, but she kept up the colony and the room always held this funny odor, like corn chips. I look around the apartment for their little cage. It's a tiny place: Living room and kitchen and a door that clearly leads to the bedroom. Jessie is standing in front of the open refrigerator.

"Soda? Beer? Milk?"

"Soda. You still have gerbils?"

"No, no more gerbils, just Bo, who's probably hiding under the bed."

"Bo's still alive? What is he, like 103 by now?"

I open the bedroom door. Jessie's clinking ice cubes into glasses in the kitchen. I kneel and lift up the dust ruffle. Sure enough, there is Bo, staring back at me with those manic yellow eyes, his fur all puffed out and his head pulled into his body like a turtle.

"Yeah, he's under the bed," I call out to the living room, then walk back to where Jessie is sitting, with two glasses of Coke and a bag of chips. We sit across from each other, silently eating for a minute, and it is then I notice that the place is spotless, kind of drab with no real decor to speak of, but dustless even in the baseboard corners. Like some poor, proud old guy with only two pairs of jeans but he makes sure the pair he's wearing is clean and his white sneakers are polished.

It also occurs to me that the couch smells like gerbils because it was Hannah's couch. The one we'd sat on and slept on about a billion times.

"And how did you get to be a nurse?"

"You're not *really* asking that question, are you?"

"I guess not." Shaking my head.

"Lots of therapy, Rose," she says, "and a little phenomenon called sublimation. You know, doing something constructive with all that experience I have caretaking. Oh and of course, cutting, being at home in hospitals . . ."

We laugh. But I know that, while she's making fun of herself, she's doing it in a way, good-natured and kind, that speaks to a sturdiness inside.

By the time Jessie walks me down to the car, it's almost 1 in the morning. The street is so silent you can hear each cricket.

"I'll call you tomorrow night. We'll be back from Brooklyn about 4 and then everyone's staying for dinner."

"Okay."

A quick hug with her hair brushed against my mouth.

Chapter 10

Tina and Claire and I stay so close to one another the day of the funeral, it's as if some imaginary thread runs through us and binds us to my grandmother's black steel sewing machine. We find ourselves in her sewing room after the funeral, our coats strewn on the twin beds, touching all her things. I sit on her chair, my feet resting on the big foot pedal of her machine, spinning spools of thread in a cigar box. Tina is on the floor sifting her hand over and over through a huge jar of buttons. Claire is rolling the chalk she used to make button marks from one hand to another, palms powdery.

The funeral is a caravan, limos in the front, other relatives in the middle, and the three of us bringing up the rear. My grandmother's sisters, Marge and Carmela, pop out of cars and run to the ladies' room after the two-hour ride to Brooklyn. Then they hop in place, tugging up their girdles, as we all rush in and out of the single stall. I'd never seen the priest, and it's too windy to hear what he says. Somehow I'm holding a rose to put on the casket. They put Astroturf over the mounds of dirt they'd dug up for the grave. I pick an acorn, cool and smooth, up out of the grass and climb back into the car.

"No one's going to drive all the way out here," Tina says, and we drive home.

By 7 that night everyone has headed home. Our house is oddly silent after being stuffed so full of people and food. Vivian has sent everyone home with grocery bags full of leftovers portioned out into paper plates, wrapped in aluminum foil. Finally, Claire, Tina and I scatter like someone has snipped our thread, and when I come downstairs, after changing out of my funeral dress and into jeans, Claire and her husband, James, are standing in their coats. I give them each a hug.

"When are you going back to California?"

"Probably a couple of days," I lie.

Tina and my father are in the living room watching some old war movie, and when Vivian goes up to change, I leave a note and drive to Jessie's.

I wake the next morning to Jessie's eyes and the warm crumples of her bed. We lie there for a few moments as sleep drifts away. A slow smile slips over her face.

"Poor Rose," she says. "You didn't move all night."

After I arrived at Jessie's house that night, we sat on the couch looking through the newspaper for movies to take my mind off my grandmother. Jessie went to the bathroom and came out to find me asleep on her couch. The next thing I knew, Jessie was shoving some pajamas into my hand and me into the bathroom.

"Sorry," I'd said, emerging a few minutes later, holding my clothes in a ball, trying to get my words out before sleep fell completely over me like some big black tarp. "I'm usually more fun."

Then there were just the comforting sounds of the whoosh of the covers as she pulled them over me, the snap of the light switch, the brush of the bedroom door along the carpeting.

That morning, as I come out of the bedroom, I can hear Jessie stirring coffee. She's opened the front door. Outside the day is waking with the clicking of women's heels on the blacktop, two little girls chanting and the bouncing of a ball.

"I called your mother last night," Jessie says, handing me a mug of coffee and sitting on the floor. "Just in case you hadn't. I figured she couldn't have changed that much."

"What did she say?"

"She asked if we'd been drinking."

"Like we're still 17."

I laugh, shaking my head.

"She said she was worried about you. That you hadn't cried once and that she knew you were heartbroken over Gail, but she thought there must be something else."

"Oh for God's sake, the woman has mental radar! I haven't told her I'm out of a job."

"Why not?"

"Because I feel like such a fuck-up. You're pathetic enough when you get left for a farmer, but then to be unemployed on top of it! It's just too much. I already feel like a 12-year-old every time I come home. I know if I tell them I lost my job, they'll start handing me twenties and the next thing you know I'll be asking for Fritos in my lunch."

"You gotta give that up, Rose. Vivian is never giving you those preservative-packed Fritos—stunt your growth."

"Oh shut up!"

We laugh, fall silent.

"What *are* you going to do?"

"I guess I'll go back, call some people, see who's hiring, what's available."

I wander off in my head, my eyes following a panel of sunlight along the carpet.

"I wonder who she got to replace me. Mark, my sous-chef, annoys her. Too pliable, she thinks. I think he's ready, but she wouldn't pick him. Marcelle offered me a few shifts at Felice Mundo to tide me over. She said she could use the break, but I think she's just being nice."

"You'll find something else, Rose. Wait and see, something even better, probably."

"Yeah."

"So tell me about this Marcelle and her restaurant. I thought you said she couldn't get a job?"

I never knew Marcelle was in recovery when I was her student at the Culinary Academy. She never missed a day, never late. Her classes were my favorites, always peppered with stories of her childhood in the French countryside, and then her marriage to an American soldier stationed in Belgium, who met her during a French furlough and whisked her away to Concord, California after she told him she was pregnant.

Years later, after the Academy, when we became friends and she was in recovery, she told me she had lied to him, that she wasn't really pregnant but knew if he left she'd never see him again. She saw her life stretch before her, mending shoes in her father's shop, an existence of holey soles, boots to lace, floor to ceiling, and even at 16 she wanted something more than being married to some farmer or, worse yet, her father's apprentice, for the good match it would make.

She laughed when she told me how she insisted she and Stan,

her new American husband, make love every night on the ship, and then as Stan lay sleeping beside her, she would pull her rosary beads from her suitcase and plead with the Blessed Mary to give her a child. She'd sit at the foot of the bunk, having the same silent one-way conversation over and over, explaining that she knew she had lied, she knew that was a sin, but suicide—the certain outcome if she had no baby—was a worse sin, wasn't it? Then she'd imagine this seed of a baby growing inside her, looking like the tiniest zucchini. But it always became a baby by the last bead. In her anxiety, the journey to the U.S. seemed to last forever. By the last day she was so agitated she started appealing to St. Christopher, patron saint of children, and even God Himself, though she had always worked from a belief that God was a busy guy with millions of prayers stacked on his desk, and that she'd get a better response from Mother Mary or the saints. Or even the apostles. They had to have less of a backlog.

Mary must have licked the flap on Marcelle's return envelope in the nick of time. She was heaving in their tiny bathroom as the ship docked.

The baby was a son. Mark, plump and pink and more pumpkin than zucchini-like. Marcelle doted on him, inhaling his baby smells and exhaling her awed joy. "My sun, my sun," she'd murmur as he shone up from his cradle at her. She breathed him in and out like life's breath itself—the more so, she admitted, because in that first year she was so lonely. America did not open its arms to her the way she did to it. She tried hard to fit in, to not be ignored, studying TV soaps as she ironed—*General Hospital, Edge of Night*—trying to learn the proper way to mingle with Americans. This was a miserable failure. The TV plots didn't work for her. She loved Stan too much to have an affair, and she didn't know anyone to steal away with even if she had been so inclined. She did have coffee a few times a week with Harriet, the Polish woman who lived next door, but Harriet was as much a stranger to Jell-O salads and canasta as Marcelle.

It was Stan who first went to the Culinary Academy. When he dropped out—so many pink welts on his hands and arms from brushing up against the racks and sides of ovens—to open an auto-body shop, Marcelle got Harriet to watch Mark during the day and showed up herself. They had paid for the full semester up front, and she couldn't see wasting the money. Besides, she'd given up on the soaps and needed a new plan.

She was a natural with a whisk, inspired with spices, and finally she found a place where her accent was an asset. Many of the students were kids, some straight out of high school, and though Marcelle was barely 18 herself at the time, they all assumed all Frenchwomen whipped up a Béarnaise Sauce or Crème Brulée like American women fixed grilled cheese sand-wiches. She picked up *Mastering the Art of French Cooking*, replaced the soaps with Julia Child's *The French Chef*, and no one was the wiser.

The drinking, she admitted, was a sneaking mystery of a habit to her. For so long she had been so happy, climbing the culinary ladder, watching her sun grow into a person, and Stan's auto-body shop did so well he'd started looking for a second spot right in San Francisco. She had a scrapbook of her reviews in the *Chronicle* and *Gourmet*. She was so overjoyed by her acceptance, she didn't pray for anything. And that wasn't from a lack of faith, she explained to me. She figured she'd been dished out more than her share of hap-piness, that she should take her overflowing plate and step aside, make room for the others. She always saw God behind a desk, cluttered with papers—so many requests for salvation.

Maybe He misunderstood her being out of touch. And maybe Mary forgot to mention that Marcelle did frequently take advantage of a lull in the dinner rush to gaze up at a particular water spot on the ceiling and whisper, "Merci, ma Mère." Once her sous-chef even turned to her saying, "What?" So she had a witness, she said, she had expressed her gratitude.

Besides, one day on the way to work, during a terrible storm, a huge cypress tree fell into the road, came straight down on her car so quickly and with such deafening force she was sure she'd be killed. Her car was totaled. She climbed out the window, not a scratch, showed up for work in a cab telling the story to her staff, scoffing, "That goddamn tree—Stan says maybe $100 we'll get for that car."

But she knew she was lucky; she was certain she was being watched.

Then one night, when Mark was 17, Stanley ran him over to the mall for a pair of Earth Shoes and on the way out of the parking lot, a VW Bus ran the red light. Mark was killed instantly. Stan hung on for 12 hours. Marcelle paced his room, tried to kneel, paced some more, one bead to the next. She told me Stan's mother was there, and his sister, but it was as if they were calling up to his sixth-floor room from the parking lot. She heard their sounds vaguely, fleetingly, like the sound of a radio from a passing car. She paced around them. When he died, in a rush of doctors, nurses and buzzing, beeping, zapping machines, she saw Mark, the shiny flax of his Earth Shoes' laces, felt his arms around her, and knew she'd be okay.

Okay, she later explained to me, is a generic and descriptively useless word. The doctor gave her a prescription for Valium, and she found it afforded her the comfort of days wrapped in a kind of fuzzy blanket, life smeared into a tolerable blur like some pastel landscape that hung in the halls of the hospital. It did nothing for the nightmares. Everyday she worked the dinner shift, one flawless dish after another. The problem was the front door, walking through it into the house, so hollow and quiet. The pain would begin to creep up her insides, it built like the strings of a symphony until one more octave and she was certain she would lose her mind in a twirling screaming way or stick her head right in the oven like that pathetic Sylvia Plath. So she just started washing down the bedtime Valium with a shot of Scotch, and then another, until the nightmares ceased. Soon being drunk or hung over was the only thing that stopped the climbing chords, the roaring crescendo of pain.

She told me plainly that she had known her work was slipping, and the last time she called in sick she knew they would let her go, even though they had been so kind and patient. After all, anyone would acknowledge the tragedy of it, but finally they had no choice. People going out to dinner expected to be fed. She knew this.

What she didn't know was how to tell anyone she had no choice. She didn't know another way to stand it, she didn't think anybody else knew either, and in any case she was too proud to admit that to anyone.

It was Harriet who brought her to her first AA meeting. Harriet's husband, Carl, was a tried and true alcoholic, who would come home from the bars at dawn singing. He would inevitably pass out on the front lawn, and Harriet would drag him into the house. Then she found Al-Anon. It took her a good six months to work up the nerve to hand her life over to a power greater than herself, but after that old Carl woke up in the hydrangea or the rhododendrons or wherever he fell. Harriet nearly needed a drink herself to go through with it, but once she did, it felt so good she'd greet Carl, as he stumbled into the kitchen the next morning, with a foaming glass of Tropicana and a high sing-song, "Mornin' dear!" that made him wince.

For Marcelle, with sobriety came depression, months of pent-up, unprocessed grief and a sponsor, Janet, who insisted Marcelle show up at the Holy and Blessed Mother Church each night for a meeting. It wasn't like she had anywhere else to go, actually. The TV was back on during the day, game shows this time, and then off to the Holy and Blessed Mother Church—or the Holy BM as Janet often referred to it, insisting that with everything she'd heard in her 20 years of recovery, she knew God most certainly had a sense of humor.

So Marcelle sat for seven months in the same overstuffed chair with the TV on. The chair cover was peach, lavender and white flowers, she told me, and slowly she started picking the most expensive item or the correct key on *The Price Is Right*. She started to consider how if it had been her name they shouted into the audience, she'd have run up to the podium and won. Started to consider maybe she had some luck left after all.

She rose from that chair, switched off Bob Barker mid-sentence, and went out and bought what was by then a dingy coffee-shop. It had been run by the same little man, an ex-jockey, for 30 years. It was in a questionable neighborhood on San Pablo in Berkeley—comfortably distant from the watchful eye of the San Francisco culinary community. She opened Felice Mundo within a month.

It was a concept that had come to her in Safeway's ethnic-foods aisle—an international theme of homey comfort foods served in ridiculous portions. She decorated with Mexican blankets and kimonos hanging on the walls, brightly colored ceramic sugar bowls on the table, piñatas hanging from the ceiling, tall glass canisters of pasta and boxes of matzos in the front window. She got a kind review in the *Chronicle* about a year after she opened, in which the reviewer mercifully buried a single sentence referring to her past midway through the review. He called it a politically correct diner, an imaginative and ambitious undertaking. He loved her quesadillas. Her matzo-ball soup was a little salty.

She has one prep cook, Joven, who used to be a Silicon Valley CFO and, after discharging from the rehab where he'd kicked his cocaine habit, decided that the only executive decisions he really wanted to make anymore were those that involved parsley or no parsley. He also kept her books. The senior waitress, Bessie, is about 203 years old and has been waitressing for all but a handful of those years. If they give out 100-year chips at AA, Bessie's got one. The junior waitress, Dee, is a Berkeley undergrad who is suffering under Bessie's tutelage. Every time I stop by the restaurant I wait to see the two of them come rolling out of the kitchen like a furry ball of fighting cats, but it's been three years and they're both alive. They should get married.

It was Jessie's idea to spend the night in Montauk, get away, clear my head. We back down my parents' driveway, leaves crunching, a brown, red and orange carpet beneath Jessie's Civic. By the time dusk comes, with the sky purple and some plane leaving a flute of white I see out my window, we are on the Long Island Expressway. I stare out and up, making sure the plane isn't crashing, and Jessie slides her hand into mine. I wrap my fingers around her palm. We drive on, wordless, my mind a circus of thoughts in all three rings and sticky as cotton candy. When I look over at her, sunglasses still on, her other hand just brushing the steering wheel, I sink farther into the seat and into a quiet inside.

"Should we talk about this?"

Softly, not sure I want to say it at all.

Jessie takes off her glasses, letting them hang from the red cord around her neck, and does what I'd stopped waiting for years ago: She looks at me.

"Yeah," she says, "later," and pulls me close, my head resting on her shoulder, smelling her, deep and warm, wrapped in the sound of the car heater.

We drive along in silence, and I can almost see this tiny version of myself sorting out my feelings. If I'm honest with myself, Jessie scares me. Not the Jessie in the car—I'm sure I don't know that Jessie—but the old Jessie, or I guess that would be the young Jessie, and my memory of her. What I think of are the bubbles kids play with, the kind with the plastic wand in the plastic bottle and the soap liquid that coats the tips of your fingers, the way when you go to pop the bubbles they're so unearthly, the slight movement of your hands enough to push them out of your reach. I know that kind of reaching, the sting of fingers clutching at empty air, the look of empty palms.

I've had enough of that, the tiny me says, but of course some other me is drawn to Jessie, still in love with Jessie in a pink-Mohawk, belly-button-pierced, I-am-who-I-am-I-don't-care-what-you-think kind of way. The stance I'm able to hold onto for about two and a half minutes every other leap year. I *know* this doesn't look good. Still, if I peer inside, that tiny one is standing there with a fistful of daffodils and a moony expression.

Don't even ask me to explain or I'll make *you* sit down and tell *me* why you love your love—every mushy line of it. I'll make you drag out those embarrassing decks of cards in the box that say *52 Things To Do for Your Lover*, or the very bad poetry. You will be made to stand up in front of us all, with a microphone and really say, "We got each other's grocery bags by mistake at the Safeway but realized in time to exchange them in the parking lot along with our phone numbers. So we knew it was meant to be." It's terrifying, the flimsy foundations on which people set up the beams of love.

Still.

After midnight we pull into a motel somewhere in Montauk, a long white building with rows of blue doors and flowerless window boxes. I can practically see the ghosts of the summer crowd, families escaping from Manhattan for the weekend, sand-dusted children wielding beach balls, flip-flops slapping the parking lot. Jessie checks us in as I wait in the car, staring at the motel sign, Montauk Motel, with VACANCY in neon red. We pull our bags out of the dark car and walk into the room. I lean back against the door, closing it. My doubts fall away like my bag to the floor, the weight of them uncurling my fingers, and we are kissing, her mouth, the length of her back, from shoulders to waist, a place familiar, like a favorite song or food or friend.

"Kiss me," she says, her hands cupping my face.

"I *am* kissing you, silly."

"No, like this," and we are up all night, a swirl of legs and my hair falling across her face. There are times I think the world is the moment you're in, and the next and the next. That the world is your love's eyes, the bottom lip she bites, a tear you kiss, still salty in your mouth as you glide along each curve, the bone of a hip, a pillowy stomach, the length of her, damp and warm, that you fall into, cold callused feet in a tangle.

I come out of the bathroom and she's sitting on the edge of the bed, fiddling with the clock radio, music and static. She stops at a Muzak station—entirely too many string instruments playing *Evergreen.*

"That's really awful."

I climb onto the bed behind her, resting my head on her back.

"Let's dance."

"Dance? It's bedtime, Jessie."

"No, no. It's morning time. It's exactly 2:23."

"It's morning time for people who actually had bedtime. Jessie!"

134

But she's pulling me off the bed and we're laughing, a tan-goesque charge around the room, Jessie singing.

"Looovvvveeeee soft as an easy chair. Loooooovvvvveeeee fresh as the mo-or-ning airrrr. Loooooovvvvveeeee . . ." And pretty soon she's got my sneaker for a microphone, full volume, and I sit, wrapped in the sheet, laughing so hard I try to sing along and can't, just grab her hand and pull her to me till finally I gasp, "Shh, that is *so* bad . . ."

"Wait, wait," she says, dodging as my hand reaches to cover her mouth, "really." She's suddenly quiet and serious, and I stop and her face is so close.

"You," her fingertip brushing the tip of my nose, "are so loved by me."

When I wake that morning, Jessie's arm is draped over me and I look at her face, her red curls smashed under her cheeks and the scratchy motel sheet wrapped around one leg. I am relieved in the way you feel after searching for a missing posses-sion and finally spotting it between the cushions of the couch. Having Jessie this near, being finally the two of us again, is a completion that settles me like coming across a glassy-surfaced pond.

I sit in bed, my knees pulled up to my chest, and watch Jessie sleep and the night give way to light. A gentle drizzle taps at the panes and I feel like I'm on a boat, sailing along lapping waves. My eyes are sore from so little sleep, the beginning of an ache in my forehead that I press at with my fingers.

I slip out of bed, careful as can be not to wake her, and step into her sneakers, big enough to accommodate the thick socks I pulled on in the middle of the night, shrug into my coat, and open and close the door quietly behind me. The air is sharp with a chilly damp, and the sky is dark gray. A survivor cricket is still chirping away. I sit on a bench outside our door that looks out onto the motel parking lot. What must it be like to be Jessie, to hurl your heart out into the world without any promise that you will reel it back in intact? As we were finally falling asleep she had whispered my name.

"Rose?"

"Yeah?"

"I meant what I said."

"What?"

"I love you." And I had rolled over to look at her, her face intent on her words.

"I love you too."

"I mean *really*."

"I know."

I remember when we were kids, sometimes I'd worry that Jessie didn't actually know where her imagination ended, the fulfillment of her wants and needs, and reality began. It was as if she believed she could make the world be what she saw in her heart if she willed it so hard enough.

I push my hands in my coat pockets and think of the feel of holding her waist, how holding Jessie is like holding a storm. I see me in her eyes when she looks at me, a face so full of adoration and joy, that I can't believe I can be the cause of that look. I think love is someone seeing your real, lopsided self and loving you just the same. I think Jessie loves like Vivian, a brave and ferocious love, a force to be reckoned with. Me, I stand crouched behind something sturdy, something I can peer over, and watch others go at it. I am not that brave.

I go back inside and Jessie is sitting up, blinking awake.

"I'm starving," she says. "Breakfast?"

But I crawl back under the covers, to Jessie, warm and waking, and we fall back. I press my ear to her chest, listening to her heart, and then laugh, thinking about her standing on the bed holding the sneaker.

"What's so funny?"

"You. You are no singer but I give you full marks for effort."

"Yeah? Well, you, my dear, are no dancer," she says, kissing the top of my head.

We go to a place called The Clam Hut, where luckily they don't serve clams until noon. We order blueberry pancakes so big they hang over the edge of the plates, pulpy orange juice, coffee. Each sip and bite is a taste too good to just be the food—the way we reach under the table to squeeze each other's hand may just have something to do with it. I smile, shaking my head.

I kick absently at the gravel in the parking lot as we walk back to the car, want suddenly to call Becky, wake her up and tell her what has happened, finally.

▼

Becky and I met at Claremont. She was in the room next to mine. About a month into our first semester, her roommate, Stacy, had a nervous breakdown.

The climax of this breakdown is Stacy pacing up and down our hall, muttering to herself that she's had it with her poli sci professor and that he's leaving her no choice but to poison him. She's particularly irritated about this because it's totally his fault that she can't just stab him or run him over with her VW Rabbit—a much easier task, as she has those tools on hand. I go out to the vending machine to get a soda when she spots me.

"Hey! Hey, you! You got any Drano?"

"No. Why?"

"She needs to poison someone."

It's Becky, leaning in the doorway of their room. She gives me a look like, Follow me here.

"Oh, well, can you use something else maybe?"

She stares at me impatiently.

"Of course not!"

"I just called Paul the R.A.," Becky says, "and he's going to stop at the Alpha Beta for us and he's gonna drop it off. Right, Stacy?"

Like Paul is also stopping at the state hospital for injectable Haldol.

"I'll call him myself," and she heads toward the pay phone at the end of the hall.

"Don't worry," Becky says, "she doesn't have any change."

She doesn't, but she starts talking on the phone anyway.

"Hi. I'm Becky Fletcher."

"Rose Salino."

Not too long after that, Paul arrives and pries Stacy away from the phone with promises of especially potent rat poison at the Thrifty Drug Store. A couple of days later her parents come for her stuff.

I move into Becky's room about a month later, unofficially, as the school never gets it together enough to rubberstamp the switch—my first brush with bureaucracy. My roommate is happy enough to be rid of me: Now she can move her Ultimate Frisbee-playing boyfriend and his various drug paraphernalia into my place.

Becky was a drama major and had grown up in town, knew the names and histories of the little town's eccentrics. Like Bert, the gray and bearded man who hung out in front of the barbershop but never seemed to get the trim he so desperately needed, who used to be a mathematics professor at the college until one day his students came to class and found him eating chalk straight out of the little cardboard box. Pica, the diagnosis was. He'd never recovered, and the college had let him go. He lived on his Social Security and his gambling winnings from the barbershop, which was actually a bookie joint.

We'd go hang out at Becky's house when we needed to get some real studying done. Her father, Max, was an anthropology professor who frequently came home from work and deposited some animal skull on the kitchen table, along with the mail, before heading into his study with a beer. Her mother, Ruth, the dean of admissions at Claremont, was the only person at the whole college who wore a suit and stockings, looking like the WASP poster child. She traveled a lot, and it was Max who usually whipped up dinner.

Dinner at the Fletcher house was usually some casserole involving cream of mushroom soup and those dehydrated onion rings, but if Max was feeling particularly inspired we'd be treated to one of his signature dishes, typically a recipe he'd learned in Asia where the family had spent Max's sabbatical in 1970. You took your chances here. It was Max who taught me to make dim sum, how to fold the papery dough with care so as not to rip it. But it was also Max who once presented us with Flaming Thai Duck, the duck body standing straight up on a stick, engulfed in flames. We were vegetarians for a good month after that. Still, Max was a good argument for exposing your kids to various cultures and lifestyles with the goal of cultivating an open mind.

It worked with Becky, who'd eat anything. This hit an alarming peak when she was about seven months pregnant with Katlin, but back in college days it was simply great fun. She'd unscrew jars of pickled herring, caviar and Kalamata olives, and pull big hunks of Stilton out of the fridge when Max left us to our own devices at dinnertime. She's still the only person, besides Tommy, who will eat sardines with me or order an anchovy pizza.

In the way I'd pedal fast to keep up with Jessie's physical speed, my mind raced with the same skipping, twirling energy to keep up with Becky. No doubt it was her father's digging and searching example, along with the genes: Becky seemed to be interested in and know something about everything, from the name of the game-show host on *Jeopardy* to the names of generals in the Korean War.

She'd keep me company late at night when I'd be at my work-study job, baking for the coffee-house, and sit up on the metal counters, reading out loud from whatever play she was practicing for at the time.

I was still reeling from the loss of Jessie, though I'd found it was actually taking most of my energy to get used to my new surroundings, the palm trees, the many blond classmates. Get used to how everyone assumed I was Mexican. Get used to being so free, so far from Vivian's and Tommy's watchful eyes. Over our freshman year I told Becky about Jessie, with alternating anger, sadness and fondness. Becky nodded kindly and said things like, "Wow," "I'm sorry," and "You never know, Rose, when you'll see someone again."

At the time her comments struck me as odd. It wasn't for some time that I figured out that the oddness for me lay in the fact she was listening, purely listening, and not telling me what to do.

I know it was Becky and the way she gave me hours of tamales and easy talking, anchovies and vivid accounts of Stonewall Jackson, who made a soft, breezy place for me so I could look at myself with the knowledge that there was at least one other person looking too and liking what was there. One night in our junior year, we were sitting in her car, in the Alpha Beta parking lot, eating a pint of rum raisin ice cream with two spoons, when I told her about my crush on a girl in my Abnormal Psych class. She just nodded as I spoke, rooting around in the pint for a spoonful with a raisin, and commented, "I've seen her in the meal hall. She's cute."

Later, when we graduated and shared an apartment in San Francisco, while I attended the Culinary Academy and she interned at the Berkeley Rep Theater, she covered for me with Vivian.

"I told her you were out with your new boyfriend, a med student from UCSF."

"You couldn't just tell her I was working late?"

"I don't think so. I think if I'm gonna lie for you, I get to have a little fun."

When Becky married Peter, a quiet bearded man who had been one of her father's doctoral students, I made her wedding cake as my finals project for my pastry class. It was an Italian Cream cake with butter-cream frosting, and at 1 in the morning I was crying into the lavender rose border. I couldn't get the petals right, kept scooping each flower off with the pastry knife and starting again, worried I'd lose her like Jessie.

I didn't.

She and Peter bought a huge fixer-upper of a house in the Berkeley Hills. After Katlin was born, I worried again, this time that she'd replace me or get too busy. Again I worried when Colin was born. By the time Laurel and Annie were born, she'd convinced me there are bonds enduring enough to always have their place, even in the chaos of walls being torn down, children to bathe, and news release deadlines.

Chapter 11

We drive home in the rain, heavy plump drops that drum on the hood of the car. The thunder explodes in the sky, and we point at the lightning that shoots in a jagged line, a lit fuse. The car windows are shut tight, but the seat, my clothes, feel like a second skin, just like everything did in the pop-up camper Tommy bought one year when Jessie and I still wore undershirts. I remember it was so hot at the campground that the dirt was cracked dry and we had to wear our flip-flops so our feet didn't burn. We'd run into the bathrooms, into the showers that always had sand and spiders in them, and run the cold water on the tops of our heads. Sometimes we'd wear our bathing suits, sometimes the undershirts and shorts.

We slept together in one of the bunks that appeared on either side of the camper when Tommy opened it up. The sheets and pillowcases felt damp, stuck to my legs.

"You feel that?" I'd whisper in the dark.

"It's clammy."

And we'd kick off the sheet and fall asleep with the night breeze making a soft popping sound as it sucked at the mesh window.

"When are you leaving?"

Jessie's voice parts my recollections and the beat of the storm like curtains pulled aside.

"Oh God, I don't know," I say, squeezing her hand.

I had sat on the bed in the motel room, listening to her shower and the rain, thinking about that question, trying to make my life fit with Jessie's. Jessie and I, the unmade bed, her sneakers with knotted socks stuffed neatly into each one, her face so close, looking down at me and my hands in her hair. I want to put her in my suitcase and take her back to California with me, or call Becky and ask her to call Goodwill, clean out the whole apartment. I'm staying here.

I'd sat on that bed, dictating a list of things to keep, my CDs, my clothes, a few favorite books, everything in my kitchen. I want to feed Jessie—solid, warm food, garlic mashed potatoes, lemon herb chicken—and I see myself popping peas from their pods, ringing the orange cake round and round with the raspberry filling and butter-cream frosting I press out of the pastry bag in a basket weave.

Becky would do that for me. She hated Gail, thought she was too self-engrossed and pretentious. Becky was a paper-doll cutter too, read the whole Tolkien series in a week in the sixth grade.

And then there is the other me, the other tiny version who sits on my shoulder like the good and bad angels in Saturday morning cartoons and chastises me for my impulsive blindness. I see her actually cleaning out the fridge with that smug smirk worn by people who regularly clean their fridge, that kind of if *–you*-made-better-life-choices-you-too-would-have-time-toresew-those-buttons attitude. Oh, the *shame* of those little silver safety pins! I hate those crisper-cleaning types, but I admit I'm a little intimidated too—maybe the telltale dried-milk puddle on the first shelf *is* a symptom of something bigger. Maybe I do need to reevaluate.

And if that's true, I could be oblivious to my unconscious hurling of myself into a life of poor choices, bad judgment and public humiliation. Sure, love's an ethereal gift, but what if Jessie relapses, sets a podiatrist's office on fire. What if one day, as I'm feeding our toddler (a little girl with carrot curls), finger franks scattered on the highchair tray, I glance out the kitchen window just in time to see Jessie hopping a ride on a VW Bus filled with fed-up, depleted CEOs heading for their llama farms in the Midwest? What could I possibly say to people? The handwriting being on the wall and all.

"I wish you could just stay," Jessie says. "Do you wish you could stay?"

"Or you could come with?" I ask, giving the tiny me a quick shove off the yogurt carton into the lunch meat drawer—heh, heh, I think you missed a spot. The thing is, she's clever. She'll pry the drawer open with a log of goat cheese.

"You know, I used to think of you, right after you left for college, when I was in the hospital again, and try to picture you there. And I never could."

And I know what she means. I would lie out by the pool in my bathing suit, reading Machiavelli, watching girls splash around in the deep end and then climb out all skimmed with water, and I'd see Jessie. And then read the same page three times, daydreaming, wishing she would fall, a sprinkle of cool drops, on an outstretched towel next to me. I don't know when that stopped. Even in Southern California it eventually got too cold for the pool, and when it warmed up again toward the end of the year, the little clean-up crew was done.

"Did you ever tell them about your dad?"

"Yeah, that second time I was in the hospital. Sara, my therapist, started to see me then, and she guessed and made me tell."

"What happened?"

"I kept telling her that it didn't matter anymore, that it didn't matter if I told anyone, that it was done and over. I remember she pulled her chair up closer and pointed at one of the cuts on my arm, at this little spot where they tied the stitches, and she said, 'It doesn't look over to me.' Then she said that my father may have stopped, but it looked to her like I was picking up where he left off."

The windshield wipers swung back and forth, filling the quiet with a steady pumping, a clearing cut from the wall of rain falling all around us.

"We had this horrible family session and I confronted him with it. At first he denied it, but eventually he said, yes, well, he sort of remembered some of it, but he was young and drunk and something about how I had misunderstood his intentions. But Hannah was screaming and crying and I walked out. I remember watching myself walk out of the room and close the door, like I was up on the ceiling, and I went into my room and took my roommate's vase of flowers, dumped the water and the flowers in the bathroom sink, wrapped the vase in a towel and cracked it on the pipe under the sink. I still can't remember after that, just that I had new stitches."

"Why would you do that?"

"At the time I didn't know. It's like something you have to do. It always felt better for a little while after I did it, like all this bad stuff got let out and I hated myself so much then, disgusted myself. It felt like I was making something right. They put me on a 72-hour involuntary hold with one of the nurses watching me all the time, even when I went to the bathroom, *especially* when I went to the bathroom. They made me wear a hospital gown and I wouldn't talk to anyone. So Sara brought me into one of the therapy rooms, and there's just two chairs and she sits right across from me and says, 'You ever play bridge?' And I look at her like, fucking bridge? You want to talk about card games? But she's looking at me totally seriously, so I say, 'No,' and she says, 'There's this thing in bridge called a finesse, and what happens is there's a certain point in the game where if you take the finesse you could lose, be out of the game right then and there, but you also have the chance to win. If you don't take the finesse, you'll stay in the game longer, but it's a mathematical certainty that eventually you will lose.'"

And Jessie smiles then, a shrug of memory.

"So, I took the finesse."

▼

I stand on the front porch, listening to the doorbell sound, five chimes rising and falling, and some young angry voice screaming, *We won't! We won't! Not us, we won't!* and a bass, loud and jolting. Hannah opens the door and hugs me, one of her complete full hugs with her arms seeming to wind around me twice.

"The Rotortillers," she says, a pleased smile. "Jules loves them."

Jessie had told me about Jules on the ride home, how it wasn't until last year that Hannah and Dr. Spencer had separated, when Hannah fell in love with the computer programmer in her ceramics class.

"You like him?"

"Oh yeah," she had said, smiling and shaking her head as if she was remembering something fondly. "Jules is a trip. Last year, he and a bunch of guys from his company started a band. I'll take you to see them. They just play here in town and at Royos in Port Jeff, but the teenagers love them. Jules writes the lyrics. I think he thinks he's the second coming of John Lennon, but he's sweet and he loves Hannah."

"Honey, come say hello to Rose," Hannah calls down the stairs. "Turn that down," she adds, fake annoyance in her voice, like a mother trying not to laugh at a naughty child. The music becomes a faint irregular bass, and Jules appears at the bottom of the stairs and walks halfway up, hand extended.

"Hi there. Nice to meet you."

I lean down to shake his hand.

His peppery black hair is cut short and spiky and he is big and round without being fat, a bear of a man with red plastic framed glasses, Levis and a faded black T-shirt.

"I'll be up in a bit," he says to Hannah.

"Don't rush, Jules, us girls have catching up to do."

It's funny the feeling a house can hold. Each room still has the look of being suddenly evacuated, books open, about 10 editions of the *New York Times*, read and refolded on the couch, coffee table and kitchen island. There are ceramic mugs where the Coca-Cola cans used to be, and a sense of more space that at first I attribute to the dogs being gone, but is really something less tangible.

Usually as people get older, they get shorter, but not Hannah. She got taller. Her hair's all gray, swinging like a cape behind her as she moves through the kitchen making us tea, large heavy mugs, minty steam rising between us. She smiles at me through a cloud of steam, her face moist, and she seems to have skipped middle age altogether; her eyes that always looked too young for her body now shine quietly, like they've found a home. They've caught up with the rest of her, in a place between wisdom and a settled resignation.

"So, the word on the street is an old flame has been rekindled," she says teasingly.

"Jessie told you, huh."

"She did, and she's pretty happy, I would say. She should have the retirement home picked out for the two of you by the time she gets off work tonight."

"Oh, I don't know about that, Hannah. It's been a long time. We're taking it slow."

"Maybe *you* are taking it slow, Rose. I know my daughter. She moves things right along once she makes up her mind, and I'd say her mind is set on you."

And we laugh, a laugh of shared fondness.

"She seems good."

"She *is* good," Hannah asserts. "It was very hard there for a few years. Hard for her. Hard for us all."

I just nod.

"There was a time when it was really bad, Rose, that I thought I would lose her."

"Me too. When she ran away I thought for sure the police would find her on the side of the road, raped and strangled."

"You know, it's strange but that wasn't the worst part of it for me."

"No?"

"I *was* thoroughly worried, frantic even at times for her. Still, in the beginning, when she was running away, it was like she had somewhere to go, some reason, however self-destructive, to live. Later, when she was home and taking pills, cutting herself, it was as if she was playing Russian roulette about life."

"She was in pain. I remember before I left for college she said she couldn't stand the pain."

"That's how it started, but it's not that simple."

Hannah's voice is clear and knowing, a tone I had never heard from her, a tone I vaguely connect to the space I feel in the room, like something you can't see but keep tripping over anyway.

"What do you mean?"

"The razors, the pills, the way she would lock herself in her room and George and I tiptoeing around as if we had some time-bomb threatening to go off. I tell you, I still don't know how much of that was because she wanted to die, and how much of that was to punish me."

"But she couldn't help it, Hannah. She was frightened and confused and what Dr. Spencer did was terrible and you stayed with him and . . ."

"I didn't protect her," she cuts in, and I catch my breath, realizing I've said more than I planned to. She goes on, slowly.

"I have to live with that. For the past 10 years I've been over it and over it, this therapist, that book, this prayer, that pill, trying to fix it, trying to make it okay for Jessie. And you know, Rose, what I finally realized is that some things you don't fix. Some things you just own up to, and forgive yourself, and try to go forward, do better and be honest with yourself.

"Jessie was very, very angry with me. She had a right to be, a right to expect her mother would take care of her, but at a certain point that anger turned a corner, became its own thing; manipulating, punishing. I took that for a while, but I was angry for the way she had us under house arrest with her constant threats of suicide. I read one day that suicide is many messages: I want to die, but also, I want you to die. That'll fix you. I want you to kill me. I want to kill you. It was all of that. You understand what I'm saying, Rose?"

I nod but I don't, really. Hannah stares out into the backyard. I wonder how many times she has said this, to herself, to anyone else. It's dark, the wind smacking the trees, and she is nibbling her bottom lip, fighting back tears.

"What, Hannah?"

"I didn't know. I should have known."

"What would you have done?"

She shakes her head slowly, brushing a tear from each eye.

"I would have left him," she says finally. "I would have taken her away from him. That's the truth."

I reach over and squeeze her hand.

"I believe you," I say, though of course I don't, can't, and I watch her, trying to find something to say that *is* true. "You know, Hannah, I was angry too, and hurt, and now I guess I worry."

"About?"

"It's like last night she says to me, 'I love you,' like she's so sure. But who knows? What if she decides tomorrow the pain, the depression are too much and she needs to take off again? I *do* love her but I feel like if I let myself love Jessie, *I'm* playing Russian Roulette—maybe I'll spin the wheel and win the Jeep Cherokee, and maybe I'll lose it all."

"Have you told her that?"

"That's not exactly the kind of thing you say to someone."

"But she's not *someone*—or at least you don't want her to be someone. Rose, I think if two people are even entertaining a life together, if such an awesome undertaking is going to work, those two people don't have the luxury of squirreling away what's hard to say. I'll tell you that one of the things I learned from my marriage to George is that you need to say and ask it all.

"I know Jessie believes she told me, even though I don't remember that, but, on some level, I knew something was wrong. Only I know the million times I went to ask both of them, but I didn't know what I wanted to ask, just that something kept tugging at me. Now I just steel myself and say it out loud."

"But she really believes everything would be fine between us."

"Maybe it would."

"But what if it doesn't?" I plead. "You're her mother. What do you think?"

"I think you owe it to yourself to give this its time. You haven't seen each other in years. I think the two of you are a beautiful possibility, and that if you stay quiet inside and listen to yourself, you'll find your path."

I try that for a moment, listening to myself, but all I hear is the dull thumping of the goat cheese against plastic. I sigh.

"No one knows the future, Rose. There are no guarantees, but what are the options? A life of what ifs?"

I get this flash of myself retrieving the finger franks from under the kitchen table where my toddler has thrown them after I've explained to her that her other mother has thrown her over for a llama.

"Maybe it's more than just Jessie you worry about," she says gently, pointedly.

I tell her about breaking up with Gail, about losing the restaurant, tell her things I didn't even know I was feeling, about how the trip home has left me even more confused as to my next step. That's the thing about Hannah now, you can tell her anything, not worry she'll judge or criticize, a woman without the luxury of stones to cast.

When I get back to the house, I put the car away and go in the door leading from the garage to the kitchen. Tommy is standing at the fridge, holding a gallon of milk. A placemat sits on the kitchen table with a mug and a package of cookies, shadows in the one dim light from over the stove.

"Want some?" he asks, motioning with the milk.

"Sure." And he pulls another placemat out of the pantry and I get a mug.

"Where you been?" he asks, pouring milk, opening the package of cookies.

"With Jessie. And then I went to visit Hannah tonight."

"How's Hannah?"

"Good. You know she remarried."

"Yeah, your mother told me. How's Jessie?"

"Good. She's gonna come by tomorrow."

"She's a good kid."

I nod, smiling fondly at his word—kid!—and we sit there, dunking our cookies.

"So, your mother told me about, ah, Gail."

I look at him, surprised to hear him say her name. We never talk about it. Even when I first came out, he didn't say much beyond, "Just make sure this is what you want."

"Yeah, the day grandma died."

"That's cold."

"That's not the half of it," I tell him. "She fired me, too."

"You're shittin' me."

"No."

"It's probably for the best," he says slowly, dunking a cookie. "I mean she was a little strange, wasn't she?"

I have to laugh. I told you, Gail wasn't winning any popularity contests.

"You need any money?" Taking another cookie.

"No, I'm okay."

"Let me know if you do."

"I will."

He drinks his milk in two quick gulps and gets up from the table. He closes up the package, puts it away. I put our mugs in the dishwasher while he wipes crumbs from the table, and we both look around the kitchen, scanning for any untidiness. He straightens the doily under the centerpiece. Vivian.

"Tell Jessie to bring that shitbox of hers to the gas station. I

153

heard something rattling around yesterday when you guys were pulling down the driveway."

And he kisses me on the cheek and I kiss him back—a lifetime of ritual all the more dear because of time, kisses and prayers at four, hurried eye-rolling kisses as I ran out the door to horn-honking at 16, another at the airport gate with a twenty he shoves into my hand even now when I visit.

▼

It's Vivian who wakes me, gently whispering, "Becky's on the phone."

Instinctively my eyes go to the alarm clock and the red numbers, 9:22—6:22 California time—and a best friend you know doesn't go to bed until 2. I'm out of the bed and scooping the receiver off the nightstand in my parents' bedroom.

It's Marcelle, she says. The ambulance roused Carl from the bushes. Harriet called to say they're keeping her for testing. Terrible stomach pains, leg pains. She couldn't get out of bed, and when Harriet got there she couldn't even move her to get her in the car. *What do they think it is?* Harriet called from the emergency room. They didn't know. *They must have some hunches.* Honey, I'm not holding out on you. I'm telling you everything Harriet told me. It's probably fine. It's probably appendicitis or something like that. *Oh yeah, then why are you calling me at 6 in the morning? See? I'll leave today.* I'll pick you up at the airport. Call me back with your flight. *Oh, Becky.* Probably it's nothing.

Jessie drives to the airport like I have water that's about to break. I drill her with questions the whole way.

"What's the worst it could be?"

"The cancer could have spread to her stomach, I suppose, but it could also be very bad gas."

"Gas!"

"Or something in the middle, not terminal but serious."

"Like?"

"Maybe a cyst in her ovaries. Maybe gallstones, maybe kidney stones."

"That wouldn't be so bad."

"Yeah. It's probably just something like that."

"Okay."

I lean back in the seat, looking out the window, feeling a warm, slushy calm stream down my insides. But no, it's too easy. "But what if it isn't?"

By the time we get to Queens, Jessie honestly can't think of another disease and we fall silent.

"Call me tonight," she says. "I want to know what happens. I want to know how you're doing."

"Okay."

More silence.

"So, Rose, what do you want to do here?"

"What?"

She doesn't even look at me, just rolls her eyes, shaking her head.

"I'm going to help you out," she says, "just this once. I'm pretty sure I've gone and fallen in love with you. I'm driving you to the airport to go back to California. I think you love me."

She pauses here for a response.

"Yes," I say, "I do."

"That was convincing."

"Oh, God, Jessie, of course I do. It just feels so quick, too quick, and I think we both need to sit with this a bit—not to mention my life feels like it's in chaos right now."

"That's fine."

"What?"

"I said that's fine. You understandably need to think about it for a while. So do I. I was just wanting a status check on where we are."

And I think about Tommy and how he told Vivian that first week he was going to marry her.

"Oh."

We kiss good-bye with one of those airport cops they've resurrected from Nazi Germany tapping on the window, his perfectly straight nose practically pressed up against the glass. I walk through the terminal doors with the two Tiny Mes doing this high-pitched duet: *I told you soooo . . . I told you soooo . . .*

Chapter 12

Katlin lunges for me, a leap into my arms that sends my carry-on bag and my purse off my shoulder and onto the airport carpeting in a heap around my feet.

"Aunt Rose! Aunt Rose! Sleep in my room tonight."

I give her a big squeeze of a hug, looking over her head at Becky, who stands smiling and holding Colin's little hand, his other hand clutching a green plastic dinosaur, a Tyrannosaurus Rex, I believe, though I still score about 50% on those nights when his bedtime stories turn into dinosaur quizzes.

Katlin is seven, wavy brown hair she insists on growing long even though she battles Becky through most shampoos. She likes me to tell the story of the time I was three and went to Europe with Vivian and would scream every time she washed my hair, like she was murdering me in the hotel room. About halfway through the trip, the scissors came out and I ended up with a pixie. I showed Katlin the pictures of me in a photo album, before-and-after shots, me with curls down my back and a big bow, then me the hair cropped to an inch all over. She stared at the photos, ran a finger across them.

"Didn't you promise not to cry?" Her face in disbelief.

"I don't remember."

"*I* don't cry anymore."

She said it like a vow.

The house has six bedrooms, three floors, and four years after they bought it, workmen still trail in and out of the house, reminding me of Jessie's brothers. It's the kind of house where you slip a robe on in the morning when you wake up to go to the bathroom because you never know if some strange man will be in there ripping the tiles out of the shower or replastering the wall lining the hallway. I was spending the night a few months after they moved in, and woke up the next morning, rolled over still half-asleep to look out the window, and this face stared back at me, this old guy with leathery skin and about four teeth. He grinned at me, mouthing, "Good morning," and then held up a paintbrush, half-white with paint, as if to prove he was not a peeping Tom. I smiled back, gave him a little wave and then slid to the other side of the bed and onto the floor, my hand reaching around the foot of the bed for my robe.

At one point the whole kitchen was torn out for a good two months, and dinner became a dizzying assembly line of kiddy TV dinners, jars of creamed chicken and rice and Cup of Noodles in and out of the microwave oven. One time I had them all to my apartment for dinner, and I swear I'm still stepping on the now pebble-like peas wedged in the carpet fibers. The morning after Gail left, I sat at the kitchen table, staring out the window, and found myself scraping flaky, caked mashed potatoes off the sill.

"Why don't you just go out to dinner, Becky?"

"What, and ruin a meal for 50 people? You must suffer for

the masses, Rose," Peter teased, sweeping half-chewed scraps of this and that into the trashcan he held up to the edge of the table.

Katlin and I have a special bond that I believe goes back to when she was two months old and I baby-sat her while Peter was on a dig in Africa and Becky went to an opening at the Rep. Katlin went to bed all sweet baby powder, her eyes falling shut by the time I pulled the fuzzy yellow blanket over her. I walked into the living room and picked up my book, thinking how dear it is, the way little babies sleep and sleep and sleep. Until 9:30, when she woke with a howl that jolted me from my book and forever from any baby illusions I had cherished up to that night.

Realistically, I know she was two months old, and so how much could she understand? But I swear to you she was hell-bent on making sure no one, especially me, was going to be having any fun in that house she wasn't a part of. She was fine for the next hour and a half as I put her in her wind-up swing and crouched down in front of her cooing and squealing as she swung up to me—*Honey! Who loves you! Big girl!*—but when I fell to the floor prying my knees straight and tried to sit next to her with my book, letting the wind-up swing do its thing, she immediately burst into a scream, a note she held for so long I was sure she was moments short of a ruptured vocal cord. Finally, at 11, when *I* was certainly ready for bed, I put her in her crib and shut the door praying, *She must be overtired. Please God, let her be overtired. She'll cry herself to sleep.* But no, she actually worked her way into a crying jag that culminated in what sounded like a gasp for her last breath and gagging clearly meant to convey that she was ending her own life, the yellow blanket half shoved down her throat, the message clear: My blood will be on your hands. So we read a book. Actually, we read close to 14 books. It was a long play.

She's much more cooperative now, but still a very watchful and demanding kid. She has my phone number memorized, so whenever Becky puts her on a time-out, she finishes her time patiently and then calls me. I come home to these messages on my answering machine like, "I hate Mommy. Can I come live with you tonight?" Or, "I need Brownie socks. *Everyone* has Brownie socks and Mommy says to just wear my white ones but I *can't.*"

Colin is five, and he's a little clingy and whiny but very sweet, likes to pat the twins and sing to them. Peter made him a sandbox in the backyard. You unravel the hose and turn it on, and Colin is your friend for life. I've seen him spend four hours straight in that sandbox with a couple of quick breaks to pee in Becky's hydrangea bush. The twins, Laurel and Annie, are just two and, you know, they were born when Gail and I first got together, and I just feel like I know them less well. I didn't spend as many nights sleeping over at the house, as much time in general, and it shows. You do make your choices and I'm not narcissistic enough to think they'll need therapy or anything, but I know I haven't been as good an aunt to them.

Katlin and I get one of those metal baggage carts, and Becky and I hoist the suitcase onto it and head out to the parking garage.

"I'll drop you off at the hospital."

"Did Harriet call you back?"

"Yeah."

"What'd she say, Becky?"

"The cancer spread to her ovaries. They operated today, did a hysterectomy, but it's in her lymph nodes."

I look down at Katlin who I know is listening but is staring off across the parking garage at some father carrying and patting a screaming infant. The cry echoes through Level B. Katlin slips her hand into mine, leans into my leg.

The Oncology floor is a dizzying scene. Various medical staff—nurses aides, patient care technicians, nurse practitioners, respiratory therapists, phlebotomy technicians—rush around the hall, practically plowing down the two or three teetering patients. All I can think when I pass one is that they look so feeble, and I try to imagine Marcelle that gray-skinned and thin. Marcelle, so stout and strong, who would hoist 25-pound bags of flour onto the marble pastry counter at Felice Mundo in one swift motion, like a mother transferring a baby from one hip to the other. How, I wonder, could anything so microscopic and deadly as a cancer cell burrow its way into such a body of strength? And more than that, I wonder, what actually is enough? I'm not a big believer in God, used to wear my First Communion rosary as a necklace, which is probably some form of sacrilege for all I know, but Marcelle certainly is a staunch believer, and I have to tell you I don't see the big payoff to all that devotion. I know it's a buck or two every Sunday in the collection basket—people spend more on lottery tickets—but still, people don't pray to the California Lottery Commission for the speedy recovery of a loved one. It's not lost on me that this all-giving and all-loving Being swiped the two people Marcelle loved the most from her and has now proceeded to tear her remission from her.

I stand in the doorway of her room at first. She's sleeping, wearing her own flannel nightgown Harriet must have thoughtfully brought her. She looks fine to me, stout and ruddy-skinned, same as always, I think as I peer at her like a gratin I'm checking for doneness. I ease my way into the room, feeling like when I was a kid and saw a *Star Trek* episode about this colony of space lepers, I couldn't sleep that night because I was certain they'd set up camp underneath my bed. I'd take a running leap off the mattress and sprint into the hall, into the bathroom, the tile cold on my bare feet—alive! Then I'd peer out into the darkness, from the safe island of the bathroom floor, to see if they had followed me. In the episode, if they touched you, you became a leper. Hospital beds, thankfully, are high and there was nothing under it, but then cancer cells are invisible to the eye. It's the same lurking feeling.

A TV is bolted in the corner, up on the ceiling. The sound is off, flashes of news that make shadows on the white walls. It's starting to get dark outside. Out in the hall there's bustling noise, but in the room I can hear our breathing. I don't know what to do with myself. The last thing I want to do after a five-hour flight from New York is sit down. It doesn't seem right to wake her. She must need the sleep, the good cells resting up to do battle with the bad cells. Luckily, Harriet walks in.

"Come on," she whispers, leading me out of the room and hugging me at the same time. "We're in the visitors' lounge. Let her sleep." She propels me out the door, which is a good thing, because the hospital, the smells, too many ghostly gowns, the brightness of the white sheets, the bedside tables whirl in front of my eyes. I feel like one of those helium balloons you see flying free over a strip mall because some kid let go of the string.

The visitors' lounge is at the opposite end of the hall from the elevators, glass-windowed, overread magazines and a Hold Everything catalog. Harriet closes the door. I breathe a sigh of relief and everything starts to come back into focus, like the lepers can't make it past a closed door. Possibly one of the staff out in the hall has a nametag that says Visitor Care Technician. I want something in one of those little paper cups they have lined up on a tray at the Nurse Station.

The whole Felice Mundo crew is there—Bessie, Dee, Joven—and they've set up a buffet: potato salad, deli sandwiches, chips and mineral water. Harriet stayed all night, went home for a shower and came back. The rest have been here since this morning. Harriet starts to fill me in, and I interrupt.

"Who's running Felice Mundo?"

Joven looks at me like he'd be happy to go up to the Nurse Station and fetch me one of those paper cups. "We closed. Why?"

"She'll want to know when she wakes up."

And I sit down on the couch and start to cry. It's so nice to lose it in a room full of recovery people. They've seen it all, know the benefit of a good crying jag, and know all these cool things to say. "Grant me the strength to accept . . ." "One day at a time." "Live and let live." "Serenity"—just the word itself has a lulling quality. Finally I'm able to listen, really hear what's going on. There'll be more chemo. Have to hope they got it all. Have to wait and see. Bessie says it's no use asking the doctors how long she'll live. They just guess: six months, a year, two years. Her mother was given a year and was gone in three months from pneumonia. Her sister-in-law's sister had a mastectomy 10 years ago. Harriet says it's a personal call on whether recovering addicts can take painkillers. "Pot's out," Joven says in a stab at humor and I elbow him, let my head fall on his shoulder.

I say I'll spend the night so they can all go home and sleep, shower, hit a meeting. God knows they could use one. We decide we'll talk tomorrow about what to do with Felice Mundo. Marcelle's clearly not going back to work anytime soon, and I say the obvious, that I can certainly fill in being as how I love her and am unemployed. We leave it at that for now.

I wander back to the room where it's completely dark. I switch on a light over the sink and it bathes the room in a comforting creamy dimness. I sit in a green plastic cushion chair and dial Becky's house with the phone in my lap and tell her I'll call in the morning. It's close to 11 New York time and I conk out in the chair, so when the phone rings it vibrates my whole body like I'm being executed. It's Vivian.

"How are you?"

"Okay," I say. "I think she's pretty sick. She hasn't awakened since I've been here."

Tommy picks up the other phone and I tell them in a hushed tone what I know, which isn't much. It's the safety I need in the middle of all this unknown danger, the sound of their voices, not even what they say.

The next morning it's the groaning bedsprings that wake me, and she opens her eyes.

"What are you doing here?" she asks, her voice hoarse. "I thought you were in New York."

"Harriet called Becky. Becky called me." Not what she was asking, but it'll do. "How are you feeling?"

"Like shit. Did they tell you, they're going to give me that chemo that makes you lose your hair again?"

"Yeah, but I think it's that chemo that helps you stay alive. We'll get you some wigs from Vivian if you want."

"Yeah, yeah," and her voice is thick. "What is this?" She's holding up the IV tube.

"Demerol." I had asked the night nurse who came in to change the IV bag. When she told me what it was, I'd said, "I'll take a double." She'd ignored me. I figure if I keep up this drug-seeking behavior, maybe I can gain entry into those AA meetings on a preventive basis. Then maybe I'll have a library of the right comforting things to say too. At that moment I don't know what to say.

When Beth Patient Care Technician comes in, Marcelle tells her she wants the Demerol turned off.

"We have to wait for the doctor."

"When is he coming in?"

"Sometime this morning."

"I don't take drugs."

164

"You have cancer. Chemo is a drug." And I'm out of the chair about to pull her little blond ponytail out of her head, but Marcelle beats me to it.

"Get out and call the doctor."

Marcelle is pretty ferocious-looking when she's mad, and the Care Woman skids out of the room, leaving the blood-pressure cuff decompressing on Marcelle's arm.

Her doctor, Dr. Myers, we all love. He's a tall thin man in his sixties and he has this sweet Mr. Rogers smile and always answers all your questions directly. Becky arrives, and we listen as he tells Marcelle that she's looking at weeks of recovery from the surgery alone, and that they'll try a new chemo. They do it monthly, in the hospital. Can't he just give her something to take at home this time?

"I know Marcelle," he says, reaching over, pressing his hand over hers, and the way he says it, looking at her straight on, so sincere in his disappointment, makes me start to tear up all over again. "The second I think it's safe to discharge you, I will, as long as there's someone to help you."

"There is," I say.

"Okay." He takes a breath, a practiced sigh that sends pins up my neck. "As I told you, we have more time, if we got it all. We'll just have to watch and wait."

"How much time?" she asks.

"Maybe a year."

Marcelle just nods like she knew this, like he said, "Your co-pay will be $500."

When he leaves, I go over to the bed and give her a hug and get her face all wet with my tears. She doesn't cry, just says, "You know I dream about Stan and Mark all the time. I miss them. I'm not ready to die, but if I do I'll be happy to see them."

I hope she's right and I'm wrong, that there is a God, a Mark

Angel wearing Earth Shoes, brand new feathery wings in a box and a place called heaven for my dear friend to live. If the place lives up to its reputation, it'll have a sunny kitchen window and her favorite skillet. Dear God, please don't take my friend.

▼

We can actually make it through the week with Felice Mundo closed, according to Joven, who pored over the books one whole evening. After that, it could get tight. I don't go home, just sleep in the chair with one of those transparent white hospital blankets flung over me. The weave is so big it's a wonder the thing holds any warmth at all, though it's not really a problem, as they keep the hospital at a nice sweltering 80 degrees for the germs to have a lovely greenhouse atmosphere to flourish in. Yes, I'm a little angry.

Marcelle looks great by Day 3, and with a little help in and out of the bed is able to use the bathroom and take a shower on her own. I have these moments of thinking Dr. Myers must be wrong, that it really *is* a bad case of gas. Then I hear his gentle voice each day talking about cell counts and using long ominous words, and I go back to the business of coping with it all.

At the end of the week, Marcelle holds a staff meeting in her room. We'll stay open five days and Joven will fill in for me if I have a job interview. Marcelle goes over the menu, checking to see if I know how to make everything, and I admit I get a bit irritable when she starts demonstrating the proper way to roll a matzo ball.

"Maybe we should just set up a hospital bed in the kitchen so you can command from on high," I tell her.

"Then," Bessie chimes in, "if you get too obnoxious we can just wheel you into the walk-in box."

"No respect for the dying," Marcelle says. We've already

started dipping a toe into sick death jokes.

The home health nurse will come check on Marcelle each day; various AA friends will drop in. I think we have it about as covered as we can, seeing as how none of us knows what to expect. Jessie calls me every day and patiently answers all my questions, but it's clear to me that no one really knows what will happen.

"I can come help if you need me to."

"I think it's okay, Jessie, but I'll call if I need help."

Becky picks me up from the hospital to spend a night at the house. It was her idea, but I would have asked. I'm not up for going back to my apartment alone. I'd left it a mess, books in piles, stacked up against the walls, clothes in heaps on the floor as most of the furniture had been Gail's. But it's more than that; it's a feeling that the minute I walk in that door I have to start putting my life back together, and I don't know where to start.

As we pull out of the hospital parking garage, I see the six-pack of generic beer sitting on the floor in the back.

"Ah, Becky," I say, holding up the beer, "generic brand? Is this another boycott thing?"

"It's for the snails."

"What snails?"

"You know how I like to have that little vegetable garden in the backyard? One morning last week I go out there, and there's snails everywhere, big hunks chewed out of my zucchini and a whole tomato plant lying on the ground. So I'm out there in my nightgown every morning picking snails out of the dirt, cursing to myself, and then lining them all up on the patio and smashing them with my spade."

"That is disgusting."

"Well, I couldn't think of anything else to do. I mean I could have put them in a plastic bag and let them just suffocate and eat each other . . . Never mind. So, I'm smashing away like my own little death squad at dawn, and I think I'm winning . . ."

"Gardening as a contact sport."

"Ummm. Anyway, then when I think I've killed them all off, like 40 members of the murder victims' extended family descend on my garden like a Sicilian vendetta. So I call Peter's father, who you know is an avid gardener and would never put up with this kind of thing, and he tells me to get some beer."

"Beer like we drink?"

"Yeah, you put bowls of beer out in the garden and the snails crawl into the bowls to drink the beer and drown."

"So, now you're waking up each morning to bowls full of dead snails? "

"Well, wait. So I thought it was working, but then a couple days ago another whole herd of them show up and these are *bigger*. Seems I only killed off the weak alcoholic snails. I was going to try to return the beer to the supermarket and then I thought maybe we'd just drink it tonight."

"I am not drinking beer that appeals to snails."

It's Indian summer, 85 degrees and sunny. We pull into the driveway. Peter is out front crouched over the upside-down lawn mower, screwdriver in hand. The lawn is half cut, the smell of cut grass everywhere as we climb out of the car. He walks over to us.

"Welcome back. How's she doing today?"

We hug and I tell him, "Okay." With a shrug.

Sue, their baby-sitter, is standing in the living room with an armful of puppets. Peter built the wooden puppet theater for the kids last Christmas; Becky sewed the red velvet curtain. The three of us had painted it one late night the week before Christmas, opening all the windows in Peter's study, up on the third floor, so we wouldn't asphyxiate ourselves. I had painted little rows of audience heads along the bottom, but they ended up looking like brown and yellow circles with multicolored triangles that were supposed to be their bodies. Katlin thought it was confetti.

"Hey, Rose," Sue calls softly, a tone that I know means the twins are napping, as she dumps the armful of puppets into their plastic laundry basket. "Someone called for you." She riffles through a pile of papers. "Jessie. No emergency. She said just call when you get a chance." I look over at Becky who looks back, eyebrows raised, a smirk.

"Don't look at me like that," I say, embarrassed.

"I want to hear this *whole* story."

"What story?" Katlin chirps.

"Aunt Rose saw her childhood sweetheart while she was home."

"Ohhh," Katlin says, mimicking Becky's face. "Is she your new girlfriend?"

"You and Gail broke up?" Sue asks.

"Yeah, a few weeks ago."

"So, is this like a Jane Eyre kind of thing, years of secret, frustrated longing?" Sue says to Becky.

"Okay, I tell you what, why don't you guys call Jessie back yourselves and quiz *her*. I'm going up to take a shower."

I let the shower run over my head, the water streaming down my face, my eyes closed, for so long I have to keep adjusting the hot water. I only step out when the knob won't turn anymore, the water lukewarm threatening to go cold.

I pull on a pair of Becky's shorts and my T-shirt out of my suitcase, get dressed and as I walk into the living room, I see Katlin lying on the couch, her legs draped over the arm, talking on the phone with the air of a precocious adolescent.

"I don't know, maybe a doctor, but the kind that helps animals . . . yeah, a veterinarian but big animals, like at the zoo . . . do you wear one of those hats . . . oh . . . I went to the hospital once when I had croup. Mommy sat in the bathroom with me with the shower going . . . Wait, wait, Aunt Rose is here . . . okay, bye!" she yells towards the receiver as I take it from her hand.

"You know, Katlin, you're going to be the first kid to get her phone privileges revoked before you're old enough to have them," I tell her. "Hi, Jessie."

"Hi," she says. "She's so cute."

"Yeah, yeah, she's a kick," I say, sitting down, tickling her. She shrieks. "Okay, kiddo, out. I want a little privacy."

She tumbles off the couch with a cushion, walking out, talking to it in a syrupy play voice, "Oh, Jessie! Oh, I love you . . ."

"Out!" And she drops the cushion and heads out the back door, the screen rattling with the slam.

"Okay, I'm back."

"How you doing?"

"Okay. I think I need a good night's sleep. I'll probably be in bed before the twins."

"So what's the game plan?"

"It looks like I'll cover for Marcelle at Felice Mundo, look for another job, try not to drive by our restaurant like a stalker."

"*Her* restaurant."

"See what I mean?"

"You know, Rose, I had this girlfriend once who traveled a lot—Tokyo, London, New York—and she'd call me every night from wherever she was, tracked me down at the hospital or at my mom's, and I really thought she was the one. I thought, Here's someone I can rely on and trust. Her hobby was bird watching, which I somehow took to mean that she was the quiet, dependable type. I saw us as old ladies, vacationing in Maine, binoculars hanging from our necks, the whole thing. Then, a year into the relationship, she calls me from Tokyo to tell me she's fallen in love with a Japanese woman, she's transferring to the Tokyo office. It was like she was there and then she was gone. I thought for a while that maybe I dreamed her up, except I was so heartbroken I couldn't sleep. I was 25 and hadn't been in the hospital for three years, but I'm telling you, that nearly sent me back. Time, tears, sleepless nights, extra meds. And eventually you know what happened? I just got sick of myself."

"I'm already plenty sick of myself."

"See? It's a process. And remember, you've got me."

"You know, Jess, that reliable factor, you don't exactly have a history of scoring high on that with me."

"That was 12 years ago, Rose."

Silence on both ends for a little while.

"You know what, Rose? Why don't you just come out and say it? Just say it, because you've been skirting around this since we first saw each other again. Why don't you just say, Jessie, you were a crazy, irresponsible mental patient the last time I saw you. I don't know the next time you're going to wig out, and I don't want to get involved with you."

"I didn't say . . ." I practically sputter.

"I'm not a fucking idiot, Rose. I can feel you pulling back, watching me for signs of I don't know what. I worked hard to be where I am today, my job, my friends, and things you can't even imagine—not feeling like I'm damaged goods because of what my father did to me. I had a year when I woke up every night in a sweat, terrified because all these memories of what he did were coming back to me in my sleep, and yet I did not miss a day of work, didn't hurt myself. You want to know who I am, ask! I have no secrets. I'll tell you everything, my diagnosis, my medication, what a bad day looks like, but if you've already made the decision that you can't rely on me, that I'm too messed up for you, then don't waste my time!"

Click.

I stand there with the receiver still up to my ear like maybe she'll pick the phone back up until it goes to dial tone. I go to call her back and then slam the receiver down. Forget it. I don't even know what I'd say. She might be right. I am afraid she's too much. That I'll be Tommy yelling into a phone for her to come home, in between picking our kid up from soccer practice and making Hamburger Helper which is all I'll have time to make because I'm spending all my time juggling one crisis after another. Just walk away from this, too messy, wasn't meant to be obviously.

But then I think about Montauk. I think about eating those pancakes. I think of us as kids in Baskin Robbins picking ice cream flavors, us lying by the side of the pool, weary and pruney, Night Diving, that hair of hers—and I reach out to touch it.

I stare out into the backyard. The twins are in the sandbox, wearing their Huggies pull-ups, Sue and Becky sitting together on the sandbox bench, just one long board nailed onto either end. I watch them, Sue and Becky chatting, and the twins, Annie scooping sand into a blue plastic pail with a yellow shovel, and Laurel sucking on the handle of her pail.

By 8 the kids are fed and in bed, Becky vetoing Katlin's plea to sleep in my bed.

"She needs to sleep, Katlin, and don't even think about sneaking in there in the middle of the night."

Becky closes the child's bedroom door and we go downstairs. Peter is up in his study. The house is the kind of peaceful quiet that's so odd in a place with children; the edges of the day are soft and fuzzy. Becky pours wine for us. We go in the living room.

"Gail came by while you were gone to say good-bye to the kids. I told her she could visit them whenever she wants. Hope that was okay."

"Sure," I say, feeling a surprising twinge. "She won't, though."

"I know."

We sit, sipping our wine.

"So," she says. "Tell me everything."

I start with the funeral, when I saw the back of Jessie's head, and wind my way through the last week, and finally to this afternoon's argument. I keep stopping, taking a sip of wine, getting embarrassed saying aloud the moments I've held tightly to, played over and over in my head since I got on the plane.

"Are you in love with her?"

"I think so."

Then I'm saying that actually I don't know. I don't know what will happen with us. I don't know what to do next. I don't know exactly what's best, if I'm acting like some infatuated teenager talking about being in love after not seeing each other for years. I tell Becky I don't know how to make this work. I tell her there's something ravenous about Jessie, a neediness and recklessness that frighten me and yet draw me to her.

"It's like she has something dangerous inside and it used to run wild and now she has it in a cage, but it's still there."

"And?"

"And I don't know. That's the problem."

"Maybe you have to trust she won't accidentally leave the cage open? Or that if she does, you can handle it."

"I don't know if I can—or if I want to."

"Well, then you need to think about that. You want my opinion?"

I nod, take a sip of wine.

"I think you tried the safe thing with Gail. And I think you found out how much Gail was not the antidote."

I fall back into the couch with a sigh.

"Just shoot me. Just go ahead and put me out of my misery."

"Am I not right? I mean, you pick this very respectable, neat and tidy person who you think is the opposite of Vivian, and she screws you over. Love is not neat and tidy, Rose. You have to take some risks."

"Okay, but there's risks and then there's feeling like you're jumping off a cliff."

"And like you realize you can't fly?"

"Exactly. I mean, I don't even know how to begin to make this decision."

"Why don't you just try enjoying it—just the way it is? See what happens."

Which is just the kind of annoyingly healthy thing someone with four children can say to you.

"Oh, I'm enjoying it. I am, can't you tell?"

"Rose, I love you, but you're the kind of person who, if Ed McMahon showed up on your doorstep, you'd be holding that big check worrying about the tax implications."

"Very funny."

Chapter 13

You know you're the one who's been left if you're the one standing in a half-empty apartment with a pile of framed photos of the
two of you lying at your feet after the breakup. Gail and I
drenched, our hair flat to our heads, big dark splotches across our
clothes from the wall of wave, a direct hit by the killer whale at
Marine World. Gail and I in Calistoga, frosty Margarita glasses in
hand, toasting the waitress we asked to take our picture. We've got
these big smiles, laughing really, in each one. I pick up the piles
and shuffle through them like mail. Pictures are deceiving, I
think. There's one of us, dusty and sweaty, after a hike up Mount
Tam, and we're all smiles in that one, too. That one I remember.
We were with six other women, and after the hike we went to
Chevy's and all ended up drunk, the heat and not enough to eat.
Those little trail bars taste pretty good after two miles uphill, but
they don't hold you. Something went on between Gail and one of
the women in the ladies' room. Gail came out with her shirt

inside out. No one said a word, but I caught each woman's attempt at a subtle glance, which you should know is nearly impossible to pull off after that much tequila. One of them was actually squinting. I could tell she was trying to confirm for herself the line of seam running down the sides of Gail's shirt. The conversation grew stilted, with everyone taking a renewed and intense interest in the pile of clay-like beans on their plate, searching for a salty place on the edge of their glass. I could feel Gail looking at me, but I kept up a conversation about henna versus permanent dye with the woman to my right, waited a good 15 minutes, took my purse and went to the ladies' room. I walked straight from the ladies' room out the front door. I could feel their eyes watching me. I left the car for Gail, walked along the residential blocks that lined Magnolia in case someone came after me. By the time I called a cab from the Sunoco station, I was almost sober. I didn't realize until then, when I was fishing around the bottom of my purse for change, that I'd taken the car keys.

That night, after we made up, we had to take a cab back to the parking lot for the car. It was late, nearly midnight, and the parking lot was empty. That was four months ago, but I think, as I put the pictures down on the couch and head into the kitchen, that I'll see that night as the beginning of the end. It's always that way with the end, a subjective point.

Becky had collected my mail every few days, and it sits in stacks on the kitchen table along with a very dead potted plant, the leaves brown and stiff. There's a cross stuck in its dirt, two yellow baggy ties Becky twisted together with a note: *I leave my pot to Cousin Flo. Please honor my memory with a proper burial.*

The kitchen looks the same because it is mostly my stuff; a couple of kitchen magnets are gone, but that's all. It's the room that feels the least empty. I'd walked in the bedroom and walked right out. She'd left the bed, which made me wince. A concrete reminder that she had another bed now.

I think the worst is when emptiness around you makes you feel hollow inside, though clutter can do that, too. I know from when Vivian got sick that first time, from Aunt Moe. I fill the kitchen trashcan with junk mail and then sit down with the last can of Diet Pepsi in the apartment and go through the rest, starting with an envelope from Gail. I slide the letter from the envelope and a check drops onto the table: $2,100, half her rent for the next three months through our lease. I had thought of the lease on the plane from New York, planned on calling Gail and demanding this exact check, feeling self-righteous, so I'll admit I'm a little disappointed. You want your ex to be a total deadbeat. The note is short, written in large script to fill the page.

> Rose,
> Here's the rent $ for the rest of the lease. I'll send you some $ towards the utilities next month. Call me if I forgot anything (427-3167). I'll be traveling for work through Oct. 28th. Sorry again about your grandmother.
> Take care,
> Gail

I leave the rest of the mail and take the Sunday *Chronicle* into the living room and sit on the floor, pull out the classified section and open it to R for Restaurant, C for Chef. There isn't much, and I know I need to suck it up and pick up the phone, call around and see who's looking for a chef. But then I'll have to explain about Gail, and I can't figure out how to stay in the professional mode—I need a job—without getting into the personal mode—she dumped me for a farmer.

I get up and go into the bedroom, start unpacking my suitcase onto the bed, making a pile of dirty laundry. Then I just stand there. The apartment is silence and stillness, just the sound of kids yelling to one another outside, hurling themselves into the apartment complex pool out back in loud cannonball splashes.

I see Gail pulling open dresser drawers, angrily shoving clothes, shoes, into her navy duffel bag. I had stood in the doorway watching her. We had fought all night, hurling accusations. She was a cheat, a liar, a betrayer. I was remote, withholding, already gone. By 4 in the morning we were done and I felt *right*. After all, *she* had had the affair. But I also felt embarrassed. How could I not have guessed? Why was someone chosen over me? Gail looked like someone escaping from prison before the guards caught her missing, couldn't get out fast enough.

That she was firing me seemed to be an afterthought she flung, like the Sunday paper pitched into the apartment on her way out the door. We yelled back and forth, with the front door open, and God knows who heard us, until she screamed, "It's my decision and I've made it!" And slammed the door. I'd stood there in disbelief. The call from Vivian saying my grandmother had died was somehow a bizarre relief. I actually gave the door a good slam myself on the way out.

The clock on the nightstand reads 10:30, and I pick up the phone to call Jessie and then put it down. Becky had made it sound so simple.

"Just call her. Apologize for giving her mixed signals. Just 'fess up and tell her you're confused. Ask her to just give you some time to think."

"I don't know."

"You're trying my patience, Rose."

"Okay, I'll do it." Smiling weakly.

But so far, I've picked up and put down the phone a dozen times. I'll just give her some time to cool down, I tell myself. She sounded really pissed off. I go in the bathroom and stand, staring into the mirror. You are such a wuss, I tell myself. Then I tell myself it's going to be okay. I give my reflection a big grin. Right!

For days, I carry the Sunday paper around like Linus's blanket and slowly circle about 20 ads. Ones I wouldn't even entertain on Sunday I'm considering by Wednesday.

Joven preps for breakfast and I arrive at Felice Mundo each morning at 7. I had stopped working day shifts years ago, graduated to the more prestigious dinner shifts, and I can barely drag myself out of bed when the alarm goes off.

Felice Mundo has taken on an odd hipness. The clientele is varied: Mothers with strollers and Snuglies having breakfast, corporate types meeting for the Berkeley equivalent of power lunches, and a clutch of UC Berkeley students who look like they've slept in their clothes. The place isn't exactly packed on a Tuesday, and I check out the patrons through the window of the swinging kitchen door.

"Don't we have *any* kind of a dress code?" I ask Joven. One of the UC girls actually is wearing her pajama top.

"You're kidding, right?" he says, not even looking up at me from the grill.

"Croque-Monsieur?" I ask, gesturing towards the grill.

"Toasted cheese sandwich for the three-year-old at Table 4."

And we make malts. I alternate from lazing in the gentle pace like I'm in a hammock, the soothing whir of the malt machine, somersaulting a quesadilla from the grill up over my head, and freezing like a possum in headlights everytime Bessie or Dee tells me a customer would like to see me. So far it's been only strangers, regulars wanting to ask about Marcelle, drop off flowers, or tell me the matzo ball soup needs more salt. But I'm waiting for the day when someone from my Gail life wanders in and finds me here, and the word gets out in the City that I'm making peanut butter and banana sandwiches.

As it is, only two people have returned my calls. Ron, owner of Zulus, calls to tell me he's not hiring but thinks he has a lead to call me back on, and he's heard about me and Gail and he's sorry. I should stop by for a drink. Faye, an old culinary school buddy, calls back to say she has a tip on an opening coming up at the Washington Square Bar and Grill—not exactly cutting edge but respectable. Then, in a hesitant, hushed tone, she adds, "Look, it's none of my business, but be glad you're done with her. She's a back-stabbing bitch."

"What do you mean?" I move towards the back screen door—like Joven is even interested! He's been busying himself all day with a recipe for borscht.

"All I have to say is, good riddance."

"Faye, now you have to tell me."

"It's really none of my business."

"Faye!"

"Well, okay. Gail was over at Zulus the other night with Old McDonald—who, by the way, dyes her hair—and she had a few too many and started bad-mouthing your cooking. Ron couldn't remember if it was that morel pasta or your blackberry flan . . ."

"The flan," I tell her. "She thinks flans are slimy."

"Well, she's the slimy one, if you ask me. No one took her seriously, but she sort of insinuated that wasn't the only problem, like there was more you did."

"Like what?!"

"I probably shouldn't have said anything . . ."

"Jesus Christ, Faye. Stop saying that. What did she mean?"

"She insinuated that you embezzled money from the restaurant."

"That bitch!"

I'm so blown away by this I nearly lose my balance and fall through the screen door.

"Like I said, no one took her seriously so I wouldn't worry about that, and quite honestly I don't think that place is gonna last two months without you there . . ."

I lean into the screen, feel the cold mesh on my check. It's way over. It is *so* way over. This is love, huh? One day you're feeding each other tastes of marinades to check for herb content and flipping through your joint phone bill, and the next thing you know that same person is publicly humiliating you. Again I think they should let me into the meeting at the Holy BM on an honorary basis. I've heard their stories over the years. I think losing a job, a relationship and a grandmother, and having a close friend with life-threatening cancer all at once must constitute some form of bottom-hitting.

I go over to Marcelle's after work.

"I *knew* it," she says when I tell her about Gail. "She is trash," a condition that sounds even more seedy in a French accent.

"Sit down," I tell her. We're in her kitchen and she's washing the dishes. She's supposed to be in bed.

"It's 2 in the afternoon. I've been in bed all day. I think I need to go back to work."

"I think you need to do what Dr. Myers says."

But I see her point. It's been over a week. Her surgical staples are out and, while she gets tired more quickly, she's got too much energy to be sitting around the house. She does take a nap after lunch, but I came by after work one day to find her playing paddleball with Colin on her front lawn. Louise, the home healthcare nurse, comes by to check on her each day. Someone stays with her each night. I'm tempted, even when it's not my night, to stay over and have to remind myself other people love her, want their private time with her when we have no idea how much she'll have to give. Some nights I stay in the East Bay and spend the night at Becky's, bring over a tray of enchiladas or blintzes.

It's not even that I'm sad, I decide in Petrini's late one night as I'm grocery shopping. Sad requires some sinking into yourself, and I'm entirely too anxious for that. I just feel lost. I'd managed to update my resumé that day and written a cover letter applying for a job in Napa, a good hour and a half from my apartment, but time and distance have taken on a whole new meaning for me. There are nights I drive over the bridge from Marcelle's house so tired, so late, that the next thing I know I'm brushing my teeth, in my pajamas, and can't remember how I got there.

Marcelle's first chemo doesn't seem so bad at first. We play poker on the bedside table and she tries to eat lunch but can't find an appetite. I watch the IV bag empty, and I feel like I've taken her here to be poisoned. I am so frustrated that all I can do is get fresh cold compresses from the nurse station that, when Dr. Myers comes to check on her and tells us that the next day will probably be worse, I snap at him.

"And what are you going to *do* about that?!"

Marcelle reaches from under the sheet to take my hand and gives it a little squeeze, which does wonders for my self-esteem. I am the most selfish being on the planet, being comforted by the cancer patient.

I fling a box of cereal with mini marshmallow dinosaurs in the cart with disgust.

Jessie had asked me twice, before our fight, if I wanted her to come help out—for a visit, she'd added quickly, no big decisions. No, I'd said, I'm okay. Between being at the hospital and keeping Felice Mundo open, I'd keep myself busy enough to get a grip.

I'm surprised and worried that she hasn't called me, and yet,

I can't bring myself to call her either. The truth is I am terrified that the minute I call her, I'll beg her to come, and when she does, I'll burrow into one of her pockets and not come out. Just the thought sends me reeling, feeling so fragile and scared, like I am spending every second of every day at the edge of the black hole I fell into the first time Vivian got sick, and again when Jessie ran away, digging my heels in, fighting to not get pushed back into that hole. I stand in the produce section, holding a zucchini, my eyes fixed on it, seeing green, seeing nothing. Luckily the store is empty, just me and some furry-looking guy with a hand-basket of avocados and quart bottles of beer and a woman in a business suit with a whole cart of health foods, obviously just off from work.

▼

By the end of the first chemo week, Marcelle is pretty beat up but is home and quickly getting her energy back. And I am an irritable, unemployed, raging insomniac. The AA group decides to move the Friday night meeting from the Holy BM to Marcelle's living room for the night so she can attend. They let me come, sit on the couch and say, "Hi, I'm Rose and I'm not an alcoholic but I play one on TV." They say, "Welcome, Rose," and then tell me to get lost, in the most loving and playful of ways.

The whole time since I got back to the apartment I've been cleaning and organizing, like I can scrub the pain away, fling the feel of Gail sleeping next to me out with a pile of old magazines. I'm done with my closets and dressers and start in on the kitchen, Tupperware stacked neatly one inside the other. I make lots of rows, rows of canned goods with the labels facing forward, rows of cleaning supplies under the sink. I've got a good 50 jars of spices and it's when I'm arranging them in rows of A through J, L through Q, that the phone rings and it's a woman who introduces herself as Marie Strand from Yellow Dog, a place in Palo Alto I'd seen written up in *Food and Wine*, offering me my first interview.

We schedule an interview for 10 Monday morning, and I get back to my spices. I'm gazing into the kitchen cabinet, admiring my work, when the phone rings again.

Jessie.

"A 15-year-old girl came in to the ER today, slit her wrists, the *right* way."

I can hear she's crying. I pull the phone cord and go out the kitchen door and sit on the back porch.

"God, that's terrible. Why?"

"I don't know. She was unconscious when they brought her in and I don't work the ER. I was having lunch with my friend Jackie and I went down there to meet her. That kind of thing is the reason I *don't* work down there."

"Why are you crying?"

"Why!"

"No, I mean, it's terrible, but I'm just asking, are you crying for her or are you remembering?"

"Remembering, I guess. I don't know."

She's breathing heavily, catching each breath.

"I'm sorry. I'm sorry. I don't mean to put this on you. I called Sara and left her a message."

"It's okay. We can talk about it."

She doesn't answer, just cries.

"This is what you were talking about, isn't it? You're probably thinking, Great, the last thing I need right now is to be involved with a hysterical . . ."

"No, don't do that. Jesus Christ, Jessie, it *is* wrenching to see some teenager try to kill themselves and it *is* close to home for you, so no, I just don't think it's so strange that it would make you upset!"

"No. But I'm okay now. Really. What are you doing?"

"Let's see, I just finished alphabetizing my spices . . ."

"You what?"

"See? You think you're such a mess. You've got some competition now. You should come by. I'm starting my Popsicle stick jewelry box this afternoon."

"With painted macaroni?"

"If you insist."

"Hey, Rose."

"Yeah?"

"I'm sorry I blew up at you the other night."

"No, I'm sorry I'm being such a jerk. My life feels like a train wreck right now, and I'm not the nicest person to be around."

"And who would be?"

"Oh, God, I hope there's people out there who handle life better than this. And you and me, Jessie, I just feel like I don't know what we should do."

"And I'm going to do my best to not take that personally and really think about whether I'm ready to take you on again."

"Take me on?! What's wrong with me?"

"Oh, like you're so perfect, Rose. You think loving you is easy?"

"Okay. I deserve that."

"Any luck on the job front?"

"I got a job interview."

"That's great. When?"

"Monday. I'll have to get Joven . . ."

Over the phone, I hear someone start banging on her door, big fist on tin.

"You need to get that?"

"UPS," she says. "I better get off. I'll call you tomorrow, okay?"

"Okay," I say, but she's already hung up.

I'm awake at 6:30 on Wednesday. For that matter, I'm also awake at 2:16 and 4:37. I just get up at 6:30 even though it's supposed to be my day off. I make huge chocolate chip cookies, the kind that fit three on a cookie sheet, twelve to a batch. They spread into each other as they bake, thick and cakey. I used to make them for the coffee-house at college, walk them up the hill from the cafeteria kitchen at night and in the back door of the coffee-house where a couple of kids sat studying in the kitchen—just a sink, a table and chairs, and a toaster oven. Coffee House Server was a coveted work-study position, pretty cushy, free food, and the servers would be sitting at the kitchen table studying, occasionally interrupted when a student at the kitchen door that opened in two, the top swinging open, the bottom with a shelf where the students put their empty coffee cups for refills, requested something to eat from the list on the blackboard: brownies, quiche, pies, and of course the cookies. I made the pies six at a time, one dozen mounds of powdery butter yellow dough, sweet and heavy. Apples I peeled in one long curl, red, thin as skin, the fruit cut into slender half circles I plopped into bowls of lemon water to keep them from going brown. Strawberries I cored and mounded whole into a brown speckled crust, glistening a deep color of tongues and poppy petals from the glaze.

I lean down and gaze through the oven door, the light inside glowing over the bubblings and meltings, and I watch the cookies like a show, my face warmed. And I think of my lie.

I lied to Becky and Marcelle, told them the interview is in San Francisco, just a BART ride away. I count silently, my lips moving, one, two, three, possibly four freeways. I have picked out my interview suit, the navy one, and a brightly flowered blouse, the sensible round-toed pumps, like I am picking out the clothes for my own execution. My heart does that pounding thing just imagining the turn of the ignition key, and I am stubborn shame.

I try to keep this secret. Only Becky really knows and even she doesn't know it all.

The truth is that it's more than distaste, not just a preference to be a passenger, no, it's the terror of turning a steering wheel too soon, too late, a light I run. Mostly, though, it's the speed. The speed that makes teenage boys covet Mustangs, and for others evokes images of hair flying back in spirited freedom, for me equals sure death waiting to happen. I can't track it all. I know I'll miss something, the car quickly cutting in front of me to make an exit, my timidity to merge smoothly, to easily become one in a large fluid row. I watch others do a dance with steps too quick and complicated. The bottom line? All I feel the whole time I'm driving is that one second when the world explodes into folding, flying metal, that one second, over and over.

One time I had wanted to apprentice at a bakery in Walnut Creek, a French pastry shop renowned for their work, and when I got there I had to sit in the car, watching the clock. I couldn't stop crying, those gasping panic-attack breaths, and by the time I did stop, I was a half-hour late and my make-up was completely off. I don't remember how I got home. I didn't go to the interview.

I remember all this, lifting cookies off their sheet and onto the metal rack, scooping and flattening the dough, the chips and walnuts bumpy against the spoon, and I am this weighted bowl of batter with my shame and fear.

It is 6:30 New York time when I call Jessie, the buttons on the receiver sticky on my cheek from my fingers. I run the cold water in the sink and fill a glass. I hear the receiver fumbled from its cradle and then, "Hello? Hello?"

I'm across the kitchen and slamming the phone back into the wall with a force that sloshes the water over the edge of the glass and down my hand. It wasn't Jessie. It was a woman's voice, but not Jessie's. My mind jumps to Jessie hanging up so hurriedly, her voice edgy as the screen door rattled in the background. I am instantly sure she has decided she is fed up with me and my ambivalence. She has fallen for someone who can make a commitment. But who? I want details, details I can later sift through in private, holding pebbles of suspicion up to the light, turning them, trying to read meaning. Then I think, Who am I to be jealous?

I'm winding up like the Jack-in-the-box of jealousy. You want some private time for this kind of third-degree jealousy. You want to pop out of that box in private where you can have your hideous fantasies play on all four walls of your living room and the volume a bit too high while you fumble through your CDs for the right soundtrack. Linda Ronstadt's *Desperado* is good, you can howl along. The Beatles' *Long and Winding Road* is also a winner *if* you've wound down to the kind of quiet crying that is just tears sliding down your face in a stream steady enough to threaten to douse your smoke.

I show up at Felice Mundo with my face swollen, sure I've been dropped. I can't concentrate on anything and burn three omelets, my mind choreographing some vile scene of Jessie and a very sculpted and tight version of this woman I caught her looking at when we were at the Clam Hut in Montauk.

Jessie calls me at Felice Mundo and is obviously trying to act like nothing is going on, probably trying to hedge her bets. I make some excuse that it's getting busy and hang up.

Marcelle, who is camped out in a chair in the kitchen depodding peas, just shakes her head at me. She's been patiently listening to my ranting all morning, time counted in aluminum bowls of hulled strawberries, peeled potatoes, the growing hill of peas.

"Don't be a fool, Rose. Love doesn't come in the mail everyday."

"I know that wasn't her voice."

"Foolishness." Then, "That's enough sage."

Night Diving

▼

Marie Strand looks like an Asian version of Betty Crocker, hair definitely set and teased, one of those ladies that used to come in the shop on a Saturday to have the week's worth of hair spray washed out, their wet heads set with those multicolored plastic rollers and sheets of roller tissue that stick to their crunchy curls after you pull the rollers out.

I arrived an hour early covered in sweat and went directly to the ladies' room. I sat in the stall, swabbing my wet face with a toilet seat cover and regulating my breathing. I'd completely lost it on the 880 freeway. Pulled onto the shoulder, turned on my hazards and crept to the next exit where I got onto the next freeway and did the same thing. The cars whizzed by and I turned up my tape player. "Don't your feet get cold in the winter tiiime! The sky won't snow and the sun won't shiiine . . .'

Marie gave me a tour of the restaurant, had me spend an hour in the kitchen observing the present chef who was leaving to open his own place and not only tried to pick me up but tried to recruit me, and then she interviewed me for a good hour and a half about my work history. When she asked me about my last position, I told her the place had burned down. She looked a little startled but just made some more jots on her pad. By then I was thinking of my drive home, little beads of perspiration gathering under my arms.

"So, we'll be in touch," Marie says to me with one of those restaurant-owner smiles that seem to say, We eat our young.

I take a final gulp from the water glass she has a busboy fetch for me, shake her hand and head out the door and to my car, feeling pretty sure I have the job, can almost envision my leisurely, future commute along the freeways' shoulders each morning, sipping my coffee, picking at my bran muffin, the comforting click of my hazards.

Chapter 14

It's 2:40 when I get to Felice Mundo, and the lunch crowd has left. Joven, Bessie, Dee and Marcelle sit around Table 7 eating, counting tips. Becky is there, too, over at the coffee machine pouring herself a cup. Joven is making out a bank deposit and Marcelle has yet another aluminum bowl in her lap. This time it's lima beans. I lean over to kiss her cheek

"These beans are shit." It sounds like sheet with her accent.

"Jim said they were great," Jim being our produce man.

"Jim has good stuff but he's a lying son of a bitch. You pick what *you* think is good."

"Scott quit," Dee says, pushing a pile of coins at Joven. "Five bucks," she tells him and he hands her a bill.

"What happened?"

"Jim Beam."

"Of course," Bessie says. "We would have fired him anyway."

Scott, the dishwasher, was a newcomer to their home group.

While Marcelle likes to help the newcomers out, even let one of them sleep in the back booth of Felice Mundo for a week after his boyfriend threw him out, she has a strict no-use policy.

"I'll get an ad in tomorrow," Joven says, getting up with the leather deposit pouch, just like the one Tommy used to have. Bessie grabs her purse and gets up to leave too. "How'd your interview go?" he asks.

"Pretty good," I say. "Fine, I guess."

"Really?"

"I don't know, Joven. It seemed fine. It's just sort of a drive."

"I thought you said it was in San Francisco. I thought you took BART."

"I know. I lied. I didn't want you guys to worry."

"Where *was* it?"

"Palo Alto."

"Palo Alto?!" All of them say it at once.

"You drove to Palo Alto?" Joven asks.

"Sort of. I mean I got there and back."

"How?"

"You know, I think I'll spare you the gory details on this, but my point is, I couldn't do it every day. It's enough of a stretch for me to drive here."

"Rose, why don't you just move back to the East Bay," Bessie says.

"Yeah," Joven says. "You're over here all the time anyway, between Felice Mundo and Marcelle. Then you could catch a ride with one of us."

"Joven, I'm not working here forever."

It comes out with more disdain than I planned. Marcelle, who has been quietly depodding beans, gives me one of those eyebrow-raised smirks.

"Well, excuse me, I forgot we were being graced by her Royal

Culinary Highness."

"I didn't mean it that way, Joven. I just meant that eventually Marcelle will feel better . . ."

"Or die," she says, not looking up from her beans.

"Could you not do that, please?" I say to her. "That's not funny."

We fall silent. Bessie leans over, puts her hand gently over mine.

"Rose, we're just a little, I mean not really, but a little because we love you, worried about you. You seem unhappy . . ."

"Bessie! I think if she *felt* like talking about it . . ." Dee says, letting out a disapproving sigh.

"Rose, we worry that you're on a self-destructive path," Joven chimes in, ignoring Dee.

"Is this like an intervention?"

"No, no, I don't think so, but we want you to just take stock here. Sure, Gail dumped you . . ."

"That was sort of insensitive, Joven," Bessie says.

"You want to do this?"

"No, Joven."

"Okay then. Anyway, you and Gail needed to follow your separate paths. I really believe it's for the best, seeing as how she was a bit, you know . . ." And he actually looks to Bessie for help.

"She was sort of loose. Not in the woman-as-madonna-or-harlot dichotomy kind of way, but she didn't respect the monogamous agreement you had together. I mean, I think you respected it. It's really none of my business . . ."

"Slut!" Marcelle practically spits into her beans. "What else you want to say? You sleep around you are what else? Slut!"

"I'm outa here," Dee says, her face a bright pink. "I mean, God, you guys."

They pause, listening for the sound of the back screen door closing.

"I agree with Marcelle," Becky says. "And furthermore you have Jessie, whom you've been pining away for since I've known you. Yet you refuse to allow yourself to be happy. I just don't get the problem."

"You know, Prozac has been helpful for me," Bessie says.

I sink into a chair, reach over for Becky's coffee and take a sip.

"I think the thing with Jessie and me is over."

"Over? It just started. What do you mean, over?"

"I called there the other day, really early in the morning, and some woman picked up."

"I've heard this," Marcelle says, getting up with her beans. "Fool," and she disappears into the kitchen.

"You're sure it wasn't her? Maybe she had a cold or something."

"I know Jessie's voice and it wasn't Jessie."

"Maybe you dialed the wrong number."

"Rose," Becky says, "could you just clarify something for me? Why don't you just call her up and ask her about this?"

"She'll just deny it."

"Oh my God, I give up. Gail! *Gail* would deny it. Jessie called my house today wanting to know if she should call you or continue to give you space, because you hadn't been returning her phone calls."

"She did not," I say. God, I sound 12.

"Yes indeed, Rose. One person in this relationship is exhibiting signs of mental health."

"There was a woman in her bed!"

"What do you have, radar or something? You can see through a phone? Maybe she had a friend sleeping on her couch," Becky says.

And I'm telling you, every one of them is looking at me like, Come down off the ledge, Rose.

"When I talked to her she certainly didn't sound like a person with her mind on another woman."

"She's covering."

"Why don't you give her a chance to explain before you jump to all these conclusions?"

"I'm not up for this," I say wearily, "especially with Jessie. I've been through this head-for-the-hills act with her before. Every time things don't go her way, she cuts out."

"Prozac couldn't possibly be strong enough," Becky says, scooping her purse up from the floor. "I think you should just talk to her, give her the chance to explain before you make yourself so damn miserable. Would you do me that favor? Maybe hold off on the divorce proceedings for a couple of days until you're feeling a bit more like yourself? Come on, I have to get home. You are still coming for dinner?"

"Yeah, okay," I say and start to get up.

"You know, Rose, not for anything but you've sort of been putting her off, it seems," Bessie says, just as Marcelle walks back out from the kitchen with yet another bowl and a bag of string beans.

"Sheet or cut bait," she mumbles, sitting down and yanking the ends off a bean.

"I heard that and it's fish," I tell her. "Fish or cut bait and shit or get off the pot."

"You love this girl?"

"Yeah but there are other things . . ."

"No, there are no other things," Marcelle says, her voice husky. "You know what there is? There is a day, and you don't know when, when she is gone. *Then* you really have time to think about all things. Today she is here. I tell you one sure thing, when they're gone, it doesn't matter if you decide you love them." She shakes a dishtowel at me. "Don't be a fool."

I nod feeling like I might cry, like Laurel and Annie overdue for a nap, cry over everything, the events of the day, the interview, my panic attack in the car, Jessie's betrayal. There's a different and distinctive pain at the base of my throat.

When we get back to Becky's house, I watch videos with the kids while she makes dinner.

"Move *over*, Colin," Katlin yells, giving him a push that practically sends him off the couch.

"Ow! Mom!"

"Give me some space!" Katlin yells and I get up, go root around in the bathroom for some Tylenol when the phone rings. I hear Katlin and Colin scurry for the phone, the sound of a struggle.

"Ow! Mom! Katlin hit me in the head with the phone."

"It's for you, Aunt Rose," Katlin calls to me.

I take the phone from her as Becky enters the room and gives Katlin the come-here-so-I-can-beat-you-within-an-inch-of-your-life hand signal.

"Hi, Rose. It's Joven. I was over your way for a meeting, but it got canceled. You want to go have a cup of coffee, maybe talk a little?"

We agree to meet over at Peets on Fourth Street, and I head out the door, kissing everyone good-bye except Katlin, who is on a time-out in her room crying and screaming, sounds reminiscent of our special babysitting night.

When I walk up to Peets, Joven is already there, sitting at an outside table.

"What is this?" I ask, taking the cup he hands me.

"Hot chocolate with whipped cream. I figured you could use a little comfort food."

"Oh, Joven." I sip the chocolate and our eyes meet. He smiles at me, shaking his head.

"What?"

"You know, Rose, when I was in the first few days of detox, all I could think about was my job and how quickly I could get back to it, how much ground I was losing by not being there. That's how crazy I was. I had lost my marriage, my kids, my self-respect, everything in fact, and I was worrying about a project deadline. I was about as far away from serenity as you can get. After a couple of weeks sober and getting my self-important butt kicked in Group everyday, I woke up one morning and thought, What if I don't go back there? And the thought terrified me. I dismissed it, but it was enough—that door cracked open just enough to consider there might be other choices. And when Carol came in that week for family night, I was finally ready to come out from behind the work excuse—the thing that always convinced me I didn't have a problem because how could I be a hot-shot CFO if I was a drug addict—and started taking responsibility for my marriage and my family. Now, you know I decided to quit and I'm not saying that should be your choice. I'm just saying maybe you want to ask who's running the show here, your ego or your heart. And maybe . . . I'm talking way too much here, aren't I?"

"No, no, Joven, you're right. I've got a lot more wrapped up in being *The Chef* than I should. I mean, it's not something I advertise, but I know that—and I guess it shows, huh?"

"A little, mostly today. And you have to hear me, I'm not here to take your inventory or anything. I just care about you, and I see you letting a good thing walk away with Jessie. And I guess I'm thankful enough to all the people in the program who helped me not to lose Carol that I just must say this to you."

"But, Joven, you're forgetting one thing: The woman who answered the phone."

"Okay, strictly speaking as the King of Rationalization Himself and Grand Pooh-Bah of I Don't Do Feelings, is there a possibility that there is no other woman? Is it maybe just possible that you're not calling Jessie to ask her straight out who picked up the phone because if you find out you're wrong, you'll have to follow your heart and take a chance? And you forget I'm in that kitchen with you everyday. I hear you humming away as you make those cream cheese cupcakes. And those oallieberry pies. I saw the way your face lit up when Dee told you that woman at Table 4 asked if she could have three pies for her party this weekend. Rose honey, what are you so afraid of?"

"It's just too many choices, and I'm worried I won't make the right choice and then!"

"And then what?"

"God, I don't know. I'll fuck up. I'll open my own place like I always dreamed of and I'll go bankrupt. I'll marry Jessie and she'll just take off on me again. I'll turn her away and I'll be 90 and wondering what if? I don't know what to do."

"I think you do," he says gently.

"I don't."

"You do."

"Don't."

"Do."

"Don't."

"Rose! I've known you a lot of years, and if there's one thing I know about you, it's that too often you do what you think you should do at the expense of what you want. And honey, this time I think life is saying to you, Rose, you need a new act."

I open my mouth and then close it.

I walk from my front door straight to the phone. I dial Jessie's number, figure I'll take Becky's standard advice and get all my crises over with in one day, but the machine clicks on with me calling for her to pick up. I envision her hand emerging from the sheets to slide the volume switch and returning, in one graceful motion, to the frenzied passionate sex I'm sure she's been having all day.

I sit in the dark kitchen eating Cherry Garcia straight out of the carton. I am sure I can actually feel the calories migrating to my thighs. I think about what Joven said, that maybe I'm the one getting in my own way. Then I think that Jessie could be not answering the phone because she's been in some terrible accident, that at that very moment the jaws-of-life could be her only hope. I jump up and call Hannah.

"How are you, dear?"

"Not so good. Hannah, I haven't heard from Jessie since Thursday and I was getting a little worried."

"Oh, Rose, she's been working a lot. One of the nurses on the unit is sick and she's been filling in." How can she ask her own mother to cover for her, jeopardize her ethics like that!

"I called at 6:30 in the morning and some woman answered the phone."

"Oh, honey, that's Jules's daughter, Maureen. She was visiting. Maureen lives in New Jersey and she always spends the night at Jessie's when she comes to visit. They're just friends."

"Oh."

I am the husband in *The Burning Bed*. There must be some psychiatric diagnosis—Pathological Insecurity? Stage-Three Jealousy?—for this. A simple outpatient referral cannot possibly address my needs. Clearly, my symptoms warrant a more protected setting, perhaps like the grassy grounds and bar-windowed place Natalie Wood got to inhabit in *Splendor in the Grass* . . . plastic utensils, those peaceful benches out on the lawn where my rocking and drooling roommate and I sit in between our E.C.T. treatments. The only thing that saves me from putting down the phone, crawling into the freezer and closing the door behind me is knowing I'm talking to Hannah here.

"Oh, Rose, Jessie adores you. I haven't seen her this happy in years . . ."

I get off the phone pretty quickly after that and dial Jessie's number. She picks up on the first ring.

"It's me," I say, and I instantly start bawling.

"What's going on? Hey, hey, it's okay, Rose . . ."

"I'm sorry," I say. "I'm just having a hard time."

"What happened?"

"You. Me. Us."

"What? Rose, wait, wait, take some breaths. Come on. Really. I mean it."

And I obey, three breaths in . . . and out.

"Okay, now try again. What were you saying?"

"I'd really like it if you could come for a visit."

"When?"

"Today, tomorrow at the very latest."

Chapter 15

"Why are you getting that tone with me?" Vivian says. I sigh, pulling the phone cord taut to sit out on the back step with my coffee. "If this career issue is so difficult for you, maybe you should go back into therapy."

"I'm considering that."

"I can send you some money."

"Do *not* send me money."

And there's this uncomfortable silence on the other end, when she is wounded, struck down by the cruelty and ingratitude of the child she carried in her womb for nine months. It's no picnic on the other end, either. Claire and I actually have a system worked out, messages we leave on each other's answering machine: *Call me. I need to debrief about Mom.*

I don't completely understand it. I used to talk about it with Becky, but of course now she plays for the other side, so the conversation doesn't go very far before we hit that roadblock of Once

You Become A Mother. The point is, if anyone else offered to send you money, even a stack of checks made out to cash, you'd think, How thoughtful. Okay, maybe not checks made out to cash unless your friend was the under-the-table type and you were used to giving him little lectures on tax evasion, but short of that, anyone else offers to help you out and it's a gesture of kindness. You thank that person, right? A mother offers to do that and it's like she's forcing you to play with Crayolas and wear those itchy plaid skirts with the four-pound pin on the front you have to drag all over the kickball field during recess.

"Oh." Clipped tone. "You don't need money? You found a job?"

"I went on an interview yesterday. A chef position out in Palo Alto."

"What about Marcelle? What about Felice Mundo?"

"I don't know. I mean, I can't do that forever."

"Why not?"

"Why not? Because I've been busting my ass for the past 10 years making a reputation for myself as a chef—not some diner cook!"

I can't even believe I'm hearing this from Vivian, who has always acted like anything short of directing the White House culinary staff is beneath me.

"If that's what you want to do. I was never really into that status sort of thing."

"Excuse me? Whose designer tablecloth dress was I wearing at the funeral?"

"Your Uncle Davey had 50 of them. He was practically giving them away. My point is that you *did* go through all that schooling, but I don't see that you should feel boxed in by that. I've always told you: You can make more money with your own place. My client, Joyce, is making a hundred thousand grand a year with that hot-dog truck of hers. She's parked on the Jericho Turnpike Exit in the morning. The cars stop before they get on the expressway . . ."

"A hot-dog truck! You're suggesting I get a hot-dog truck?!"

"I'm just saying there's different ways to make money."

"I am not getting a hot-dog truck, okay?"

"You're missing my point. Take a chance."

"And do what?"

"Whatever you want—just don't shoot too low is all I'm saying."

"Wait a minute. You were concerned when I was going to be a chef, remember? That I was going to starve?"

"You know what, Rose? That was eight years ago. When your child is 22 years old, you worry about her choices, but at this point I personally don't see why you need to pressure yourself like this. You have a friend who needs your help and you want to help. Do that for now. I think there's a bigger picture here. Then later you can open your own Russian Tea Room."

"You are hopeless," I say, finally laughing at her stubborn belief in my ability to be Culinary Queen—if I only didn't have such low self-esteem!

"So?"

She's laughing too.

"Wait a minute. You're actually telling me to do this?"

"I'm not telling you to do anything. You are a 30-year-old woman. If you want to pick bananas in Cuba and you can make it work, you should do it. I certainly never let anyone tell me what to do."

Now there's one of life's great truths.

"I was thinking," I say, tentatively. "Maybe a bakery, something like that. I'm a little scared but I want to."

"Of course you're scared. You think I wasn't scared when I

opened the first hair salon? And you don't have two kids to support."

"You, scared? You never acted scared."

"Well, Rose, you don't go to your children and tell them you're scared you can't pay your lease. Believe me, there were times I was scared, but if you don't take the risk, you end up staying in the same place all your life. And that's a choice too. Some people are too afraid and they do the same boring job all their lives, and I'm not putting that down. Sometimes I think it would be a lot easier to just go to work and come home, being some robot, doing what you're told."

Vivian is nothing if not even-handed.

"I've been to some of the finest restaurants in Manhattan and your cooking is just as good . . ."

"Well, I wouldn't go that far!"

"There you go, selling yourself short again. You are so talented, and I'm sure, if you put your mind to it, you could be right up there with the best of them. You know, one of my clients is in the restaurant business and I could make a few calls. I'm sure . . ."

"No! And how did we get from a hot-dog truck on the Long Island Expressway to the Russian Tea Room?"

"Do what you want, Rose. You don't need my permission."

The way she says it, like she's thrown up her hands with me and my obstinate stupidity, gives me that old little-girl feeling I keep hoping I've gotten over. There's a long silence.

"Rose, honey, why is life so difficult for you?"

A sigh.

"But you know what? You'll figure it out. You'll see."

"Thanks."

"I'll call you from the shop tomorrow. I love you."

"I love you, too."

We hang up, and I call Marcelle. I can hear pots and pans

being knocked against burners, the loud sizzling that several pans going at once make.

"Listen," I tell her. "Don't worry. I'm just going to stay and work as long as you need me."

"I wasn't worried."

"I called Jessie. She's coming today to stay for a week. We're going to talk."

"Good. Don't be a fool. You feel better now?"

"I'm okay." Okay, one of those vague, noncommittal words and, I remember, not one of Marcelle's favorite words. I think, am I okay? Am I going to be okay? How can I make things okay? If I listen to Becky and just wait, ride the wave, will it end up okay or will the tidal wave come and wipe everything out? Though it hasn't yet, I consider.

I pull on my suit and head out to the pool, lie in a lounge chair, let the splashes and someone's radio lull me into a nap. I wake with a start to the tinkling of the ice-cream truck, the thumping of bare little feet on cement running past me.

"Rose?" I look up to see a man standing over me. "Rose Salino?"

Something about the voice is familiar. I sit up, trying to focus on his face.

"Rose? Rose, it's me. Alex?"

"Alex? Alex!"

"I thought it was you!" And he chortles as I stand up to hug him. He's still short, maybe four inches shorter than me.

"What are you doing here?"

"I'm visiting my wife's niece."

"Do you live here?"

"We moved here about a year ago. I'm with Lawrence Berkeley Lab."

"Oh, Alex." And I can't say anything else.

"Chris!" he yells over my shoulder. "Come here, please. I'd like you to meet someone."

She walks toward us, a woman with hair pulled back in a ponytail and a big smile.

"Hello," she says, extending a hand.

"This is Rose," he says. "You know, Rose and Jessie I've told you about from junior high."

"Oh, of course. It's so nice to meet you. Alex has talked about you several times."

"So, Rose, I wondered if you were still out in California."

"Yeah, I live here, and you'll never guess what. Jessie is flying in today. She should be here any minute."

"Oh, Alex," Chris says, "we really need to go right now to get Phil."

"Our son," Alex says.

"You have a son?"

"Three sons," he says, rolling his eyes. "Here," he fishes around in his wallet, hands me a business card. "Give me a call at work and we'll meet for a drink while Jessie's in town, or maybe you can come over for dinner one night. Where are you working?"

"In Berkeley, over on Fourth Street."

"Oh, where?" Chris says. "We live in North Berkeley."

"Felice Mundo."

"Oh, isn't that funny! My mom's group meets there for breakfast once a month."

We walk out to their car, chattering away. I hug Alex goodbye twice, I'm so happy to have found him again. I wave, watching their car pull out of sight, and then walk back to my place, looking at Alex's card. It figures Alex would grow up to be a scientist.

"Hi."

I look up to see Jessie sitting on my front steps. For a moment all I can do is just stand there, sort of swaying like I'm catching my balance.

"I'm from the local visiting nurses chapter," she says, getting up, one smooth motion from sitting to hugging. "You the lady who called for a nurse?"

"Yeah, psychiatric nurse. I don't think it's your area."

"Well, how about a lay person with years of psychiatric experience?"

"I'll consider that."

She pulls back and looks at me, hard and close and full, and I don't let go, slide my hands down her arms to rest at the crooks of her elbows. A tingly coolness showers over me like the fan of drops from the sprinkler Tommy would turn on in the front yard and Jessie and I would stand near, watching its water sway back and forth, gasps and giggles as it hit, the water wiped from our faces as the cooling fan cleared us and fell to the other side and then started back toward us. Feelings are like that, coming toward you in cool drops, and feelings are anticipation of what you've felt before.

And I'll tell you something about kissing your love with your eyes open to the sun, the world a blur, fuzzy and luscious, like a stuck sprinkler, cool drops that fall and fall, the moistening ground that sucks at your bare toes, brings you sinking down, green spiky grass blades tickling the tops of your feet.

We stop, halfway up the stairs, and I reach for her face, fumbling in the darkness my eyes make as they struggle to adjust from the bright sun to the covered stairs, yellow flakes of sun flashing in front of my eyes. And I kiss her again.

"I love you," I tell her then, my hands sliding down to hold her hands that hold my waist. And I lean back against the rail to look at her, want to tell her I won't let her out of my sight again, won't let her go.

I lie in bed that night, Jessie sleeping, and I see myself throwing garlic and olive oil and zucchini into a pan, making a recipe my grandmother made that I forgot I even knew. In the morning, the breeze coming through the back door screen whips around my ankles; Jessie emerges from the shower, her head wrapped in a towel. She sits in the kitchen chair, a can of Pepsi balanced and sweating on her knee, and I am a clear, crisp-edged calm.

You never can tell where you'll find your way.

"I'm throwing a 60th birthday party for Hannah next month," she says that night. "Maybe if Marcelle is doing okay you can come. Maybe we could go back and forth for a while till we figure this out."

"I'd like that."

I put the plates of zucchini on the table. We eat. Talk. I can't stop smiling.

I don't know what will become of us. I lie staring up at the ceiling and play that kitchen picture over and over in my head. I don't want to forget it, the sudsy pan in the sink, even the shadow her bent leg made on the seat of the chair. If I remember it well enough, the good feelings will stay put. I don't understand me sometimes, but tonight I don't care about figuring much of anything out.

Besides, I'm so tired, the kind of tired that has nothing to do with sleep, the kind of tired that gets you up in the middle of the night to kneel on the couch and look out your front window into the darkness to see what the street lamps light up.

I think if you happen to love a woman who can teach you to climb rooftops, pull a trembling watchful you up with one swift arm to see stars and everything sparkling, you've got yourself one full life.

Night Diving

▼

"Wake up, put this on!"

She does and I lead her outside and around the back, open the gate and the pool is dark, almost black at the shallow end, with the deep end lit in a funnel of blue that spreads into darkness. We stand, the concrete edge lining the pool cool and gritty to the soles of our feet. And for just that moment we are 14 again, Night Diving, a whole life of tomorrows before us. It is Jessie, of course, who dives first, aims herself into the blue. I watch the pool swallow her and then she pushes off the bottom, rushing toward the surface, and I dive into the dark. I let myself float slowly up, watching her legs tread water. She looks like she's dancing.

▼

Joven, Dee and Bessie won't let up, tease me mercilessly about my black-and-white plaid pants and the white uniform top. Joven cooks in a pair of Levis and the same three stained T-shirts. I think once a month he throws them all in the wash together and they take on the same grayish hue. I come home from Felice Mundo one day, gather all my uniforms in a heap on my bedroom floor and then cram them into a Hefty bag. I swing the bag up over my head and into the dumpster, walk back into the apartment feeling like I just burned my bra. The next day when I show up in my Just Do It T-shirt, I expect, at the very least, a little toast with our morning coffee cups, but what I get is Marcelle bursting into the kitchen yelling, "That dishwasher's a fucking madman. Where the hell did you find him?"

I'd hired him and, okay, so he talked to himself, occasionally froze mid-rinse, staring off into space, but it's not like you're going to get some Harvard grad to wash the dishes. I guess Marcelle's alone with him in the kitchen on my day off, and he starts doing this zombie walk toward her with the big chopping knife. The week before he'd disappeared, and we'd found him standing in the walk-in box having a conversation with the tub of salmon. But this is Berkeley, after all, and you learn to let certain things go. Anyway, she says to him, "Hey, Kevin, put that thing down before you hurt yourself," and he keeps coming at her. "I said put that thing down. Hey!" And she picks up the cleaver. That snapped him out of it.

"That's it, you crazy, you're fired!" And from what Bessie says, Marcelle didn't put the cleaver down until he was out the door.

"I have enough to worry about with this cancer without having to worry about some madman dishwasher. From now on *I* hire the staff."

We're getting a routine down with the chemo. Last month Jessie was out for a visit and took care of Marcelle while I was at work. Louise, the home health nurse, still comes by once a day the week of the chemo. She and Jessie went to Fourth Street and bought Marcelle all these brightly colored caps. She's lost most of her hair. I thought she'd get thin, but she hasn't. She looks different in a way I can't describe, and she has this smell, like medicine and vitamins. It's a comforting smell. Sometimes, I get a stab of fear all of a sudden, and I reach down and give her a hug, inhale her deeply, and I feel calmer, like I can smell a healing going on inside her.

Dr. Myers is a straight-shooter and sometimes the news isn't good. Sometimes I wish he would lie. It's been one year and 14 chemo treatments and still the cancer spreads. In April we had a real scare, and she was in the hospital for weeks, so weak, so much pain, she couldn't get out of bed, and the blend of IV painkillers they were giving her made her look miserable. That was the first time I thought in the secret of my own head about when it's okay to die, and like Marcelle could read my mind, she says to me, "I'm not ready to go but last night I saw Stan and Mark."

210

"Mark still wearing those Earth Shoes?"

"Yeeesss!"

"Next time you see him, you need to tell him to spring for a new pair of shoes already."

Three days later she has this incredible turnaround and she's back home again. Two weeks later, she's back at Felice Mundo. We go to the same unit every time she has the chemo, and the staff just bring a cot for us to take turns sleeping on. There are nights that I'm jolted out of sleep by the loudspeaker and all these feet running down the hall for a Code Blue. The next morning I'm in the little kitchen behind the nurse station making a pot of coffee, and one of the nurses tells me the woman in 61 died last night. The second one this week. Then she says death always comes in threes. I'd like to get my hands around the neck of whoever made up that little piece of morbidity. We were out of there by the end of the week, so I can't tell you what happened. I don't plan to ask.

I see Jessie every month or two. I go there or she comes here. It's an in-between that we've made comfortable. There's a certain sense of accomplishment to getting everything you need for a week in a carry-on bag. I wear her clothes. They're big on me and I roll up sleeves and swim in them. The last trip, she bought a pair of shorts and pajamas on sale at Macys and said, "I'm just leaving these here, okay?" She can't squeeze into a single thing of mine. And then she says, "You know, Rose, I could do with us both being in one place."

I had bought the same pajamas in blue and was sitting on the bed, pulling off the tags. I just sort of looked up from what I was doing and said, "Me too."

"I like it here," she says, sitting down next to me. I can't tell you most of what else we said because it wasn't as romantic as you'd hope. Finally, two hours later we're still talking, changed into our pajamas.

"I want a ring, Jessie."

"Like an engagement ring?"

"Something like that. Not like Liz Taylor's hunk-o'diamond-mine kind of ring but something."

"Me too! Come on, let's go right now!"

"Now?"

But we did. We had an hour to throw on our clothes and tear down to the Village. We got the same thin gold bands with a sprinkling of diamond chips that we picked because they look like the stars from up on a roof. We stopped for ice cream and sat out on the curb with our cones. My grandmother told me that when she and my grandfather got married, they didn't have money for a wedding or a honeymoon, so after the city hall ceremony, they split a box of Jujcyfruits on a park bench. Like that.

The next day Jessie has to catch her plane and when I get into work, Joven tells me Marcelle has to go back in the hospital. It's spread again. I know it's bad. I go out the back door, pace around the empty parking lot in the stench of the dumpster. I look at my ring catching the sun and cry angry tears. After a while, Joven comes out with my purse and my car keys, and I go and spend what turns into a month at Marcelle's, with Louise and then the Hospice people.

One day she wants to get out of bed and she looks suddenly stronger, like she can sometimes, and makes me get her recipe file. She flips through it and pulls out a piece of paper so crisp with age it falls apart at the folds when she opens it. The recipe is written in French, so she sits at the kitchen table and reads ingredients and amounts off to me. I watch her still-thick arms push and churn a circle of dough, stubby fingers sprinkling flour, and we talk about her death. People will do that if you let them, open the door to their hell, and share it with you like cups of coffee at a kitchen table. She tells me she hopes I have the kind of love with Jessie that she got to live with Stan and Mark. She tells me that I've been like a daughter to her, that she loves me, that I am scared like a bird sometimes, that I need to make a nest. She says she will watch me, and that really sets me crying.

"But I'll miss you so."

"You will and it will hurt dull and sharp, but if you be still, quiet, especially early in the morning and late at night, you'll feel me there. I know. Those are the best times to feel your loved ones."

And in this way she teaches me how to make a Kuchen, a sweet yeasty cake you pour into wax-papered coffee cans to bake and glaze white, a single pink rose placed on the top. It looks like a wedding gift.

Chapter 16

"Look, I don't know how you do things in California, but in New York we sit at weddings, so when we order tables and chairs we expect them to arrive some time *before* the ceremony . . . Let me speak to your supervisor . . . I'm working with a real brain surgeon here."

I head back into the bathroom where Jessie is standing in front of the mirror. Her hair has clearly lost to the can of hair spray on the bathroom counter, the right side of her head stiff and sticky. Her reflection in the mirror looks at me, a vision of panic.

"I'll send in Vivian when she's done with the chair man."

A quick kiss. I go back out to the kitchen to check on Hannah, to whom I have assigned the fruit salad, a clear and contained task, after finding her the day before, when she was supposed to be making the place cards, wandering through the apartment, an Eddie Bauer catalogue in her hand.

"Rose, what do you think of this blouse?"

"Hannah!"

I peer into the bowl. It is heaped with fruit cut into a gazillion half-inch squares. I hold up one of the squares to her.

"This is a wedding, Hannah, not Bingo Night at the convalescent home."

But you know how it is, by the end of the day you're still just as married.

▼

Marcelle left me Felice Mundo in her will. We never even talked about it, but we both just knew she would. Joven does breakfast. I do lunch.

And we just opened a little take-out place next door. I named it Four and Twenty Black Birds. I got these great cards: Little black birds flying out of a pie in the upper right-hand corner. Everyone had a different idea for the name, and there was the fear that the animal rights people would take offense, but I just really liked it and Becky was the one who finally asked, "Do you really *want* a clientele with no sense of humor?"

I bake pies, mostly. I still make cakes, and cookies too, but it's the pies I'm known for: thick crust that shatters at the edge when you slice it and berries I always mix; strawberries with blackberries, blueberries with raspberries and no sugar—honey or maple syrup. I like to make the lattice crusts, but one year I cut little hearts and now that's pretty popular, a heavy, bubbling Valentine.

I make quiches in tart pans and I just don't call them quiches anymore, partly because Vivian took a little informal poll at the shop and quiches just aren't "in" anymore, and partly because I usually make it up as I go along and use whatever looks good at the Farmer's Market—Italian Table Cheese, Havarti with Dill, the Fresh Mozzarella in water that's just becoming trendy in California. One day I threw in some endive and now I have to make one kind with endive all the time.

▼

I get up early, just before dawn, because there are some things that just aren't as good the next day. I put on a CD and sift and roll, cleaning berries, though a few stems never killed anyone and with the way things are going with the whole homemade craze, I figure I'll be baking in the little plants, roots and all, by the end of the year. And you get to think. Well, *I* get to think. You're probably sleeping.

I think about all sorts of things: Bills; a story Jessie told me the night before about Lee, this nurse she works with at Marin General, who's sleeping with her daughter's husband; if we should have a baby; where I last saw my sun glasses. Doughy dawns and how I think I see Marcelle in a puff of flour, can feel her watching me making her dream my own. There's something about that time of day, a whole life that goes on in the dark, people whose days are over at 2 in the afternoon.

Vivian usually calls a couple of mornings a week. It works with the time difference, the rates are low, and God knows she's up. She got sick again last October, and we flew her out. I'm so used to being the only one up in the house, just me and the coffee. I'd walk into the kitchen and she'd be sitting there, in the dark. I still watch her eyes. I peer in the same way I push on the oven light to check on my pies because sometimes the crust goes brown fast, even though I always set the timer the same. It's one of those little things that remind me life is not a recipe.

At first she was the teary softness. But pretty soon, after I started taking her to the restaurant with me, she began perking up, rolling crust, writing the breakfast specials on the blackboard we hang in the front window, giving Joven a haircut out in the back parking lot.

"I do hope you're not claiming all that money you made yesterday," she says one morning. And a week or so later she was much better. I told her the truth. I try to do that with her now. Jessie does the bookkeeping and I have an accountant, Craig, who does all the money stuff. And yeah, I claim it all. It's not like I'm up for Scout Master or anything. I take every business expense I can. It's a big joke with my friends. Becky and I will go to lunch and she'll rip the stub off the check, hand it to me and say, "I believe we talked about berries over this lunch."

The bottom line is, I have to sleep at night, and Vivian and I just have different tolerances. For instance, I'm supposed to keep all my receipts. But I forget. Jessie fishes them out of my dirty laundry and stuffs them into the special envelope she made tacked to the fridge with a magnet, by the back door of Felice Mundo, where the deliveries come in. I think you have to be more organized than that to commit a felony.

By the end of her visit, I put Vivian to work icing the witch cookies for Halloween, bowls of black and orange icing, cookies on every surface, and I look over her shoulder, shaking my head. "You know, I'm just not getting the productivity out of you I was hoping for."

"Fuck you, honey."

A few weeks later she went back to Long Island, almost 100%, as Tommy said, and she sold one of the shops, trying to pare down. Pies as therapy.

I'm trying EMDR, this therapy where you sit in front of a bar of flashing lights. Becky told me some people are having great luck with it for traumas and phobias. It's gotten so I barely drive anymore, but one day I wanted to go to a new restaurant supply store in Hayward, which is about three different freeways, and I just couldn't do it. I got in the car, turned on the ignition, and had my panic attack right there in the driveway. Jessie came out, opened the driver's side door.

"Move over. Come on, I'll take you," she said, which was as much for her as for me. She still walks around most of the time secretly fearful that something, especially me, will be taken from her, like God's waiting for her to hit her pinnacle of happiness so He can destroy it in one swift and efficient blow. I remind her, more than you'd think, that I'm not to be taken away, little notes I put by the coffeemaker in the morning before I leave for the store, messages on the answering machine, reminders I still exist, we still exist, even when I'm not right there in front of her.

In return, she drives everywhere and never brings it up in front of people, because even though I've only said it a couple of times, she knows it embarrasses me.

Love is a lot of things, different for different people, but if there's one thing I'm sure of, it's that love is not the string orchestras and rose dozens. Those are just the symptoms. Love is knowing a person's tender spots, the places where the skin is transparent, not fully formed, like the clear membrane that holds a yolk round even after you separate it from the white. Love is standing guard over a beloved's yolk.

Jessie still has nightmares. Most every morning she wakes up frightened. She chips away at it, but it's slow, the kind of tedious, steady work that only shows results if you walk away and come back later, much later, like the biggest cake in the world, a decade from batter to frosting.

The kitchen gets the morning sun. I had three little pots of herbs—blue, green and pink—on the windowsill. And oh, the slaughter and carnage those pots have seen. I'm sure they hold their own little grief support groups in the evenings after I lock up, maybe invite in other pots for the open house they run monthly for pots without plants, weekend workshops on survivor's guilt. If the world was really a just place, all of this would be subsidized by Mr. Malone, the owner of the Franklin Nursery, who I believe has recently completed that addition on his house, solely funded by my personal losses, the little plaque inscribed with the dedication, "Rose Salino, so many plants in so little time," mounted above the doorbell. And it's not for neglect. I water them. I talk to them. I sprinkle little offerings of pie crust over their dirt. But they all die, some slowly, wasting away with plenty of time for me to consider the life support versus euthanasia question, while others just drop dead suddenly, their perfectly lush and green leaves drooping over the rim of the pot one morning, like Camille.

"They're not getting enough light, Rose. They need to be able to do photosynthesis," Vivian tells me, that Dr. Salino Medicine Woman tone in her voice.

"They're getting plenty of light. I bake in here in the mornings. A little dirt tucked around my feet, a little Miracle Grow, and *I* could do a better job."

"And I think you need to wait a little longer before you harvest them," she adds.

But I don't know, one leaf apiece seems sufficient to me for a plant with some healthy initiative, truly interested in future opportunities, with the ability to be a team player.

"Bad attitude," I say. "I can't prove it but it just feels passive-aggressive to me."

A longish pause.

"Maybe some nice silk plants, Rose."

So now I just buy my herbs from the Farmer's Market. I think it's important to know your limits.

I've started swinging by Becky's on Saturday mornings and picking up Katlin. She stands out on the front porch with her backpack and her hair shoved under a baseball cap. I got her these individual aluminum pie tins from the restaurant supply for her eighth birthday, and she promptly announced to everyone at the party that she was going to live with her Aunties, quit the third grade and become a baker. So this is a sort of compromise. Becky threatens from time to time to order in a supply of these pie tins for all the kids, tiny bite-sized ones for the twins, and have all four of them parked out on the front porch one Saturday morning. The truth is, Katlin's my favorite. I don't know if aunts are allowed to say that. I know mothers aren't. The thing with me and Katlin reminds me of this *New Yorker* cartoon where this old banker-type guy is sitting at a huge cherry desk, his finger on the speaker button of his phone, and the caption says, "Marge, bring me in someone who reminds me of myself in my youth."

Katlin does, and I don't believe for a minute that the cartoonist and I are the only ones who do this, find comfort in catching a glimpse of our reflection in another. I think that was what Jessie was doing when we were kids and she guarded old Alex, and what happens when she dissolves in tears and snot every time she sees an animal dead on the side of the road. I think we all see parts of our fragile hurt selves out in the world, and we try to care for and watch over these parts, out in the light where we can get a better look and enough in the distance so we can stand what we see.

Some people, like Jessie, just hide it less well. Some people make a career of it, but we won't even go there.

Hannah and Jules moved to California, near Mt. Shasta, which is supposed to be one of the spiritual headquarters of the planet and a meeting place for anyone abducted by aliens, a kind of Ellis Island for abductees to study their suspicious birthmarks. Usually you don't get taken just once, I'm told. They pick you up and drop you off a couple of times, maybe to check on your birthmark. One woman actually planned for this, had her baby-sitter on call for extra duty, as this is not something you get to schedule like a touch-up. "I need to reschedule my abduction for next week, in the morning if you have anything." I don't make this stuff up. I was told by the woman sitting next to me on the plane to Redding, who certainly seemed to know about such things.

Hannah had all her catalogues forwarded there, a task whose scope I tremble to imagine. The Williams-Sonoma catalogues have been arriving in a steady stream since I opened the store, complete with multicolored post-its marking the pages and Hannah's loopy-script comments: "So tasty!". . . "A real class act!" . . . "Fresh lemonade to go with the pies!" beside a $300 juicer. I sent that back with a little note that said, "How sweet of you! I'll take it," and the next week it came back with a little note that said, "Ask your angels." A little wit goes entirely too far with me.

Jules took me fly-fishing, seems he used to do it about 50 years ago when he was a boy in Kentucky. I went with him once and all I can say is, it's a damn good thing I have a sense of humor. I'm standing in the stream, reaching deep inside, accessing my inner Brad Pitt, mimicking my memory of the little wrist-flipping action, and I about stabbed myself to death. Death by fuzzy fish hook. What was worse is that Jules just threw them all back in. We had this ugly little scene where he attempted to wrestle my one and only trout of the day from me. I was okay with throwing them back in if I got something in return, a little trout chip for instance, that I could cash in later for a Mt. Shasta back scratcher. Of course, Jules tried to tell me how the real prize was less tangible, the essence of the experience. We don't like the same music, either.

I recently started naming my pies, a chocolate cream pie I call Tommy Pie, and a pie of green Jell-O and Cool Whip I call Thumbelina Pie, because I can and because when it's cut, it's bright as Kool-Aid and the neon blue of a pool at night. It isn't a big seller. I don't take it personally. My friend Darren, who grew up in Nebraska, where he tells me Jell-O is like the fifth food group, says it's a sign of the times. His mother calls him regularly from back home and assures him the world is ending, in a sneaky underhanded kind of way—not a decent Tupperware party in years—and Jell-O just isn't the glue of families it used to be.

My most successful is Grandma Pie, which is really a pizza. You grease the pan with Crisco and spread the dough and then drain a can of tomatoes and crush them with your fingers, a little salt and pepper, basil and olive oil, a good handful of Locatelli. At first the people would come in, the regulars, and wanted to know how long to heat it up. They were nothing short of jubilant as I insisted they serve it cold, tried to explain how we always liked it best cold, Claire and Tina and I, sneaking into the kitchen for the last pieces we'd eat out on the front porch after school, too little to know we were filling more than our tummies.

It's not something you can really explain. Sometimes I convince myself that I've sold them a piece of what I remember, and that's why they sail out of the restaurant with a smile of relief, but I know they're just happy to have one less thing to do—like Vivian always said, another plate to wash and all. Besides, I know they have their own childhoods to contend with, without having to deal with mine.

I had that nightmare again last night, the one with the giant wave on the beach, and I woke up around 3. I propped my head in my hand and watched Jessie sleep, the tiniest little snores that can drive me crazy on nights I lie awake. I'm a light sleeper and I can't nap in the day. I see Jessie, as I used to see Tommy, lying on the couch, watching TV, and the next thing you know, they're out. I wish I could do that. Still, there's something so dear, so intimate, about watching a loved one sleep. She always ends up on her back with her hands behind her head. I've been awakened more than once by an elbow knocking me in the skull. I push her over on her side, but she never wakes up.

I want peace for her. I want peace for Vivian. I think I am the witness, the other in their struggles. I cannot imagine what it must be *to be* them—or Hannah, in bed all day. What is that moment like, cutting your own skin, watching it split, or waking one morning to your world a fog with no hope of a sun that burns it off, not a single other place or room you can go to for a clearing? But then they don't know what it's like to watch, to be in the front row all the time. Sometimes, when I don't sleep, I think that's why. I have to watch; I can't leave my post. When I have that wave dream like this morning, or my panic attacks in the car, I try to think of what I'm scared of.

I was thinking again of having a baby and I thought, what if I drop it? What if I drop it on that soft spot on its head and I end up with a vegetable baby? Am I strong enough to raise a baby like that? What if I'm not watchful enough and it eats Ajax? What if learning baby CPR is like learning to ride a bike, and I just can't ever get it quite right? You don't exactly have time for a huge learning curve with that kind of thing. And then I think I'm not even vaguely healthy enough to be someone's parent. I can't even keep a plant alive.

I told Jessie what I'd been thinking. She put her arm around me.

"You'd be a terrific mother."

"But don't you worry, Jessie?"

"Sure. I worry that it will have too many needs!"

"It's a baby. It's nothing but needs!"

I don't think either one of us can do that much therapy in nine months, so we're putting off the baby thing for right now. But, I have to tell you, I'm really worried that if this keeps up, I'll end up like one of those people I see in Berkeley, riding their bikes with gas masks on, afraid of the air.

So anyway, I still haven't figured it out, what I'm scared of.

Night Diving

The other night, over Kentucky Fried Chicken, Becky, Jessie, even Katlin, kept telling me how everyone's afraid of something and that fear is a spectrum. I can buy that. Some people have a few small, well-defined fears; some of us are the Olympic Gold Medalists for the U.S. Terror Team. We stand, quivering, on top of those podiums, our heads bowed as the judge slides the ribbon over our heads, all the more touching because our eyes or mouths are doing that little twitching thing.

Seriously, I think the key is, first, to know your scared place or your wounded place or your empty place or whatever you call it. Make sure you know what it looks like, so you don't accidentally sit on it or put it out with the recycling. Then, you need to find a few people—and quality is more important than quantity here—who'll respect your place, not people who tell you they've seen plenty of places like yours and it's going to take a hell of a lot more than a little 409 to clean it up, that it's clearly beyond repair. You want people you would trust to baby-sit your place, bring it some cocoa with those mini marshmallows on those unscheduled alien abduction days, for instance.

I think that if you can pull all that together, you're pretty set and you can go about your business of tending to your place with a clear head. I think that's really the most you can ask for.

Other Titles Available from Spinsters Ink Books

The Magister, Sally Miller Gearhart $14.00
Martha Moody, Susan Stinson $10.95
Modern Daughters and the Outlaw West, Melissa Kwasny . $9.95
Mother Journeys: Feminists Write About Mothering,
    Sheldon, Reddy, Roth $15.95
Night Diving, Michelene Esposito $14.00
Nin, Cass Dalglish $12.00
No Matter What, Mary Saracino $9.95
Ordinary Justice, Trudy Labovitz $12.00
The Other Side of Silence, Joan M. Drury $9.95
The Racket, Anita Mason $12.95
Ransacking the Closet, Yvonne Zipter $9.95
Report for Murder, V. L. McDermid $10.95
Roberts' Rules of Lesbian Break-ups, Shelly Roberts $5.95
Roberts' Rules of Lesbian Dating, Shelly Roberts $5.95
Roberts' Rules of Lesbian Living, Shelly Roberts $5.95
Silent Words, Joan M. Drury $10.95
The Solitary Twist, Elizabeth Pincus $9.95
Sugar Land, Joni Rogers $12.00
They Wrote the Book: Thirteen Women Mystery Writers Tell All,
    edited by Helen Windrath $12.00
Those Jordan Girls, Joan M. Drury $12.00
Trees Call for What They Need, Melissa Kwasny $9.95
Turnip Blues, Helen Campbell $10.95
The Two-Bit Tango, Elizabeth Pincus $9.95
Vital Ties, Karen Kringle. $10.95
Voices of the Soft-bellied Warrior, Mary Saracino $14.00
Wanderground, Sally Miller Gearhart $12.95
The Well-Heeled Murders, Cherry Hartman $10.95
Why Can't Sharon Kowalski Come Home?
    Thompson & Andrzejewski $12.95
A Woman Determined, Jean Swallow $10.95
The Yellow Cathedral, Anita Mason $14.00

Spinsters titles are available at your local booksellers or by mail order through Spinsters Ink Books. Call 1-800-301-6860 to place an order today. A free catalog is available upon request. See also www.spinsters-ink.com. Please include $2.50 for the first title ordered and 50¢ for every title thereafter. All credit cards accepted.

Spinsters Ink Books is one of the oldest feminist publishing houses in the world. It was founded in upstate New York in 1978, and today is an imprint of Hovis Publishing Company, Inc. in Denver, Colorado.

The noun "spinster" means a woman who spins. The definition of the verb "spin" is to whirl and twirl, to revert, to spin on one's heels, to turn everything upside down. Spinsters Ink books do just that—take women's "yarns" (stories, tales) and enable readers to see the world through the other end of the telescope. Spinsters Ink authors move readers off their comfort zones just a bit, pushing the camel through the eye of the needle. These are thinking books for thinking readers.

Spinsters Ink fiction and non-fiction titles deal with significant issues in women's lives from a feminist perspective. They not only name these crucial issues but—more importantly—encourage change and growth. We are committed to publishing works by women writing from the periphery: fat women, Jewish women, lesbians, old women, immigrant women, poor women, rural women, women examining classism, women of color, women with disabilities, women who are writing books that help make the best in our lives more possible.

Spinsters Ink Books
P. O. Box 22005
Denver, CO 80222
USA

Phone: 303-761-5552   Fax: 303-761-5284

E-mail: spinster@spinsters-ink.com
Web site: http://www.spinsters-ink.com

Michelene Esposito is a clinical psychologist with a private practice in Northern California. She uses humor in her work and focuses on the intrapersonal and intepersonal dynamics of relationships in the development of her characters. *Night Diving* is her first novel. She published short stories in *Teen* and *Young Miss* prior to beginning her career in psychology.

"I always wanted to write a novel. I think this novel is like many first novels, part of the best work you can do at the time and part therapy."

Her literary influences include Hemingway, Fitzgerald, Anne Lammot and Wally Lamb. "When I was in the fifth grade I found a copy of *Catcher in the Rye* in my grandparents' basement. It was summer, hot and humid, so the basement was a great place to be. I sat under this bare lightbulb all day and devoured that book. I think Salinger's prose affected me more than any other as it felt close to my own voice—emphasis on sarcastic, self-effacing dialogue.

"Now I'm a mother of a one-year-old and I haven't read a novel in over a year. I'm just trying to eke away the time to brush my teeth and work on my second novel (doing okay, thankfully for all, on the teeth, failing miserably on the second novel)."